MARGO HANSEN

Irena's
Bond of Matrimony

• A Newly Weds Series •

TATE PUBLISHING
AND ENTERPRISES, LLC

Irena's Bond of Matrimony
Copyright © 2012 by Margo Hansen. All rights reserved.

No part of this publication may be reproduced, stored in a retrieval system or transmitted in any way by any means, electronic, mechanical, photocopy, recording or otherwise without the prior permission of the author except as provided by USA copyright law.

Scripture quotations are taken from the *Holy Bible, King James Version,* Cambridge, 1769. Used by permission. All rights reserved.

This novel is a work of fiction. Names, descriptions, entities, and incidents included in the story are products of the author's imagination. Any resemblance to actual persons, events, and entities is entirely coincidental.

The opinions expressed by the author are not necessarily those of Tate Publishing, LLC.

Published by Tate Publishing & Enterprises, LLC
127 E. Trade Center Terrace | Mustang, Oklahoma 73064 USA
1.888.361.9473 | www.tatepublishing.com

Tate Publishing is committed to excellence in the publishing industry. The company reflects the philosophy established by the founders, based on Psalm 68:11,
"The Lord gave the word and great was the company of those who published it."

Book design copyright © 2012 by Tate Publishing, LLC. All rights reserved.
Cover design by Rtor Maghuyop
Interior design by Mary Jean Archival

Published in the United States of America

ISBN: 978-1-62147-798-3
1. Fiction / Christian / Romance
12.09.20

Irena's
Bond of Matrimony

To:
Arlene Nygaard
Jon & Betty Stende
Virgil & Fay Nygaard
Delores Hanson

In memory of:
Millard Nygaard
Palmer & Olive Stende
Stanley & Eldora Lunde
Richard Hanson
James & Doris Finnerty
Hazel Bennett

And
To Bruce, my love, always

Acknowledgments

As my fictional *Newly* family has grown through the years, so has my real family. Each new addition is a blessing, and I realize that my family could never have been complete without each one. Every person brings his own special talent or gift to a family.

Because the *Lord Jesus Christ* instituted the family unit, to Him is the praise for these stories about family.

Because *Bruce* heads up our family so well, always striving to please God in how he leads us, I thank him for the inspiration to write about family.

Because *my children* and their families remind me of how life changes and how quickly time is passing, I thank them for their stability in the Word and in the unchanging Grace of our Lord.

Because I was fortunate to grow up with cousins, I thank *Carol, Steve, Collene, Ann, Alan, Pam, Sue, Denise, Geri, Wes, & Kyle* for all the wonderful childhood memories they provided me. And my cousins-in-law,

Sue and Dennis, have also become part of my life and make it complete.

Because friends are such an important part of my life, I again want to thank those who pray for me and who continue to encourage me to write.

And, because I couldn't accomplish this without my publisher, I again thank the *Tate Publishing* group for their support and guidance in completing this story. A special thanks to Amanda, my editor, for all the fun and helpful comments along the way!

Sand Creek

Russ and Sky Newly
Tyler (m. Jadyne Crandall)
Lucy (m. Buck Riley)
Dorcas (m. Cavan Nolan)
Emma (m. Simon Chappell)
Rex
Abel

Hank and Randi Riley
Buck (m. Lucy Newly)
Dugan (m. Melody Wells)
Mallory (m. Michael Trent)
Jethro
Parker
Rodney
Ross

Jonas and Bridget Nolan
Rooney
Bernadette

Jasper and Martha Riggs
Percy Scott (m. Rebecca Tunelle)
Peter Scott (m. Robin Tunelle)
Dexter (m. Esther Trent)
Bernard (m. Pearl Maddox)
Clayton
Rhoda
Penny

Evan and Ella Trent
Michael (m. Mallory Riley)
Gabriel (m. Leigh Sheldon)
Esther (m. Dexter Riggs)
Martha (m. Rob Tunelle)
John

Duke and Angelina Tunelle
Rebecca (m. Percy Scott)
Robin (m. Peter Scott)
Ralph (m. Philippa Gray)
Ray (m. Cora Macardle)
Robert (m. Martha Trent)

Harry and Gretchen Nolan
Annie (m. Monty Davies)
Cavan (m. Dorcas Newly)

Taylor and Violet Gray
Philippa (m. Ralph Tunelle)

Bert and Gertie Davies
Monty (m. Annie Nolan)

George and Janet Spencer   Clyde and Belle Moore
    MALACHI

Gerald and Bertha Nessel

Grandville

Tyler and Jadyne Newly   Michael and Mallory Trent
    EDMUND   MARCY
    PAMELA   MARTIN
                                         MILLARD

Buck and Lucy Riley   Bernard and Pearl Riggs
    MOLLY   THOMAS

Ralph and Philippa Tunelle   Ray and Cora Tunelle
                                         MINERVA

Malcolm and Hermine Tucker   Palmer and Hazel Granville
    PAUL   SIDNEY CRANDALL
    MARK
    JESSE

Way Station

Gabriel and Leigh Trent   Dugan and Melody Riley
    ADELE   JASON
    ARLENE   JANELLE

Norris

Simon and Emma Chappell
    TROY
    TRUDY

Chapter 1

London

The letter rustled in her pocket when Irena rubbed her hands on her apron, reminding her that it was awaiting her attention. *As if I could forget it,* she thought as she quickly grabbed a towel and began drying the tall stack of dishes before her. Her red hands still stung from the hot water that she used to rinse the many glasses, cups, plates, and silver from the Cavendish family's evening meal.

The letter had arrived in yesterday's post, quite disrupting the orderly events of the day and making Irena the object of unwanted attention by the family and staff alike. Unwanted, because any attention usually meant more work. Irena had learned long ago that being inconspicuous kept her from the numerous little tasks that the housekeeper or cook found for anyone who didn't appear busy enough to suit them.

Not that Irena wasn't a hard worker. No one could say that. As scullery maid, she did all the tasks assigned to her thoroughly and efficiently. Much too efficiently, she found. As soon as one task was finished, she was given another, then another. Irena ran and worked from sunrise to sunset with only short rests as she took her three meals at the little table in the kitchen.

Conrad, the butler, was quite put out with her, but how was she to know a letter was coming for her? She hadn't heard from her aunt and uncle in six years; she could hardly have known they would write to her now or ever. But a letter had come, and not only that, but it had come with the Cavendishs' mail. Conrad had unknowingly put it on the silver platter with the other mail and delivered it personally to Mr. Cavendish, just as he had been delivering the mail for thirty years.

It never crossed his mind that a letter for the scullery maid would appear in his employer's hands. All the downstairs help knew to have their mail sent around back, but Irena hadn't given it any thought. After all, it had been six years and nothing had ever come for her. Even though it wasn't her fault, she was the one who eventually suffered for the mistake.

Mr. Cavendish had shown his disapproval to Conrad, who in turn had given a dressing down to Mrs. Pitney, the housekeeper. She then had scolded Cook, and Cook had vented her ire at Irena with a tongue lashing, extra chores, and no supper.

All because of the letter. The papers in her pocket crackled again as she lifted the dishes up to the shelves and put them away. Being short didn't help any, but she was used to reaching and stretching for things. She didn't believe she had grown any taller since she first arrived in London when she was only twelve. Her body hadn't changed much in other ways either. She frowned slightly, thinking of the letter. *Would that matter?*

The food she was given to eat was good but not plenteous. After the Cavendishs were served their fancy meals, the staff were allowed to eat, starting with the highest-ranking members such as the butler, the housekeeper, and Cook; followed by the maids, the groomsmen, the groundskeeper, and finally the scullery maid. Irena didn't mind being last and eating alone, but sometimes there just wasn't much left over, and if Cook was in a foul mood, Irena wasn't given much time to finish what there was. As a result, Irena was slender, and the hard work had made her muscles firm. Her feminine shape was barely noticeable under her plain gray dress and white apron.

Irena had hoped to be promoted to maid one day. After all, scullery maids were usually the younger girls. The older girls were supposed to move up like Constance had. Irena worked with Constance for two years before Constance was promoted to maid. *But Constance is pretty,* thought Irena. *And I'm plain and look like a child still. No wonder they don't want me for maid.* Irena shrugged. Maybe it was just as well.

Even though the maid's tasks were easier, she had to be around the family, and just the thought of having others watch her work made Irena shiver with fear. *And the family wants pretty girls as maids,* she reasoned to herself. *They wouldn't want to be embarrassed in front of their friends by a plain girl like me.* Then she stopped, and her hand went to her pocket again where the letter impatiently waited. *Would that matter?*

Irena rapidly and with smooth efficiency finished cleaning the kitchen for the night. She banked the fires and finished emptying the dishpans in the drain running along the edge of the street outside the kitchen door. The uneven stones and bricks making up the pavement used to make her trip, but she was so accustomed to them now that she could move nimbly over them without mishap.

Almost done, she thought.

She was anxious to get to her room by the kitchen and read the letter again. Because of Cook's anger the night before, Irena barely had time to skim the contents before Cook had demanded her candle be put out, and there had been no time all day today to read the shocking message again. Irena wondered if she had somehow misread the words her aunt had penned to her. They had shaken her so badly that maybe she had misunderstood.

Quickly she pulled off her apron and hung it on its hook. Then she slipped out of the rough, gray dress and into her simple nightgown. She pulled her hair down and with experienced fingers re-braided the blonde strands into two long braids. She flipped them over her back, and in one easy motion she sat cross-legged on her small bed with the envelope and letter before her on her lap.

She stared for a few moments at the envelope. Gently she rubbed her finger across the words on the front. Her name. How long had it been since she had seen her own name in writing? School in Norway had been a long time ago, and no one here used her full name. She was either called *Irena* or *girl*. Sometimes when she was sent to the market they called her *miss*, and it made her feel almost like a lady. Irena blinked her eyes. There it was—*Irena Aarestad*.

Slowly she pulled the letter out of the envelope and unfolded it. She inched closer to the candle so that she wouldn't miss a thing it said. Silently and carefully, she read through the two pages. Then she read them again.

Irena sat in deep thought for several minutes before she replaced the letter and blew out the candle. She lay on her bed with open eyes, staring at the darkness.

Nels Jenson wanted her for his wife.

Chapter 2

London

Nels Jenson. Irena closed her eyes tight, trying to picture him. Vaguely she recalled a time when Mr. and Mrs. Jenson and their son, Nels, had come to the Torkelson farm about some livestock. She had been ten or eleven at the time. Since her parents' death when she was seven, she had lived with her aunt and uncle, and her job was to help with chores and care for the children that kept coming into the family year after year.

She had been taking care of them that day, too, when she saw Nels. He was a man already, or so it seemed to her. She remembered him smiling at the children before hopping out of the back of the wagon and going into the barn with her uncle. She thought she remembered him as being tall, but then, if she had only been eleven, anyone would seem tall to her.

Irena rubbed her hands over her face and tried to concentrate before sleep took her. Her aunt said that Nels and his parents immigrated to America two years ago, and now his parents wanted to find a good Norwegian woman to be their son's wife. They remembered the Torkelsons' orphaned niece and wondered if she was at the right age for marriage and would join them in America.

A yawn interrupted her thoughts as she tried to stay awake a little longer to sort things out in her mind. Her aunt hadn't made the idea of marriage a request. Her letter was blunt and full of instructions Irena was to follow as though Irena had no say in the matter.

But Irena was used to instructions. She knew of nothing else but following orders since the day she set foot in her aunt and uncle's house. As soon as the Torkelsons' first daughter was old enough to take over Irena's chores, Irena had been shipped off to England and employed as a scullery maid.

"Mind you, I don't need more mouths to feed," her aunt had said as she waited for Irena to board the ship that would take her away. "You're old enough now to be earning your own keep. I've done my best by your parents, God rest their souls. I've got another baby of my own on the way and Ruby can handle your work now. You'll thank me some day for giving you this opportunity." There were no hugs, no kisses, just good-bye. Irena had told the little children good-bye at the farm and had felt panicky at never seeing their young faces again, but she kept her fears to herself. No one else wanted to hear about them.

Irena was up and about her chores early the next morning, but her thoughts were on her future. *America!* The thought astounded her. Sure, ships sailed from England to America. She had heard about people booking passage and leaving their birth countries behind for a fresh start in a new land. A "land of opportunity" some called it.

Irena had no opportunist dreams of her own. The most she hoped to achieve was maid or cook or maybe even housekeeper someday. She would have enjoyed being a governess, for she loved children and was good with them, but governesses were from a higher social class. They had schooling and were considered ladies even though they had to work. But Irena had heard that in America things were different. To think that she could become a wife and live in her own home on her own land—well, her husband's land—was something she hadn't dreamed to be possible.

"Quit dawdling over those dishes, Girl! There's baking and shopping to do before dinner." Cook's orders were sharp, but Irena didn't hear the anger in her voice any longer, so she ventured a question to the older woman.

"What do you know about America?"

"America!" The buxom woman snorted. "A wild, untamed country with thieves and cut throats in every city and nothing but woods and beasts beyond. Just ask the Swede at the butcher shop about America. His son is there and has a huge amount of land to homestead. What on God's green earth would you do with a lot of wild land? You'd get lost or cut down by savages, I declare."

Irena looked around at her tiny bedroom off the kitchen. Land! Her uncle's farm had been small, and she had never been allowed to roam it. Her work there tied her to the house and barn. Here, London kept her confined to the kitchen and back alley of her employer's house with an occasional trip to market. Just the thought of wide, open spaces staggered her mind. Slowly, an inkling of possible freedom began seeping into her.

At Cook's instructions, Irena was sent off to market for the food supplies. She made haste as always but with a special intent today to speak to Swede.

Arriving breathless at the butcher shop, Irena gave her order, choosing the best of what was offered. Irena revealed shrewdness in her bargaining skills even though she spoke very little. She sensed that the Swede enjoyed haggling with her over price, but to her it was all business.

"Mr. Swede," Irena asked, timid now that the bargaining was over. "Could you please tell me about America?"

At Swede's astonished stare, Irena ducked her head then forced herself to look at him.

It was well known that Irena never conversed with the shopkeepers. There was never time for anything more, and quite honestly she had nothing to say. She could see that Swede was delighted to finally hear her speak of something other than her meat order. He smiled at her to put her at ease.

"What would you like to know?"

Irena swallowed, aware that time was getting away from her. She decided to get right to the point. "How would I go about getting there?"

Speechless at her amazing request, the Swede stopped wrapping her meat purchases to study her again.

Irena's quiet plea, "Please, Mr. Swede, Cook needs to prepare dinner," prompted him to continue what he was doing while he questioned her.

"Why would you go to America?"

Irena hesitated then plunged on. "My aunt has arranged for me to marry a Norwegian man in—Minn-e-sota." She stumbled over the word. "She's sent me some money for passage, but I know nothing about ships and such. Can you help me?"

Once again the Swede was forced to stop what he was doing, and Irena wondered what he might be thinking.

"Listen, I'll do some checking for you, and you come see me tomorrow or when you can get some free time, and we'll talk then. Any idea how much money you have for passage?"

Irena breathed a sigh of relief and quoted him the sum her aunt had sent her. She was startled when he frowned. "It is not enough? I have a bit of my own as well."

"No, don't worry," he cautioned when he saw her face. "Just come back as soon as you can and we'll talk."

Irena thanked him and hurried away with her purchases to the other vendors.

The Swede watched her progress through the market place while an idea grew in his mind.

His son wanted him to come to America and live with him and his wife on their homestead in the Dakotas. Always before when he asked, Swede had thought it impossible—not that he was too old, but more that he didn't want to get in their way; but maybe… The thought of seeing his son again and maybe someday his grandchildren was very appealing. He could go to the States and help the girl as well. After all, how could a little thing like her survive on her own? He wondered if she was even old enough to get married.

Chapter 3

Grandville

"Oh, come on, Ty! It would be so much fun!"

Tyler Newly felt like he was being ganged up on. His wife, Jadyne, and his sister, Lucy Riley, were pleading their cause to him while Lucy's husband, Buck, watched on in amusement.

"It's their twenty-fifth anniversary, Ty, we've got to do something special."

"It's *all* their anniversaries. Twenty-five years ago the mail-order brides came to Sand Creek. We've just got to have a celebration for them." Lucy added to Jade's plea.

Tyler scratched his chin while he considered the idea. "What do you think, Buck?"

"I'm all for it." Buck held his six-month-old daughter in his arms while they visited in the Newlys' lovely home overlooking the valley. Eddie, the Newlys' four-year-old son, was busy pushing toys around on the floor, and their nine-month-old baby, Pamela, lay sleeping in the parlor off the sitting room.

Lucy smiled gratefully at her husband then turned to her brother again. "The way Jade and I have it figured is that there are still twelve couples in Sand Creek we could honor; Roy and Nola Hill moved back east several years ago, but we could send them an invitation. We could have a huge meal and invite everyone in Sand Creek to it, but wouldn't it be fun to keep it as a surprise?"

"I could bake the cake!" Jade exclaimed. "And all the ladies in Grandville would be glad to furnish food and baked goods. And—"

"Whoa!" Tyler stopped the excited planning. "I have a question. Where will this shindig be held? And if it's going to be a surprise, how are you going to get everyone to it?"

"*Where* is a problem," admitted Jade. "If we have it in Sand Creek, we have to haul all the food there and it's a two-day trip. It would be easier to hold it here in Grandville, and we could do it at the hotel, right?" she questioned Buck and Lucy.

"Well, we could set up in the hotel," Buck suggested, "but we would have to set tables up outside too for that many people."

"Okay," said Tyler, "that solves the *where*, but, again, how would you get twelve couples and their families and friends to travel two days to Grandville without telling them the reason?"

The foursome sat and looked at each other while ideas were considered and discarded one by one in their minds. Finally Lucy spoke. "What we need is a wedding that they would want to attend."

"A wedding?"

"Whose?"

Lucy laughed. "I don't know whose wedding. I'm just saying that an event like a wedding would bring people together and all dressed up to boot." She grinned at her own cleverness. "Now all we have to do is find someone who wants to get married. Is Rex courting anyone yet?"

Chapter 4

Sand Creek

Rex Newly sat astride his horse looking over the land he and his father had discussed the night before—two hundred acres bordering the Newly and Trent homesteads, beautiful land, with plenty of room for horses, cattle, and the crops to feed them. His eyes roamed over the area, but he really didn't need this perusal to make up his mind. He knew the area well, having lived nearby it all his life. He'd hunted it and fished in the lake beside it and ridden through it many a time. And now it could be his.

Rex got down and dropped his horse's reins, letting it graze while he sat down on a fallen tree to think and pray. Fifth of the Newlys' six children, Rex was quiet and stayed in the background during family gatherings and social events. Maybe having three older sisters had something to do with it. Sometimes it felt like he had four mothers instead of one.

His older siblings had often bossed him about, and he'd usually put up with it without complaint. Occasionally he got annoyed, but he learned to just go about his business and get his work done and generally they all got along pretty well. Maybe if he had been closer to Tyler, his older brother, he'd have learned to put his sisters in their place once in a while with his brother's backing.

Tyler was a leader, a doer. He didn't usually take orders, he gave them; Rex had always been on the receiving end. And Tyler had been out on his own starting a new settlement when Rex was just sixteen and still at home. Rex hadn't seen much of his older brother in the last several years.

Then there was Abel, his younger brother. Abel had handled his older sisters in a much different manner than Rex. Abel was their favorite, the baby of the family. Rex smiled as he shook his head. Abel could get away with anything. He was a tease, a constant joker, but despite that, he made life pleasant for all of them. Rex still couldn't believe Abel was going away for two years for more schooling. He had thought Abel hated school with all his wisecracks about it, but it turned out that Abel had jumped at the chance to study medicine in Boston, where their sister Emma had connections in the city through her in-laws.

Rex got up and gave a short whistle to his horse to follow him as he walked down one of the deer trails on the property. It was going to be different without Abel around the place. Maybe this was the time for Rex to start on a house of his own on this property. He discussed it with his parents. His mom, Sky, didn't like it much, but she knew it was time for Rex to get out on his own.

There were things they hadn't discussed too. Rex knew they wondered if he was interested in getting married. A lot of decisions would be made for him if he were. Then he would build a house right away, and his mom wouldn't worry about taking care of him. Rex smiled at the thought. His mom thought his getting married would take care of things, but he felt nowhere near being ready for the responsibilities of a wife at this point in his life.

There *was* Bernadette Nolan.

Rex grinned. She was as talkative and vivacious as her Irish mother. Rex had never gone calling on her, but when he was around her at church or in town, he never had to wonder what to say or do. She did all the talking, and he enjoyed listening to her.

And she liked him.

He could tell.

He could tell from the secretive looks she sent his way and the appealing smiles she gave him. It made him hot and uncomfortable when she did that. Rex's sister Dorcas was married to Cavan Nolan, Bernadette's cousin. They had a son now named Leon, and once Bernadette had told Rex, "You're Leon's uncle and I'm practically his aunt. Maybe someday I really will be his aunt." She had fluttered her eyes at him and walked away with a giggle.

Rex was astounded at her bold suggestion, but it made him think about it. *Maybe in a couple of years...*

He let that thought dangle in his mind a few moments before he shook free of his wayward thoughts and got back to the problem at hand. He'd buy the land. It was a sweet deal, really. He'd be near enough to his folks to continue to help his dad with the ranch, and he'd be able to start developing his own place. He had a few ideas to discuss with his father yet. What he'd like to do is keep all the horses at his folks' ranch and start some dairy cattle on his property. He'd been helping out at farms around Sand Creek since he was a boy, so he knew he could start a good dairy and beef business of his own.

He had some money to get started and could use some of his mother's inheritance money too. Maybe he'd go to Grandville and see Palmer Granville at the bank for his advice. And there was that Norwegian family near Grandville—Jensons, he thought. They had a start on some dairy cattle. Maybe he could buy some from them or at least get some advice from them.

Although he had been praying about these decisions for several months now, Rex turned to the Lord again for guidance.

"Lord God, things seem to be falling into place," he prayed. "But if I've somehow gotten off on the wrong track, please steer me right again. I pray that you'll keep opening and shutting doors along the way to direct my paths."

It was with a peaceful heart that Rex rode his horse back home a while later.

Chapter 5

New York

Irena and Swede pushed their way through the crowds of noisy, smelly people to the immigration line directly off the ship in New York Harbor. Swede saw the pensive expression on his traveling companion's face and asked, "What's wrong, Irena?"

She shrugged, and her disappointment showed as she pointed to the rows and rows of buildings in the city. "It's just like London. I guess I thought it would be different—cleaner." She wrinkled her nose at the offending odors around her.

Swede chuckled and patted her arm in a fatherly gesture. "This is a city, Irena, and aren't all cities alike? People, noises, smells, buildings, and garbage! It's not like this where we're going, child. You'll see."

Irena nodded, grateful for his encouraging words. How she would have ever managed this trip on her own was beyond her! What could her aunt have been thinking? In the first place, the Jensons had not sent nearly enough money for her passage, let alone for the trains that Swede told her they would need to take to Minnesota. She was shocked when he told her his plan to go along with her and see her safely in the care of the Jensons before going on to the Dakotas where his son was. No one had ever done anything for her before in her entire life.

Swede had taken care of everything. After getting the information about ships going to America and passage fares, Swede had promptly sold his meat business and begun making arrangements for the two of them. Knowing that Irena's passage money and her meager wages from the past six years were not going to be enough, he inquired and found a family willing to pay half her fare if she watched after their children on the journey. Irena had been very pleased, loving children as she did, but she was also very nervous about meeting her employers.

"What if they don't want me taking care of their children after they meet me?"

Swede didn't understand her concern. "Why wouldn't they?"

Her face, flushed with embarrassment, Irena motioned with her hands for him to take a good look at her. "I'm plain, I'm poor, and I'm not well educated. I'm not exactly governess material."

Swede brushed aside her concerns. "The family needs someone to watch their children, not be a governess to them. You'll do fine, Irena girl. God will make a way."

Irena glanced sharply at the older man. More than once he had mentioned God while talking to her, and she was curious. No one had ever talked about God in the Torkelson family. She had only heard a preacher once in her life and that was when one of her aunt's babies had died shortly after birth and a funeral had been put together in haste.

Strange words were spoken over the small wooden box, and Irena had watched the proceedings with a mixture of awe and confusion. Her heart had ached for the lifeless little body being put into the cold earth but had also been somewhat comforted by the preacher's reassurance that the little girl was now being held in God's arms.

She shook the memory from her mind as Swede led her to stand before two elegantly dressed people. They were in front of one of London's finer hotels where the family was staying until their departure. The children were not with them.

Swede introduced Irena to Mr. and Mrs. Foster. The couple didn't speak immediately as they looked her over, and Irena wanted to cringe when she saw the distasteful expression on their faces, but she lifted her chin higher while they continued their appraisal.

"She's just a child herself," Mr. Foster spoke to his wife in concern, but Mrs. Foster looked at Irena more closely.

"How old are you, Miss Aarestad?"

"I'm eighteen, almost nineteen, madam." Irena was proud that not a quiver was evident in her voice although her whole being seemed to shake.

Their looks were doubtful, but the Fosters peppered her with more questions. They seemed pleased to hear of her experience taking care of children, and it was Mrs. Foster who gave the first sign of accepting her.

Arrangements and instructions were given rapidly after that, and before Irena knew it, she was saying good-bye to the household staff at the Cavendish home. There was little to no emotion involved other than Cook's warning that she'd be sorry about going into that "wild American country." She had already been replaced by a new girl, and her absence would practically go unnoticed. It hurt Irena less to leave her London employment than it had the Torkelson farm. Her heart hadn't been involved here as it had with the children. Still—it had been her home for six years.

The ship's voyage had been a somewhat pleasant surprise to Irena. Instead of the cramped quarters she had expected with the other poor immigrants, she shared sleeping quarters with the Foster's three children and had a bunk completely to herself. She was amazed at the whining and complaining of the children and the Fosters themselves over their cramped space, the rocking motion of the ship, the heat, the cold, or what they considered poor food. Irena couldn't believe that anyone would complain about their conditions—they were better than she had ever known.

The Fosters certainly could not complain about her care of the children. Irena spent hours entertaining them, taking them for walks when it was allowed, reading to them, singing to them, and even acting comically for them. The staff from the Cavendish home would not have known that this animated, funny girl was the quiet, unassuming, hard-working scullery maid who slept in the little room off the kitchen.

Irena's love for children had been her salvation when at only seven years of age her parents had been taken from her and she had been thrust into a home with three little ones who needed her care. The simple hug around her neck when she picked up the two-year-old had melted the cold brick in her chest, and the trusting looks and unconditional love the children showed her provided her with an outlet for her emotions, and she threw her whole being into their care and happiness.

Dagne Torkelson never knew the treasure she had in her young niece, her sister's daughter. As the babies kept arriving, Dagne kept giving them into Irena's capable, young hands, and she went about the business of running her home and feeding her growing brood. Irena's heart had been torn when she was sent away from the Torkelson children, and she wondered daily how they were and how the new baby was and if there had been more.

Swede earned part of his passage fare by helping in the cook's galley. His skill as a butcher was welcomed, but he also helped with washing dishes and cleaning the galley. He and Irena rarely saw each other on the voyage, but once Swede had seen Irena on deck with the Fosters' children, and he had been utterly amazed at the change in her as she talked and laughed with them. True, his conversations with her had been few and brief and almost always in a business way, but somehow he had never pictured her with a smile on her face or a twinkle in her eye as he saw her then. *Why, she's a pretty little thing!* he thought in astonishment.

It had been very hard for Irena to say good-bye to the Fosters' children at the end of their voyage, but she steeled her heart against the pain. She knew it would come, but it still hurt.

She had been absolutely shocked when Mr. Foster had pressed some bills into her hand and told her she had "well earned it" and even more so when Mrs. Foster had given her a brief hug and told her how much she appreciated all the extra things she had done for the children. She stood speechless beside Swede as the family moved away from her and could barely lift her hand in a wave when the children turned to wave at her.

"They liked you a lot."

Irena turned her amazed eyes on Swede. "He gave me extra money," she said in disbelief as she held it out to him. "Here, you take it."

Swede hesitated and then took the money to add to their dwindling supply. "It should rightfully be just yours, Irena, but I have to admit that it will come in handy for the rest of the journey. We need to buy some food for the trains, and we'll barely have enough for fares as it is."

"You must keep track of what I will owe you," Irena insisted. This was still a sore point between them. Irena's money wasn't sufficient to get her all the way to Minnesota, Swede knew, so he had planned to help her with what little was left of his own money. Irena was too sharp, though, and had found out. Insisting on paying her full way, she had almost backed out of the trip, but Swede had convinced her to go along with his plan now, as fares were only sure to increase and her wages as scullery maid would never keep up.

Irena didn't have much in this world, but what she did have was hers; she owed no one. To be indebted was very humbling for her, and Swede was well aware of that.

What kind of husband is she getting if he can't even send her enough money to get to America, let alone travel over half the country? Swede had pondered that thought in his mind several times on their journey. Sometimes he had even wondered why Irena was willing to go, but it hadn't taken him long to realize that Irena had never really been given choices in her young life. She seemed to know nothing but subservience.

It was Swede's hope that they could catch a train headed west immediately so as to avoid lodging costs for even one night in the city. They could sleep on the trains, he told her, although they would have seats that only the lowest fares would allow. No berths for them.

His fifty-four years were showing on his face as he and Irena plodded along the back streets, taking the directions from the men at the docks. Fortunately, neither of them had much to carry. Irena's possessions were few and fit in the beat-up carpetbag he had found for her. His filled a larger case that he easily carried in one hand. They would need some kind of basket for food supplies, he thought.

He glanced down at the young girl beside him. She hardly seemed weary at all; she even seemed more rested than she ever had back in London. He wondered then how bad her life had been and if that was why she was willing to leave. He sighed wearily. He hoped that sometime on their journey they would finally have a chance to talk. There was so much about her that he wanted to know, and he felt a special burden for her as if God was telling him that this child needed his attention.

Chapter 6

Grandville

"You look especially beautiful today, Mrs. Trent." Michael Trent flirted with his wife, helping her into their buggy with one hand while with the other he held their newest son, Millard.

Mallory smiled sweetly at her husband and thanked him politely, albeit with a twinkle in her eye and a look of a promise for later as she took their son from him. It still amazed Michael how his wife had transformed into such a lady. Growing up together, Michael had only seen Mallory as a tomboy who could out-ride, out-shoot, and out-hunt him and her brothers. But he loved her anyway, and when she was dressed up and using her feminine charms on him, he was completely lost.

He took a moment to check on Marcy and Martin in the back of the buggy before he climbed up beside Mallory. "All set?"

At her nod, he called to the horse and flicked the reins, and they started off for church. "It was nice of Buck and Lucy to want us to come to lunch after church. It will give me more time to gaze at my beautiful wife in her Sunday finery."

Mallory thoroughly enjoyed the attention she was receiving, but a thought occurred to her. "Mike, did you mind me wearing my buckskins yesterday?" Michael had watched the kids for her while she went out for a long ride.

Michael heard the concern in her question and immediately reassured her. "Not at all, sweetheart. If you'll recall, I found you very attractive in them." He grinned when she blushed and looked away. Indeed, when she returned from her ride with her hair flying in the wind and her cheeks flushed with exhilaration, Michael had taken one look at her and had promptly put the children down for their naps.

"I love you, Mal, no matter what you're wearing, but I have to admit that there's something about seeing you in your Sunday best that gets me right here." He placed his hand over his heart. "Don't get me wrong, you're beautiful in whatever you wear. Why, I'd love you if you weren't wearing anything!"

He said, "Ouch!" as his wife slugged him.

Then Mallory sat back to enjoy the ride to church with a satisfied look on her face.

Lunch at the Rileys' hotel was a pleasant time. Michael and Mallory were pleased to see Tyler and Jade and their children, as well as Buck and Lucy and their daughter, Molly. They sat at one table in the hotel dining room while a few customers filled the others. On Sundays, Buck and Lucy served a light lunch but a larger supper for their guests. That way they didn't feel so rushed after the Sunday service to prepare a huge meal.

After they had eaten their roast beef sandwiches, potato salad, pickled beets, dill pickles, and applesauce, they returned to Buck and Lucy's home, an addition right off of the lobby of the hotel. Clean-up from the meal was taken care of by Cora Tunelle, a neighbor and friend who had worked for the Rileys since they opened the hotel, and Mattie Morrison, a girl they had recently hired.

Lucy served coffee and chocolate cake in the parlor as soon as the little children had been put in the bedrooms for naps.

Mallory had been watching Lucy and Jade, and as Jade reached for a paper, pen and ink, she asked, "So what's up? You two are plotting something."

Buck laughed at his sister's expression. "We could never get away with anything around you, Mal. You better tell her quickly, Lucy, before she explodes with curiosity."

"Maybe us men folk better get out of the way while you ladies start your planning." Tyler made to rise, but Jade pushed his shoulder back into the chair.

"You stay put, Tyler Newly. This involves your parents too."

"What's going on?" Michael questioned.

Jade's eyes sparkled with excitement as she turned to Michael and Mallory. "In September it will have been twenty-five years since the mail-order brides arrived in Sand Creek, and we want to hold a twenty-fifth wedding anniversary celebration for all of them."

A moment passed as this news sunk in. Then Mallory spoke, "What a great idea!" Michael nodded his head in agreement.

"Now tell them about the complications," Tyler suggested dryly.

Both Lucy and Jade gave him a dirty look. "We want it to be a surprise party, is all," Lucy explained. "And we need help figuring out how to do that. Plus, we want to include everyone that we can in the planning so that no one feels left out."

"That means we'll have to put together some ideas and circulate them without the twelve couples knowing what's going on," Jade explained.

"We'd like to do it here in Grandville," Buck put in, "so we could use the hotel and prepare the food right here. If we did it in Sand Creek, we'd have a two-day trip to carry everything."

Michael and Mallory digested this news; then Michael asked the inevitable. "How would you get everyone to come to Grandville if it's a surprise?"

Tyler chuckled. "Lucy thinks someone needs to get married so everyone will come all dressed up."

"Wouldn't that be great? We could have a photographer ready to take pictures and everything," Lucy exclaimed.

"A wedding? Is there someone you have in mind, Lucy?" her cousin Michael asked.

Tyler chuckled again. "My sister thinks we should see if Rex is courting anyone."

A couple of days later, the women of Grandville gathered at the hotel where Lucy, Jade, and Mallory presented them with the suggestion for an anniversary surprise party.

"Who are all the couples again?" Cora Tunelle asked. "I mean, I know who most of them are, but in the four years I've been here, I've only been to Sand Creek twice and that was to visit Ray's folks. I wish we could see them more often. I do want Minnie to know her grandparents better and this baby too." She patted her swollen front. "They are the only grandparents our children will have."

"It *is* hard being away from our folks," agreed Lucy, who had called the meeting together at the hotel. All the women who were related to one of the original Sand Creek couples were invited, and even Leigh Trent and Melody Riley from the stagecoach way station had been able to get away for a few days to join them. The husbands had readily agreed to let the ladies begin the planning without them. Lucy employed Mattie Morrison and her sister, Grace, to watch the many children while the ladies discussed their plans.

"Let's see," Jade began. "There's Russ and Sky Newly—that's Tyler and Lucy's folks."

"And mine, don't forget," Emma Chappell chipped in. Emma and the twins had made a special trip on the stage from Norris to help with the anniversary planning. "I wish Dorcas and my other brothers could be part of the planning too," she added.

"I know!" Lucy agreed. "But the best we can do is make some plans and then write to the others to see what they think. We're going to run out of time if we don't make some things definite soon."

"You're right." Emma nodded. "So there are my folks." She wrote that down. "Who's next?"

"There's Evan and Ella Trent." Jade read from her list. "Evan is Sky Newly's twin brother," she reminded the ladies. "Next are the Rileys, Hank and Randi."

Jade waited while the others wrote down the names. "Good." She checked the paper in front of her. "Next we have Taylor and Violet Gray."

The ladies all turned to Philippa, who shrugged and said, "I hope we can find a good reason for them to come. My mother isn't very sociable and hasn't been very nice to the Sand Creek ladies." Philippa sounded apologetic, and the others knew it was because she had been the same way with them until she started walking with the Lord about six months ago.

Philippa and Ralph's marriage had been on the brink of disaster. Then, being made aware of her sinful condition and accepting God's forgiveness, she became a changed woman and their marriage had been restored.

In fact, sometimes the other ladies teased her about acting like a newlywed again.

"Don't worry," Emma advised her friend. "The Lord will provide a good reason for your mother to want to come."

Philippa smiled. "I believe he can, Emma, but somehow I doubt Mother would travel here just for someone's wedding. She doesn't like anyone enough to do that."

"We'll pray with you that your mother and all the others will be convinced to come to Grandville," Lucy encouraged her. "But one thing at a time. Who's next, Jade?" She was prepared to write the next information down.

"Bert and Gertie Davies," Jade announced. "Then we have George and Janet Spencer." Jade paused while everyone wrote. "Their son Malachi is still at home too."

"Has he courted anyone yet?" asked Philippa. "I just wondered. After all, he is twenty-three now, and we're looking for a wedding." She grinned.

"I don't think he's seeing anyone," Lucy hesitated, not wanting to gossip. "He seems awfully bashful." She glanced at Jade to continue.

Jade understood and moved on. "Then there's Duke and Angelina Tunelle." She smiled at Philippa and Cora, because these were their in-laws. "And Jasper and Martha Riggs."

"I wouldn't be at all surprised if Clayton didn't marry soon. He's courting a new girl in Sand Creek," Pearl Riggs said of her husband's brother.

"But we need the wedding to be here in Grandville," Lucy pointed out then reddened as she realized what she said. She ducked her head.

"Okay." Jade took a deep breath. "Then next are the Nolan brothers and the O'Donnell sisters." She smiled along with the others. "Jonas and Bridget Nolan and Harry and Gretchen Nolan."

The ladies were busy writing when Pearl asked Cora, "Your cousin, what was her name—Winnie? I thought she and Rooney Nolan would have paired off."

Cora sighed. "Winnie appreciated Rooney's attentions, but she was determined to get back to *civilized* life after she saw that I was staying here in Grandville. She's married now and back in Boston."

"Is Rooney seeing anyone?" someone asked.

"How about Bernadette?"

"Have you noticed how pretty Mattie Morrison is?" said another as she indicated the girl watching the children in the other room. "One of the young men in the area is sure to snatch her up soon."

Lucy realized that her wedding idea had started speculation and gossip about all the single men and women in the area and that it was her fault. She had to put a stop to it.

"Ladies, I'm sorry. It was my suggestion that a wedding would be the perfect excuse to get everyone together for this party, but I can see now that it was a mistake to suggest it. We have no business discussing everyone's romantic lives, do we? I think we better find another solution to that problem and move on with the business at hand, shall we?" She looked imploringly to Jade once again.

"Let's see. Next is Clyde and Belle Moore, who have no children. Mr. Moore is still Sand Creek's blacksmith. And then there's Gerald and Bertha Nessel. Mr. Nessel is the barber in Sand Creek, and they have no children either. And the last couple is Roy and Nola Hill, but they moved away several years ago. And that's all I have on my list. Anything we should add?"

Lucy waited, but when no one spoke, she said, "As you can see, with family and friends we could have over a hundred people at the party. Next we need to discuss accommodations, food, and we still have to figure out how to get them all here."

Chapter 7

Train

Irena watched out the window as the sun began to rise and lighten the countryside around her. Her days and nights were all confused, and her body did not seem to know what time it was anymore. She had slept for a little while when she and Swede first got on the train, but not until after she had calmed her quaking at the speed with which they were moving. She gripped the seat with both hands for fear of flying off when the train lurched forward and began to pick up speed. She was somewhat comforted to see that Swede was experiencing much of the same reactions.

Swede still slept, and Irena was glad, because he seemed so exhausted. She was relieved to feel as rested as she did, because now, at last, she could let her mind think of what was to come. She had put the thoughts of marriage to Nels Jenson away, back in a corner of her mind, and shut the door firmly on them. There had been too many other thoughts to deal with first in just preparing for the journey. Then there had been the ship and the children to care for, then food and transportation west. She hadn't stopped, not once, and opened that door to her thoughts, though she heard a persistent knocking in her mind as if the thoughts were requesting release.

Nels Jenson. What would marriage be like? Irena barely remembered her parents. She could recall a small house and being with her mother. Her father she saw only briefly in the evening before being tucked into bed. She knew they had loved each other. She remembered seeing them embrace and hearing laughter. She felt that they had loved her too.

She shifted her position a little, careful not to disturb the man sleeping on the seat beside her. She wrinkled her brow, trying to remember if she had ever seen affection between her aunt and uncle. Her aunt was always working in the house and cooking, and Irena only saw her uncle at mealtimes where he wolfed down his food without saying a word to her aunt or the children.

They had a baby nearly every year that Irena lived with them, and they already had three children when she came. Irena had been on a farm long enough to know where the babies came from and had even been called upon to help her aunt during deliveries, but much of it was still a mystery to her.

Other than that, she had only glimpses of married couples when she went to market. Sometimes she heard angry words spoken between a man and woman;

occasionally she saw special looks pass between others. She was very confused about marriage and what was going to be expected of her.

Sometimes one of the young men who provided outside help at the Cavendish house would try to catch Constance's attention. Irena recalled watching with curiosity the looks that would pass between them. No one had ever looked at her in that way, and she had to confront the fact that she did not seem to appeal to men. Not that she'd ever cared, but it was worrying her now as she faced the idea of marriage.

What if Nels Jenson didn't want her after he saw her? What would happen to her then? Or what if he did decide to marry her? She couldn't decide which she preferred. She was fearful of marriage and what would be expected of her, but she was also fearful of being left alone in a strange country with no money.

She heard Swede stir beside her and tucked her thoughts away, knowing that soon they would have to be faced again. The older man rubbed at his face and whiskers and winced in pain as he began moving his stiff arms and legs.

"How long have you been awake, Irena?"

"I watched the sunrise."

He nodded and then stared, fascinated, out the window. "Have you ever seen so much land?" His voice was dreamy. "It's just like my son said, but I hardly believed it could be true. He says he has acres and acres of land, plenty of room for me to have my own little place on a corner of it. Ah, this is grand, Irena. I'm so glad you needed to get to America, or I'd never have made it myself. 'Thank you, Lord, for this blessing.'"

"Why did you say that?"

Swede pulled his eyes away from the scenery and looked at her. "Say what, child?"

"'Thank you, Lord.' Why did you say that?"

Irena saw astonishment cross her traveling companion's features.

"I'm speaking to God, Irena. Have you never heard of God, the Creator of us all?"

Irena was not used to conversation, having rarely been asked anything, just having directions and orders barked at her. She took her time in speaking, evidence that most of her thoughts went on in her head and she only spoke out loud a few of them.

"God is in church, right? How can you talk to him here on a train?"

Irena was unaware of the silent prayer Swede uttered to his heavenly father as he reached for his bag and pulled out a well-worn book.

"This is God's book to us, called the Bible. In here is the whole story of God and also the story of you, Irena, and what God wants you to do."

Irena was surprised. "Me? I'm in there too?"

"Well, all of us are, child. Here let me tell you the story from the beginning, and you stop and ask me any questions you like."

Miles clicked by on the rails as the train raced them to their destination, but the two on the train hardly realized it as they talked on and on, starting in Genesis with the wonderful creation of mankind and working their way through the patriarchs of the Old Testament and the prophecy of the Messiah, the birth of the Lord Jesus Christ, his life, his miracles, and then his death; and on to the salvation of Saul later named Paul and the special revelation of the Mystery God dispensed to him to share with Jew and Gentile alike that all can be saved from sin by grace apart from any work.

It was nearly dark again, and they were having trouble seeing the words in the Bible, but Swede knew so many of them by heart that he continued anyway. Irena had asked questions—mainly "Why?"—when she didn't understand something, unaware the older man was praying for wisdom in his answers, and now tears appeared in Irena's eyes. After a few moments, she voiced the question in her mind.

"But why did they kill him if he had done nothing wrong? Why did he have to die?"

"This was his whole purpose in coming, child. Remember the blood sacrifices we talked about in the Old Testament? These were all pictures of the final sacrifice for sin which would be the sinless, perfect Son of God. And he gave his life freely, Irena. He was a willing sacrifice because he loved you and me and all he had created, and he wanted to give us the opportunity to accept his sacrifice on our behalf so we could be with him for eternity."

Irena was not used to being emotional, so she was amazed when she brushed tears away from her eyes. "That's so sad."

"It is sad," Swede agreed as he closed the book, "but there's a happy ending, child."

She looked at him in expectation.

"Remember I read to you that he didn't stay dead. Three days after they buried his body, he arose again. He talked with them, he showed them his wounds. Death couldn't hold God, Irena, and because he lives again, we can have life too—eternal life. Listen to what it says to us in Romans 10:9-10, and with confidence Swede quoted, "'That if thou shalt confess with thy mouth the Lord Jesus, and shalt believe in thine heart that God hath raised him from the dead, thou shalt be saved. For with the heart man believeth unto righteousness; and with the mouth confession is made unto salvation.'"

Swede watched her in the fading light. "You can have him as your savior, friend, and Lord too, Irena, just by believing that he did this wonderful thing for you and accepting it as his gift to you. If you could earn your way to heaven by doing good deeds and being a good person, Jesus would not have had to die. But you couldn't earn heaven because you are a sinner. Do you understand this, Irena?"

"I…I need to think."

This was what she had longed for all her life. Someone to love her the way she was without expectations. Swede made it sound so simple, so easy, but how could that be? Her life to this point consisted of earning others' approval, of being a servant to their demands. Did this Jesus not have demands of her as well?

He wanted to give her a gift? As far back as she could remember no one had given her a gift. The closest was the extra money the Fosters gave her after their voyage, but that was still something they thought she had earned.

A gift.

But why would God want her? Why would this Jesus give his life for her? She was nobody.

Irena felt no pressure from Swede to make her decision, yet she knew it was important to him, and she was beginning to accept the fact that Swede cared about her well-being. That, in itself, was new to her. She glanced at the older man sitting beside her and wondered why he would take so much time to explain this to her.

She rubbed her forehead as thoughts swirled through her mind. He said she could have a new life in Christ Jesus. This trip was the beginning of a new life for her, a new country, a new home, a husband. There was so much fear in her of the unknown, and Swede told her that with the Lord by her side, she'd never have to be alone again. She could take her fears to him.

She didn't understand the love that motivated God to offer her this gift, but she knew she desired it more than anything else.

A look of yearning crossed the young woman's face, and then a smile appeared, causing a transformation. "This is the most wonderful thing I have ever heard in my life, Mr. Swede. I *do* want to accept this gift and have a friend like Jesus with me always. How do I do it?"

A tear appeared in Swede's own eye at her eagerness. "I believe you already have, child. Though it's not necessary, you may want to pray and tell the Lord what you're thinking and tell him thank you too."

She paused. "How?"

"I'll show you." Swede began, and Irena watched as he closed his eyes and bowed his head. She bent her head forward but kept her eyes on him. "Father, Irena wants to be your child. She says she understands about your sacrifice for her sins and wants to accept your forgiveness. Help her, Father, to learn more and more about you so she can learn to please you with her life. In Jesus' name, Amen."

Irena was silent for only a moment, and a teardrop slid down her cheek when her small voice began. "Father—God—I believe in you. Swede told me about what you did for me, dying for my sins. Thank you. I'm so glad you're alive again. I want to be your child too, and I'm glad I can go to heaven now. Thank you. Amen."

She was hesitant to look up but then laughed out loud when Swede pulled her into a bear hug.

The next several days were tiring and exhilarating for both of them. Travel weary, they often lost track of the time or even the day, but they continued to study the Bible together, and Irena was thirsty for every lesson.

As they shared their lunch supplies from the basket, which they replenished whenever the train stopped or they had to switch trains, Irena brought up the subject of her marriage to Nels Jenson. As usual, she had thought through her words carefully before she spoke.

"You say that believers in Jesus shouldn't marry non-believers—that they would be *unequally yoked*. I don't know if Nels Jenson is a believer. What should I do?"

"Then you shouldn't marry him."

Irena was startled by his words, so Swede attempted to explain. "You have become like a daughter to me these past weeks, child, and the thought of you being committed to marriage with a man you don't even know bothers me."

"But..." She paused to think over her words. "He paid for me to come here."

"That doesn't mean he owns you, and you have to 'obey God rather than man' it says in the book of Acts. So my advice is that you don't agree to a marriage until you know if it's what God wants for you."

There were questions in her eyes, but she remained silent. She wasn't used to making decisions, and she wondered if she would be able to stand up for herself in the days ahead.

Chapter 8

Way Station—Grandville

Rex felt very satisfied with himself as he rode along but humbled also as he realized how God was blessing him. The papers had been signed and the land was officially his! He felt both the heady excitement of being a landowner and the heavy responsibility of seeing to it that he used this gift wisely for the Lord. He was on his way to Grandville to talk to Palmer Granville and get some advice about his plans for a dairy business. He would do most of his banking in Sand Creek, but Palmer was a lawyer and almost a relative, being Jade's stepfather, so Rex wanted to talk to him first. Besides, it was a good excuse to see some friends and relatives in the process.

He stopped for lunch at Dugan and Gabe's way station and had a great time with his cousin's children, Adele and Irene, and with Dugan and Melody's two kids, Jason and Janelle. The children seldom saw their uncle Rex, but they took to him with no trouble, especially since they knew he had a horse ranch. The older three pounced on him for horsey-rides and when he was worn out from that, he took a turn holding little Irene and cooing and talking baby talk to her. Melody and Leigh watched with amusement and delight, and his cousin Gabe couldn't help teasing him.

"When are you going to get married, Rex, and have some kids of your own?"

A speculative expression crossed the women's faces, and they gave each other a knowing look that wasn't lost on Rex, though it confused him.

"In God's good time, Gabe. Meanwhile I'll just enjoy rough housing with these rascals and then I'll give them back to you when they get crabby. I never know what to do when they start crying. You should have heard Leon the other day when Bernadette was holding him. He didn't settle down until Dorcas had him again. Babies must know their own mothers or something."

"Bernadette? Have you started calling on her, Rex?" Melody's question was asked in innocence, but Rex felt his answer was very important to her.

"No, she was just visiting Cavan and Dorcas the same time I was there is all." He left it at that. A short time later he got a fresh horse from Gabe to continue his ride to Grandville.

As he rode, Rex recalled the suspicious glances that had passed between the two women. *I wonder what those two are up to,* Rex thought. *Seems like they were hoping Bernadette and I were courting or something.* He pondered some more on the way Melody and Leigh had acted then shrugged it off.

He couldn't shrug off the feeling being around the children had given him, though. Rex loved his nieces and nephews, and being with them gave him a longing for children of his own.

Maybe you're trying to tell me that it is time, Lord, that I marry and start a family. He prayed silently as he rode along. He stopped his horse and just waited while the thought took hold in his mind.

Who, Lord? Is it Bernadette? he wondered. Rex was thoughtful as he continued his ride. He wasn't sure who the Lord had in mind for him, but perhaps he should reconsider his thoughts on getting started on a house when he got back to Sand Creek. He wanted to be ready for whatever the Lord had in store for him.

Rex bypassed the town of Grandville and rode straight to Tyler and Jade's beautiful log home. He stopped to admire the structure before riding up the hill and into the yard. Eddie heard his horse and came running from the back of the house.

"Mama! It's Uncle Rex! It's Uncle Rex!"

Jade swung open the door and hurried out with Pamela resting on her hip. She flung her free arm around her brother-in-law. "Rex, we didn't expect you until tomorrow. Didn't you stop at the way station?"

Rex laughed as he enjoyed her exuberant welcome while with one swift motion he swept his niece into one arm and lifted Eddie with his other arm. "I stopped for lunch, switched horses, and headed straight here. Is it a problem?"

"No, not at all. You just surprised me. Tyler will be home soon. He and Mike are busy filling a lumber order for some people south of town. They keep busy all the time, it seems, but I guess that's a good thing. Come on in. I'll get you something cold to drink, or would you rather have some coffee?"

"Whatever you have is fine." He looked at Eddie. "What would you like, Eddie, coffee or something cold?"

Eddie laughed, so Rex looked at the baby. "How about you, Pamela? Interested in some coffee?"

Eddie laughed uproariously at his uncle.

"Pamela and me don't drink coffee, Uncle Rex. You're silly."

"Then I guess it will have to be something cold," he informed Jade, "because Eddie and Pamela will have to join me."

They all trouped into the house together, and Jade watched as Rex cradled the baby gently while bouncing Eddie on his knee.

"You're great with children, Rex. You ought to have your own." The words had no sooner left her mouth than she saw a peculiar look cross Rex's face.

"Did I say something wrong?"

"That's not the first time I've heard that today," he admitted.

"Don't tell me. Melody and Leigh said it too, right?" Jade looked a little apprehensive, so Rex explained.

"They seemed very interested to know if I'm courting anyone."

"Oh no! Oh, Rex, I'm so sorry!"

"Why? What's the matter?"

Jade proceeded to tell him of the plans for the surprise anniversary party and Lucy's comment about needing a wedding.

"Lucy tried to backtrack and to warn about meddling in other people's affairs, but I'm afraid it was too late. Everyone started guessing who would be a good candidate for marriage. Lucy is going to be so upset when she hears this."

Rex laughed. "Don't let it worry you or her, Jade. No one is pushing me into a marriage before the Lord shows me I'm ready for it." He said it with such confidence that Jade couldn't help herself.

"*Are* you calling on someone?"

"*Jadyne Kathleen Crandall Newly!*"

Tyler's voice caused Jade to clasp her hand over her mouth, but merriment shone from her green eyes as she saw Rex laugh at her.

"Are you pestering my little brother with this wedding nonsense?" Tyler teased. He had walked in on the end of Jade and Rex's conversation, well within Rex's view but not Jade's.

"Stop sneaking up on people and scaring them half to death, Tyler!" Jade squealed as Tyler pulled her into his arms for an embrace. Rex felt something stir in his heart.

Rex had always felt content with his life. He often thought that if he had been with the men who started the town of Grandville, he would have opted not to get a mail-order bride. He wanted things to move at a slower pace, and he wanted to be very sure of each new step he took. That's why this land purchase was no surprise to his family. They all knew that he had studied the matter and prayed about it for a long time.

Now, his brother Tyler was a quick mover. Once Tyler decided on something, he went ahead and did it without wasting time on second thoughts. *And that's the way you made Ty, Lord.* Rex thought as he handed the baby over to her father for a cuddle.

Once, Sky Newly had said, "I dearly love all my children, but Rex was a little easier to raise than the others because he thought things through before he acted."

"So what brings you to Grandville?" Tyler's words interrupted Rex's musings. The telegram Rex sent had only said he was coming, not why.

"His horse brought him, Pa," Eddie informed his dad.

"That's right!" Tyler laughed.

"Well, not *my* horse, Eddie. I left mine with Gabe at the way station. Jason promised me he'd take good care of him for me, and Gabe lent me this horse."

Eddie's eyes lit up at the mention of his friend's name. "Can we go see Uncle Rex's horse, Pa?"

Tyler laughed again and pulled his son up on his knee. "Any time the way station, horses or Jason is mentioned, Eddie gets all fired up to go for a visit. We can't go for a while, Eddie." Tyler looked into his son's eyes. "But I promise we'll get to the way station for a visit sometime this summer, okay?"

Eddie reluctantly nodded, and Tyler gave him a squeeze. Then Tyler turned his attention back on his brother.

"I'm here for a couple of reasons," Rex explained while Jade passed out glasses of lemonade. "I bought the property between Pa's place and Trent's." He didn't have to wait long for his brother's response.

"I thought you would. It's a nice piece of ground, but we kind of hoped you might want to settle here in Grandville. We've got plenty of logging work for you. Mike and I could use the help, and we'd be able to pay well."

Rex grinned at his brother's words, but he shook his head. "Thanks for the offer, but I'm not a logger. I'm going to continue helping Pa on the horse ranch, and I'm planning to turn my land into a dairy farm—milk and beef."

Tyler didn't seem too surprised that Rex turned him down. Rex had always been a rancher, and Tyler knew he'd do well in farming too.

"I'm here to see your stepfather, Jade. I'm hoping Palmer can help me with some of the financial issues, and I also want to go to the Jenson farm west of town and see if he has any advice for me or maybe even some cattle to sell."

"Jenson…Jenson…isn't that the Norwegian family, Jade?" Tyler asked. At her nod, he said, "We don't see much of them in town except for their daily milk delivery to the store. How long have they been here?" he questioned his wife again.

"Let's see. Eddie was already walking, so I guess it's been a couple of years at least. I remember because Mr. Jenson—the father—had given Eddie a piece of candy from Tunelle's store. He was such a nice man. Too bad he passed away last year. It's just Mrs. Jenson and her son on the farm now, and he must be in his thirties, not married, really quiet. Lately they've been in town a lot, come to think of it. Buck said they sit out front of the hotel and watch for the stagecoach. I wonder if they're expecting someone."

The two men listened with amusement as Jade rattled off this list of information. She saw their looks and stopped in embarrassment.

"I'm sorry. I don't mean to gossip; it's just that, well, there aren't that many people in Grandville, and we all kind of keep track of each other and..." Her voice faded away.

"It's okay, Jade. I appreciate knowing a little about them," Rex assured her. "Can you give me directions to their place? I'll probably go there day after tomorrow."

Chapter 9

Grandville

As the stagecoach rumbled its way down the road, Irena could only stare and stare out the small window. The land was a fascinating mixture of farmland, woods, lakes, and rivers. How long had it been since she had last seen green grass? The Torkelson farm paled in comparison to the expanse of land she was now viewing.

She breathed deeply, enjoying the pine-scented air. Then she glanced shyly at her traveling companions to see if they noticed. Swede's head was nodding on his chest, and Irena sympathized with his weariness. He, too, had stared long and hard, drinking in the sights and sounds of the Minnesota woods until exhaustion had overtaken him. The others in the coach seemed bored. The men stared out the windows but with unseeing eyes, and the only other lady on board was rapidly weaving knitting needles in and out of the wool she pulled from the basket at her feet.

Irena stifled a yawn and once again wondered when her body would recover from the rigors of traveling. She heard the driver call to the horses and saw that buildings were now coming into view. She leaned toward the window again, completely mesmerized by the small town. She and Swede had stopped at many small towns along their journey but only to fill their basket again and then quickly re-board a train.

At Freesburg they found themselves at the end of the train route and had boarded the stage coach for the remainder of their travels. Irena had been delighted to see the children at the way station, but she had been too shy to speak to them. Mixed with her anxiety over finally arriving at their destination was relief, for their traveling money was all but gone.

Swede stirred beside her, and she smiled at him as he rubbed the sleep from his eyes and stroked his bearded chin. He grinned back at her.

"Looks like we're finally here, lass," he stated, and the finality of his words caused Irena's heart to pick up its pace. There was worry in her face, so he tried to distract her, at least until they were out of the coach and away from the scrutiny of the other travelers.

"Look at all that lumber." Swede pointed. "Every building and all the walkways are of wood. Quite a bit different from the stone and brick work in London, eh?"

Irena nodded and noticed some curious looks from the others, but no one had spoken for so long that they apparently didn't see a need to start now, and the silence continued until the coach came to a stop and someone opened the door. Irena and Swede allowed the others to exit before them, and Irena's mouth went dry as she took the hand extended to help her descend from the coach.

So this was Grandville. She moved out of Swede's way as he stepped down, and while they waited for their bags, Irena looked around her, taking in the sights, sounds, and smells of the little town. Her eyes wandered up and down the street where hitching posts and water troughs lined both sides. A boardwalk connected the stores and businesses and was wide enough for benches or chairs for those wanting to rest and visit as several people were doing.

She noticed a young boy come out of a building where the sign read "Tunelle's General Store," and he had a piece of peppermint candy sticking out of his mouth. She was thrilled when he smiled at her, and she responded with a pleased smile back at him. Behind him came a tall man she assumed was the boy's father. The man took the boy's hand to cross the street but quickly dropped it and wiped his hand on his pant leg. Irena hid a smile. Apparently the little boy's hand was a bit sticky.

As they headed in her direction, she turned shyly away from them and noticed for the first time that the coach had stopped in front of the hotel. The wide porch in front was bustling with activity as people were greeting the coach travelers and bags were being handed down to them. Wonderful food smells from within greeted her nose and caused her stomach to rumble. She and Swede had enjoyed a hot meal at the way station, the first in many days, but her stomach told her it was already time for another.

All the chairs and benches were filled with people who seemed to have nothing better to do than stare at the passengers of the coach. Irena dropped her gaze from their interested looks and turned aside to calm herself. She noticed a man leaning against the side of the hotel but who seemed to have little interest in the coach activities.

Instead, his attention was taken by a young woman who was shaking rugs in the alleyway between the buildings. Irena watched as the girl looked up and smiled at the man, and Irena saw a look pass between them, much the same as the look she had seen pass between Constance and her male admirers.

Irena looked away, not wanting to be caught staring, and her eyes locked with those of an older woman who was sitting stiffly on a bench in front of the hotel. The woman was tall and thin and was dressed all in black. She held herself ramrod still, and she was scowling at Irena.

Irena drew in a sharp breath when she saw the woman from the porch rise and point at her. She almost took a step back, but Swede turned to her at that moment.

"I'll put our bags inside the hotel for now, Irena, until we can find out where the Jensons live and decide what to do next." He rubbed his beard. "I'm afraid we're about out of money, but don't worry, child. I'll see about getting some work to pay for our lodging." He saw that she was about to protest, so he forestalled her. "Why don't you rest on the porch there while I look around? Be back soon." And he climbed the steps to the hotel.

Irena saw that the woman from the porch was headed her way, and something inside her made her want to flee. She turned aside and nearly knocked over the little boy with the peppermint stick. She reached for him before he could fall.

"Oh, I'm so sorry. Did I hurt you?" She held him by both his arms and smiled into his blue eyes.

"Eddie!" The man behind the child reached their side in a moment, and Irena saw the same blue in his eyes as in the little boy's. "I'm sorry. Did he bump into you?"

"No. I'm afraid I bumped him. I am sorry." She noticed a curious expression cross the man's face when she spoke.

"That's okay," Eddie told her. "Did you just come in the coach cuz that's Gabe driving and he's my dad's cousin and Adele and Irene's daddy, Jason and Janelle live at the way station too, and Jason is my friend, he has horses."

Irena was enchanted with the rapid-fire speech and shared confidences of the child. She knelt to his level and said, "I saw a little boy when I was at the way station, but I didn't know his name was Jason."

Eddie's eyes lit up, and he was about to tell his new friend more when the man with him spoke.

"Your accent—are you by any chance from England? Pardon me for being so forward, but you see, my mother was raised in England, and I haven't heard anyone but her speak quite like that."

Irena stood again and brushed down her wrinkled gray skirt. Speaking to children was one thing, but speaking to an adult man was quite another. She cleared her throat. "Yes, I'm from London."

"I'm Rex Newly." Rex swept off his hat. "And this here is Eddie. Welcome to Grandville and the United States."

"Thank you." Irena struggled with the nervous quiver in her voice. "I'm Irena Aarestad."

"I thought so." A voice beside her spoke, startling Irena. "You are late." The woman's words sounded forced, as if speaking English was difficult for her. Then the woman broke into Norwegian. "Nels and I have wasted every other day this week watching the stages. Why did you not telegram the date of your arrival?"

Irena's heart sank. The woman from the porch was Mrs. Jenson—tall, sturdy build, graying, but with a determined look in her eye. There was no friendliness in her manner, and it made Irena worry about what Nels was like.

Irena hadn't spoken Norwegian in years; it simply wasn't allowed in the Cavendish house in London. Her education in English had been swift, with little allowance for mistakes. But the words came back to her with ease, and she realized her thoughts had always been in her native tongue, and she had translated to English unconsciously.

"We had no money to telegram," she said.

"We? You are not alone? What do you mean you had no money? I sent Dagne Torkelson the exact amount necessary."

A tug at her skirt prevented Irena from a reply. She looked down at the boy named Eddie, glad of the respite while she gathered her thoughts.

"You talk funny," the boy stated, wide-eyed.

"Eddie!" Rex put a hand on the boy's shoulder. "Miss Aarestad is speaking in a different language. Will you excuse us? It was nice to meet you." Rex smiled at Irena and nodded to the older woman. Before they could move away, however, Eddie had one more question for Irena.

"Will you be in the new school? Miss Pike is going to be the teacher."

At Irena's puzzled look, Rex explained. "Eddie is very interested in the school starting, although he won't attend this year. Perhaps if you're staying in town, you'll be attending in the fall." With that he and Eddie moved on, and Irena was left with the realization that they both thought her much younger than her now nineteen years. Crimson flared in her cheeks as she turned back to find Mrs. Jenson's speculative appraisal of her.

"How old *are* you?"

Irena held her small frame erect. "I'm nineteen. I had my birthday on the voyage."

Mrs. Jenson nodded and took Irena's arm, leading her forward. "I've already spoken to the minister, so he's expecting us." They walked past the hotel, and the older woman motioned to the man still leaning against the building there. He moved to join them, and Irena was startled as Mrs. Jenson introduced her to her son Nels. This was the man who was so clearly interested in the woman shaking rugs!

Nels tipped his hat at Irena but barely looked at her. Irena saw that he was tall also like his mother, but other than that, there was nothing familiar about him.

They were still moving along the boardwalk when Irena suddenly realized what Mrs. Jenson had said. *She has already spoken to the minister!* Irena stopped, but it took a few more steps by the others before they noticed that she was no longer with them. They walked back to her, and Mrs. Jenson was frowning.

"We don't have all day. Nels has chores on the farm to attend to." She motioned for Irena to come with them.

"Where are we going?"

"To the minister, like I said. You and Nels need to get married so we can get back to the farm."

Irena clutched at the folds in her skirt, willing herself to have the boldness to speak. The thought of praying for help entered her mind briefly, but she wasn't accustomed to doing so and wasn't sure how to do it. Mrs. Jenson was becoming irritated, and though Nels appeared to be relaxed, Irena could see that his face was set as though he were steeling himself for what lie ahead. Surely he didn't wish to marry her. Not when his interest was so obviously in another!

"I just wondered if we could wait. I could stay in town until we—"

"Wait?" Mrs. Jenson folded her arms in front of her ample bosom and stared down at Irena. "I paid good money for a Norwegian wife for my son, and I expect to see him married today. You wouldn't be here unless you used that money, and I intend to see that you complete your end of the bargain. Now, come along."

Years of subservience and submission compelled Irena to move forward. It was true she was indebted to these people for some of her fare, and by coming to America she had agreed to the marriage. Her thoughts were confused as she was led inside a building and before a kind-looking man who was inside.

He was holding a book in his hands, and after a short conversation with Mrs. Jenson, Irena and Nels were led to stand in front of him. The man began speaking. Irena tried to listen to the words through the thunder of thoughts going on in her mind. Swede had told her not to be unequally yoked, and she knew that meant to not marry an unbeliever. How could she know if Nels was a believer or not? She hadn't even spoken to him.

Some familiar words brought her thoughts back to the man with the book. He was reading words that Swede had read to her from his Bible. For some reason that thought comforted her.

"Irena Aarestad, do you take this man…"

Irena looked up as her name was spoken and tried to follow what the man was saying. Confusion, weariness, and hunger gnawed at her, and she struggled to concentrate on his words. Mrs. Jenson tapped her on the back, and Irena turned to her.

"You say yes now," she whispered in Norwegian.

"Yes."

"And do you, Nels Jenson…"

Irena peered up at Nels beside her and heard his reply to the minister. She saw him turn to his mother, and Mrs. Jenson pulled a ring off her finger and handed it to her son. He held it out to Irena, and after a moment's hesitation she reached for it and held it in her palm. It was much too large for her small finger, she was sure, but the others were waiting, so she slipped it on and curled her fingers around it to prevent it from sliding off.

"I now pronounce you man and wife. Shall we pray?"

Irena bowed her head but didn't hear the words being spoken. Instead, she made her own plea to God. *I don't know how this happened, Lord God. I wanted to do what Swede said and wait until I knew Nels Jenson. I know he cares for another woman. What am I supposed to do now, Lord?*

A lingering silence made Irena aware that the others were again waiting for her. She raised her head and met the kind, concerned eyes of the minister.

"Our community is small but very friendly. If you ever need anything, you have only to ask. I'd like to invite all of you to our Sunday services here in Grandville. We'd enjoy having you worship with us."

Nels shook hands with the preacher and motioned for Irena to precede him out of the church. From the corner of her eye, Irena saw Mrs. Jenson hand the minister some money before she followed them out.

Irena felt she was in a fog as she walked with the Jensons back down the boardwalk toward the hotel. Nothing felt real, and she was so very tired.

"Where are your things?" Mrs. Jenson asked. "We need to get back to the farm."

"I—I don't know." Irena broke off her words as she saw Swede approaching, looking both relieved and concerned.

"Irena!" He took her hands in his, oblivious to the two people who stood beside her. "There you are, child. I'm sorry it took me so long, but I was with the hotel owner Buck Riley. He was showing me the horse corrals and giving me instructions. I can work there for our room and board until we get you settled. Supper is being served now, and then you can get a bath and some sleep in a real bed for a change." He was beaming, the weariness from the travel barely visible, and Irena could see how pleased he was with his arrangements. She didn't reply right away; she just looked at Swede until he realized that something was wrong.

"What—?"

"Irena is married to my son," Mrs. Jenson spoke up.

Swede looked at the tall woman and at Nels behind her then back to Irena, who was still watching him.

"You're married already?"

Irena nodded but still didn't speak.

"But why, Irena? I thought you were going to wait."

"She came to get married," Mrs. Jenson spoke harshly. "We have no time. You tell him," she instructed Irena in her broken English. "We wait in the wagon."

After they moved away, Irena finally spoke to Swede. "I wanted to wait, but Mrs. Jenson insisted. She said they sent all the money I needed. I wonder if Aunt Dagne kept some of it for herself." She rubbed at her forehead. "Anyway, I am so sorry, Swede. You've spent your own money to get me here, and I have no way to repay you yet."

Swede shook his head at her. "That's not important to me, Irena. What concerns me is what you've gotten yourself into. I still don't understand why you didn't tell them you wanted more time." He looked down at her bent head and sighed.

"You've been so used to taking orders all your life that I suppose I shouldn't be too surprised." He took a deep breath and looked at the two who were waiting impatiently in the wagon. "I'll stay in Grandville for a while and work because I need to earn some money for the rest of my trip but also because I want to make sure you're all right. If they mistreat you in any way, you must tell me. And I'll be praying for you, child. Remember, you'll never be alone again; the Lord will always be with you." He patted her arm. "I'll go for your bag now."

Irena stood still while Swede went into the hotel to collect her bag. People moved about her, and she was painfully aware of the impatient looks from Mrs. Jenson. A few moments later Swede returned. He held her bag in one hand and in the other, his Bible.

"I want you to have this, Irena. You know so little yet about the Lord, but you have a great thirst to know more. Read something every day, and what you don't understand, ask the Lord for the answers. He'll provide someone to help you."

Irena felt tears in her eyes at the gesture. She wanted to protest, but she knew Swede would insist, so she didn't.

"Thank you, Swede. And thank you for all you've done for me."

"This isn't good-bye. I'll be out to see how you're doing soon as I can afford to rent a wagon." He tilted his head toward the Jensons. "You best go. They seem impatient."

Irena surprised both of them by flinging her arms around the older man and giving him a brief, hard squeeze. Then she turned and walked away. As she approached the wagon, Nels jumped down and took her bag from her. He set it in the back then held out his hand to help her up.

Irena glanced at his face, but though his eyes were on her, they told her nothing of his thoughts. Mrs. Jenson was sitting in the middle of the wagon seat, so Irena sat on the edge, and Nels walked around the wagon and climbed up on the other side. As they drove out of the small town, Irena saw Rex Newly on horseback with Eddie held in front of him on the saddle. They waved at the wagon as it passed them.

Irena was prepared for a silent ride based on what she had seen of Nels and his mother so far, and she would have enjoyed some silence and time to think about what she had just done and what was ahead for her future, but the day's surprises weren't over yet.

"Nels has chores and the milking to do when we get to the farm." Mrs. Jenson spoke in Norwegian, and Irena was relieved to hear the impatience was no longer in her voice. The older woman took a long look at the small woman beside her. "You're hungry and I imagine tired, so we'll fix a cold supper tonight and get you right off to bed. Tomorrow we'll decide what duties we will share around the house. I'm sure Dagne taught you household skills."

Irena didn't respond immediately. She supposed she should have known that Mrs. Jenson would live in the same house as she and Nels, but as events were moving so quickly, she hadn't really considered it. She was somewhat relieved to know she wouldn't be left alone with this stranger who was now her husband. But at the same time she discovered that her dream of having her own home would not be fulfilled.

"I took care of my aunt's children, including the newborn babies, until I was twelve years old. Aunt never had me cook; she preferred to do that, but I cleaned the house and did laundry chores. In London I worked as a scullery maid."

Mrs. Jenson studied Irena with interest. "You have a love for children. I hear it in your voice. That is good. I expect grandchildren. As for the cooking, I can teach you that, and you can teach me to speak English better."

Nels shifted his position on the seat, and Irena kept her head down to hide her blazing cheeks. *Grandchildren!* She was saved from replying as they rolled into the drive that led to the farm. Irena noted the weathered wooden boards on both the house and the barn. No money for paint or no time? She hadn't expected the Jensons to be wealthy or poor, and it seemed they were neither. But what they had and what they offered her was a home, a place to call hers. Despite the circumstances that brought her here, she was thankful for a home at last.

Chapter 10

Jenson Farm

The thunder is what woke her, or at least Irena thought it was the thunder. There was a blinding flash of light then a few moments later another loud boom shook the house. Irena remained curled in the position she had been sleeping in while she tried to recall where she was. The many days and nights of travel had left her confused, but something felt different here. Something was very strange.

She turned in the bed just as the lightening pierced through the house again, and what she saw in that moment made her heart leap to her throat. She screamed and scrambled out of the bed. The man who had been lying in the bed beside her also jumped, and even though the thunder that followed the lightening was deafening, Irena distinctly heard a thud as his body hit the floor on the other side of the bed.

Irena heard a groan, then, "It's okay! I'm Nels Jenson, your husband."

Irena's hand flew to her mouth while she tried to quiet her pounding heart. "Oh! Oh, I'm sorry. I forgot where I was, and the storm woke me and…"

She heard Nels light a match, and her eyes followed the flame as he lit the lamp on the table beside the bed. She turned away from him as soon as she saw that he was dressed only in his undergarments, and she clutched at her nightgown in embarrassment.

"Nels!" A voice called from somewhere in the house. "Is there anything wrong? What happened?"

Irena heard Nels move to the doorway of the room and call down the stairs to his mother. "Everything is fine, Mother. Irena was frightened by the storm."

"Oh, for goodness' sakes. *Uffda!*" Irena could hear Mrs. Jenson's muttering fade away as the woman returned to her bed. Nels moved back to the bed and sat down with his back to Irena.

"Are you all right now?" he asked over his shoulder.

Irena nodded then realized he wasn't looking at her, so she said, "Yes, I'm sorry."

"We should get some sleep," was all he replied as he leaned forward to blow out the light. The room was dark for only a moment before lightening flashed through it again, and Irena saw that Nels was lying down and turned away from her. She slid beneath the covers but kept as close to the edge of the bed as she could.

Another boom of thunder rattled the window, and rain began to beat on it in earnest. Irena was terrified of storms. There had never been anyone to comfort her or reassure her that all would be well.

In the Torkelson family she had been the one the children ran to for comfort, and somehow she managed to quell their fears while hers remained. In the Cavendish home she had always endured the storms alone, quaking and quivering in her bed. As she lay now, trembling with fear and uncertainty, she felt Nels turn toward her, and she was amazed at how much more frightened she was of him than of the storm.

"Irena?"

Irena swallowed and whispered, "Yes?"

"There are only two beds in the house." And having said that, Nels turned back and said no more.

Only two beds in the house. In other words, thought Irena, *he had no choice but to sleep with me.*

Chapter 11

Jenson Farm

Irena dozed fitfully on and off for the rest of the night, and she was wide-awake when Nels rose. She kept her back toward him and lay so perfectly still that she was sure he was aware that she, too, was awake, though he said nothing.

As soon as Nels left the room, Irena got up and hastily dressed. Then she quietly made the bed and took stock of her surroundings more thoroughly than she had the night before.

Irena sat on the bed and ran her hand over the bright patchwork quilt—Mrs. Jenson's handiwork, no doubt. She spotted her traveling bag and decided she better get settled and get used to the fact that she was now married and shared a room and a bed with a man. It didn't seem to matter that neither of them appeared to want to be in this situation. The fact was, they were.

Irena hung up her only other work dress—gray and ugly like the one she was wearing—put away her undergarments in an empty drawer she found in the bureau, and then took Swede's Bible and returned to the bed again. She opened it to where she and Swede left off the last time he read to her and she re-read a few verses. Then she bowed her head and asked her new friend for help for the day ahead.

A noise downstairs made her head jerk up, and she listened carefully to sounds coming from the kitchen. Time she made an appearance, she guessed. She opened the door and tiptoed into the small hallway at the top of the stairs. Another door across from hers made her curious, so she stepped toward it and opened it for a peek. She was a little startled at what she found there.

A rocking chair and a baby's cradle were the only furnishings, but it was enough to convince Irena of her purpose in being brought to America to be married to Nels. A Norwegian wife to produce Norwegian grandchildren! She found that she was shaking, and she leaned against the doorway to settle herself. How had she gotten here? How had she even agreed to marry a man she didn't know?

Even as she questioned herself, Irena knew the answer. She had wanted an escape, an escape from being a servant. And she wanted a home, a place she could call hers. And while she stood with her eyes closed, breathing in the pine scent from the doorframe, she recalled a verse that Swede had read to her while his face glowed with joy: "Then we which are alive and remain shall be caught up together with them in the clouds, to meet the Lord in the air: and so shall we ever be with the Lord."

Her life changed on the trip to America, she knew. The things she had once thought so important were no longer what determined her happiness. Now she had Jesus as her savior to give her a home and to be her friend, and she knew that no matter where she was, she would always be in his hands.

Irena felt her heart calm, and she wrapped her arms around herself as if to hug the good feelings in closer. Now she felt ready to face what lie ahead, and as she heard another noise from the kitchen, she reminded herself that she may not have her own home or a husband who loved her, but she had the God who created her living inside her. What was there to fear?

The stairs creaked as Irena descended toward the kitchen, and when she reached the bottom, Mrs. Jenson turned from the stove. "You're up sooner than I expected, what with your being so tired last night and then being awake during the storm. You can help me finish breakfast and then we'll show you around the farm." While she was speaking, Mrs. Jenson examined Irena from head to toe with a critical eye. "Isn't that the dress you wore yesterday?"

Irena shook her head. "No, ma'am. But it is just like it. These are the only two dresses I have. It is all any scullery maid has."

Mrs. Jenson shook her head and muttered something, but when she spoke to Irena, her voice didn't hold the malice she was obviously feeling. "I sent Dagne Torkelson enough money for your trip and for necessities such as clothing." She indicated Irena's dress. "I was under the impression that you still lived in Norway with your aunt. I had no idea she had sent you away."

The younger woman didn't know what to say to this revelation, but after a moment's thought, she replied, "Aunt said she couldn't afford to feed me, and Ruby was old enough to do my chores, so she found me employment in London. The money she sent me for the trip was only enough to cover half of it. I used all my wages as scullery maid and worked on the voyage for the other part of my passage. I'm afraid I still owe Mr. Swede money for the rest."

When she saw Mrs. Jenson's scowl, she quickly added, "I do not expect the money from you. I will find a way to earn it and pay him back."

Mrs. Jenson went back to muttering and working at the stove. Over her shoulder she said, "The wash stand is out on the porch."

Irena found the path to the outhouse and returned with haste to wash and prepare to help with the morning chores. She heard noises from the barn and assumed that Nels was milking already. *Nels.* She paused while drying her hands on the rough cloth.

He hadn't touched her last night; for that she was grateful. But she was his wife now and they shared a house, a room, and a bed—eventually.... She let that thought linger a moment then pushed it aside. She didn't know much about being a wife, but she knew how to work. She wouldn't be a burden to the Jensons.

Irena saw that the dishes were stacked on the table when she returned inside the house. She arranged them for the three of them to have their breakfast. The smells from the stove were making her stomach rumble in anticipation, and she wondered what more she could do to help until it was time to eat.

She looked past the kitchen and saw a sitting room and a parlor and what appeared to be another doorway beyond that. Mrs. Jenson's room, no doubt, and right beneath the one Irena shared with Nels.

"Here comes Nels with the milk can now, so we can eat. You pour the coffee," Mrs. Jenson instructed her.

Irena moved to do as she was told, aware that Mrs. Jenson watched her closely. As she did most things, Irena moved quickly and efficiently then stood awaiting more instructions. Years of being a servant to others were evident in her actions, and her new mother-in-law nodded her approval.

Nels washed up outside then entered and sat down at the table without a word to either of them. Mrs. Jenson motioned for Irena to sit, and after setting the last of the food on the table, she joined them. Irena was surprised when they bowed their heads, but she bowed hers, and she was even more surprised when Nels began to pray. She had to listen carefully, for he spoke very softly, but it seemed to her that he was thanking God for the food. She was very pleased. Maybe the Jensons knew the Lord after all.

The food was delicious—hot oatmeal with fresh cream, eggs, bacon, and fried potatoes. The coffee was strong, but Irena liked it. She felt a little uncomfortable sitting at the table and eating with the Jensons. She had eaten alone for so many years that she wasn't sure if her manners were correct or not. Not that it seemed to matter to Nels; he never looked at her. Mrs. Jenson finished eating then spoke to her son.

"When do you leave for town? I have a few things I need today."

Nels took a drink from his coffee cup, and Irena wondered how he didn't burn himself. Hers was still so hot she could only sip at it.

"Soon as I hitch up and load the cans. Do you have any butter ready?"

"Yes. I'll get you a list, and Irena can clean up here."

They both stood, and Nels left the house without a backward glance. Irena began gathering the dishes and found a pot of water already hot on the stove so went right to work while Mrs. Jenson disappeared into her room. Irena was nearly done when her mother-in-law returned.

Mrs. Jenson appraised Irena critically again. "I think soft colors would look best on you, maybe blues and greens."

Irena was puzzled. "Ma'am?"

"There's a woman at the General Store—Mrs. Tunelle. She's very good at choosing fabric for me if I tell her about what I want. I'll have Nels drop this note off for her, and we'll see what she sends back with him. Then we can make you some presentable dresses to wear. Do you know how to sew, Irena?"

Irena found that she was staring at the older woman, and she had to force herself to answer, "No, ma'am."

"Well, we can work on it in the evenings when chores are done." She looked Irena up and down again. "You're not very big, are you? Have you ever driven a wagon?"

Again, Irena replied in the negative.

"*Uff-da.* There is much to teach you. Finish up here while I go speak to Nels, then I'll get started showing you around."

Irena stood still in the kitchen after Mrs. Jenson left. New clothes. She hadn't expected that. Maybe they were embarrassed by her appearance. She ran her hand down the rough gray cloth of her dress. Mrs. Jenson's original harshness seemed to have disappeared, but Irena still wasn't sure how her mother-in-law felt about her. Then she remembered the room upstairs, and her cheeks grew hot. *She wants to make me more attractive to her son.* The thought almost made Irena angry. How could Nels Jenson be interested in her when he was already drawn to that pretty girl in town?

But he's married to me now.

Irena pushed at the braids in the bun at the back of her head. She couldn't worry about that now. She had a kitchen to clean, and if there was one thing she knew how to do well, it was clean.

Chapter 12

Grandville

"No, it's true. Pastor Malcolm performed the ceremony yesterday."

"Well, Grandville is known for its mail-order brides. We shouldn't be too surprised."

"But this is different. At least it seems that way to me." Lucy tried to express her feelings to Jadyne, but a knock on the door connecting her home to the hotel drew her attention. "Excuse me," she said to her guest and went to see who it was.

"Hi, Lucy. Sorry to bother you." Mattie Morrison held a stack of linens in her hands. "You said you wanted to press these before I put them away?"

"Yes, thank you, Mattie. Won't you come in and have coffee with Jade and me? You look like you could use a break." She smiled kindly at her employee.

"Thank you. I'd like that." Mattie joined Jade in the parlor and promptly picked up baby Molly and snuggled her close while she admired Pamela, Jade's baby, sleeping in the corner. She looked around. "Where's Eddie?"

"He's going to be sorry he missed seeing you, Mattie, but he's with his Uncle Rex again. He just loves all the attention and he feels like he's doing *man stuff* when Rex takes him along on his errands. He's going to be one sad little boy when Rex leaves tomorrow." Jade laughed.

Mattie sat down in the rocker and cooed to the baby while she rocked her. "Well, tell him I said hi anyway. Maybe I'll get a chance to see him later."

Lucy rejoined the ladies, carrying a cup of coffee for her newest guest. "Jade and I were just talking about the latest marriage in Grandville, Mattie. Jade, what would you think about having a small reception for them here at the hotel? Not too many people know the Jensons, and that way they could meet Nels' bride too. I know I'm dying to meet her."

"That's a great idea, Lucy! Why don't we plan it for after church on Sunday, and all the ladies could bring food."

"I've seen the Jensons come to church, but they never stay around to visit. Do you think they'd agree to a reception?"

Jade thought a moment. "Doesn't Nels come to town every day to deliver milk? Maybe we could ask him. I wouldn't want to put together a party and then not have the guests of honor come."

"You mean like our plans for the anniversary party?" Lucy laughed. "We still have a few details to work out there."

"Like getting the guests of honor to come!" agreed Jade with a smile. "Well, one event at a time. What do you think, Mattie?"

Both ladies turned to the young woman and were startled to see tears in her eyes.

"Mattie, what's the matter?" Lucy moved to her side and knelt by the rocker.

A bewildered expression on her face, Mattie murmured, "Did you say that Nels Jenson got married?"

Sympathetic understanding passed in the look Jade and Lucy shared, and Lucy put her arm around Mattie's slumped shoulders. "I'm so sorry, Mattie. I didn't know you cared for him."

Mattie brushed away a tear with a shaky hand, and her small laugh was anything but mirthful. "We never even spoke, but the way we looked at each other. I mean…I thought…" Her words ended in a sob. "How can he just marry someone else like that?"

Jade reached for Molly as Lucy took the sobbing girl in her arms. "I'm so sorry, Mattie, really I am, but I want to tell you about something that happened to me, and I want you to listen." She took the cloth that Jade handed her and passed it to Mattie to wipe her eyes. Seeing that the young woman was now calmer, Lucy continued. "You weren't here when the mail-order brides arrived in Grandville."

Lucy paused and smiled at her memories. "I was a young woman very much in love with one of my brother's best friends. I ate, slept, and dreamt with him on my mind. It was only a matter of time, I thought, and he would fall in love with me too."

She looked at Mattie. "But he didn't. Instead he chose one of the brides without giving me a second thought. At first I was devastated." She paused. "Like you are now, but then God showed me why he hadn't been answering my prayers the way I thought he should all those years. He showed me that Buck Riley loved me, and he showed me that I had love for Buck in my heart too.

"You see, Mattie, even though this seems like a terrible blow right now, God has something and maybe someone even more wonderful waiting for you. This pain will ease, and one day you'll look back on it and thank God for it. Just keep trusting him to know what's best."

"We're not trying to make light of your feelings," Jade added. "We just want you to know that things will feel better if you give them time to sort out and let God do the sorting."

Mattie nodded. "Thank you," she murmured. She took a deep breath. "I guess I better get back to the kitchen."

"No, you go on home and rest up. Come back tomorrow if you feel up to it," Lucy instructed her. "We'll be fine for the rest of today."

Again Mattie nodded her thanks, and before she left, both ladies gave her encouraging hugs.

After she was gone, Lucy turned to Jade. "As sad as I feel for Mattie, I think I feel even worse for Nels Jenson's new bride."

Nels was just on the outskirts of town when he saw Mattie Morrison's buggy coming toward him. One look at the distraught woman holding the reins told him that she had heard the news.

Mattie pulled on the reins when she saw Nels then snapped them again to move past him. Even though Nels watched her, she avoided looking at him, and a moment later she was gone.

It's what I deserve, Nels thought. He mentally chastised himself for allowing his attraction to Mattie become known to her. He always knew in the back of his mind that a girl from his homeland was the only wife his parents would accept into the family. It was his father's plan, really, to write the Torkelson family about Irena. Just days before his father died he had spoken to Nels about it, and Nels had tried then to change his father's mind.

"You need a Norwegian wife, Nels. Keep the blood line pure, I say." His father wiped at his brow while they paused in their evening chores.

"But we're in America, Father, and it is our country now, not Norway!"

"We may live here, but Norway will always be our true home. Promise me that you'll marry a woman from home, Son. Don't forget your ancestry like so many have who come here."

And I promised him, Nels remembered. But that was before he had seen Mattie and had begun thinking what a good wife—what a *pretty* wife she would be. He closed his eyes and saw in his mind the drab, small form of Irena. She was like a little gray sparrow with huge, frightened eyes. He recalled the shock and fear in those eyes when she found him in the bed with her.

"Believe me, it was the last place I wanted to be," he muttered as he flicked the reins and moved the wagon on its way to the general store. He honored his parents' wishes by going through with the marriage, but he didn't care how much his mother wanted grandchildren, there was only so far he was willing to go.

Nels pulled up behind the store and was greeted by Ralph Tunelle, who came out the back door to help him unload his milk cans and the butter his mother had made. Together they placed the items in the icehouse behind the store. After their business was through, Nels walked to the front of the store and handed Philippa, Ralph's wife, the list from his mother. She looked it over then smiled at Nels.

"Looks like your mother is planning on doing some sewing. I'm sure I can find some fabric that would look very nice on her."

Nels rarely spoke to Philippa, all his business was usually done with Ralph, but he felt he better clarify his mother's wishes or he'd be returning the dress goods the next day.

"They won't be for my mother. They're for my wife." He found it difficult to even say the word *wife* out loud.

"Oh!" Philippa turned curious eyes on him. "I didn't realize you had gotten married. Anyone I know?"

The way she asked the question and the sparkle in her eye made Nels wonder if she knew of his interest in Mattie. *Who else had seen it?*

"No. She only arrived yesterday," was all he said.

Philippa appeared startled by this news but recovered herself with politeness. "Well, congratulations, Mr. Jenson. I hope to meet her soon." She glanced down at the list again. "Maybe you could help me, then, with my selection of fabric. How tall would you say she is, and what color hair and eyes does she have?"

Nels gave Philippa a blank stare.

"Mr. Jenson?"

"Uh—" Nels motioned with his hands. "She's about this tall, I guess—shorter than you, and—uh—her hair is brown, no—blonde, I think. I don't know what color her eyes are. I'll be back in about half an hour to pick up the order." And he escaped out of the store.

Nels hastened down the boardwalk, although there was no place he needed to go. What he really wanted to do was get back to the farm and get busy on his fencing. His father had been the one to take the daily milk wagon into town, leaving Nels to keep up with the farm chores and the crops, but since his father's death, Nels had to take time out of his work every day to do it, and he was falling behind. Crops would be ready for harvest soon; some of his hay nearly was already, but here he was wasting time in town, waiting for dress goods for a wife he didn't even want.

This foul mood was displayed on his face when a woman walked toward him with a baby in her arms. She had a smile on her face as she stepped into his path. "Good morning, Mr. Jenson."

Nels almost didn't see her, but then he paused and tipped his hat and would have continued on, but the woman put out a hand to stop him. He obeyed politely, but his expression was guarded.

"I don't know if you remember me, Mr. Jenson, but we met at church one Sunday. I'm Jade Newly and my husband is Tyler. He and Michael Trent have the lumber mill by the river."

Nels only nodded.

"We understand that you just got married—"

The stunned look on his face stopped her for a moment.

"It's a small town, Mr. Jenson, please don't be offended that Pastor Malcolm passed on the information. In fact, the reason I stopped you is that we want to celebrate with you and your new wife by having a dinner for you here at the hotel after church this Sunday. Please say you'll be able to come." She kept the smile on her face, although a scowl crossed his.

Nels glanced at the building he and Jade were standing in front of—the hotel. He hadn't even realized where he was when he was stomping down the boardwalk, but being by the hotel reminded him of Mattie and his farce of a marriage.

"That won't be necessary," he replied curtly and moved to pass her.

"Wait!" Jade put a hand on his arm then removed it to reposition Pamela on her shoulder.

Nels watched her and knew that he was being rude.

"All the women in town would love the opportunity to meet your wife and include her in our sewing circle and Bible study. I'm sure she would like to make some new friends here."

Nels was about to refuse again, but the appeal in her voice and eyes made him pause. He needed a good relationship with the town people to market his dairy goods, and though he detested the idea of celebrating his marriage, he cautioned himself that he shouldn't do anything to jeopardize his business.

"After church, you say?"

"Yes, that's right. All the ladies will prepare food, and we'll eat here at the hotel. We'll see you Sunday, then." She gave him one more smile and went back into the hotel.

Nels nodded to her and moved on again a little slower this time. He noticed the older man who had traveled with Irena was out in the corrals behind the hotel, brushing down a horse. Nels ducked past to avoid being seen by him. He didn't need another discussion involving his wife right now.

After speaking with Bernie Riggs at the blacksmith shop, Nels decided he'd given Philippa enough time to fill his order, so he headed back to the store. He entered from the back door and saw some items stacked there that he assumed were for him, but he had to make sure. He found Philippa at the front of the store saying good-bye to a customer, and he waited until she was through and looked his way.

"Oh, Mr. Jenson, your order is ready, but I want you to tell your mother that if she doesn't like anything that I've chosen, she can send it back with you, and I'll be glad to exchange it. But I think both she and your wife will be pleased. We just got in some new things, and they are quite lovely but serviceable too. I know your mother doesn't care for frilly things." She picked up the account book and walked toward him. "See, here are the charges, and I've subtracted them from your dairy account with us. Is that satisfactory?" She waited while he examined the figures.

She's already costing me money! thought Nels. He didn't even know he was frowning until Philippa asked, "Is something wrong with my figures, Mr. Jenson?"

"No, everything seems fine. Thank you. I'll be back tomorrow." He tipped his head at her and slipped his hat back on as he headed for the door to load his order. His frustration increased on the way home as he thought about being behind on his work and having Irena's unwanted presence in his home on a daily basis.

Lunch was ready for him after he had unhitched the horse and unloaded supplies. He sat down at the table without a glance at either of the women, said his quiet prayer, and began eating. Silence reigned throughout the meal.

As Nels ate, he began noticing some changes in the kitchen. Nothing was moved out of its usual place, he concluded, as he surreptitiously inspected the room, but things were definitely different. Things were...he struggled to define the change. Things were *cleaner*.

Nels stole a glance at the women and caught Irena looking at him, but she quickly looked down at her plate. Later when he was working on the fence posts, he considered what he had seen. His mother was a good housekeeper but didn't spend a lot of time on the cleaning. She was an excellent cook, but her favorite *chore* was her handwork. She loved sewing and knitting and crocheting. He had no doubt that his mother would assign Irena the household cleaning chores so that she could have more time for her projects, and the way his mother looked through the dress materials he brought home, Nels knew she would get started immediately.

Nels stared at the ground for a moment then shrugged. If his mother chose to hand over the harder chores to Irena, why shouldn't she? She was getting older, and Irena obviously knew how to clean. He had noticed the scrubbed floor, the polished look to the silverware, the shine on the dishes, and the overall tidiness in the room. He experienced a small twinge of guilt in seeing Irena treated as a servant rather than as a wife, but he quelled it at the thought of Mattie's tear-stained face that morning. He dropped a heavy post into the hole he just dug. And it wasn't as if Irena had anything to offer other than her cleaning skills. He scowled again. She wasn't attractive at all to him, and he was stuck with her.

Chapter 13

Jenson Farm

Rex walked his horse into the Jensons' farmyard while Eddie clung to the saddle in front of him, pride on the boy's face at being allowed to come this far from home with his uncle Rex. Eddie's shadowing of his uncle was an amusement to all, but Rex didn't mind. He was enjoying the time to see all his nieces and nephews in Grandville and knew he was going to miss them when he left tomorrow. His business with Palmer Granville had gone well, and now he had only to see Nels Jenson.

Eddie was looking forward to seeing Miss Aarestad again—or Mrs. Jenson—Rex reminded himself. He still couldn't believe the young girl he met the day before was old enough to be someone's wife, but Jade had assured him it was so. He also hated disturbing the newlywed couple the day after their wedding, but since he had plans to leave the following day, he felt he had no choice.

"Whoa!" Eddie called to the horse as Rex reined in at the front of the Jensons' house. As Rex swung down from the saddle, he took in the house, barn, and outbuildings with a measured glance. *Buildings look in good shape,* he thought. But the lack of paint and care was obvious.

Eddie ran up the steps to the porch and knocked on the door while Rex waited by his horse and watched in amusement. Eddie's energy amazed him, but he was delighted with it as well.

Mrs. Jenson stepped out on the porch, and though Rex was surprised to see Nels's mother, he was pleased to see her smile kindly at the young boy in front of her, though the smile disappeared when she turned her attention toward Rex. "Good afternoon."

Rex removed his hat. "Good afternoon, Mrs. Jenson. My name's Rex Newly and this is my nephew Eddie. I was wondering if I could speak with your son Nels."

"What about?"

Rex was surprised by her abrupt question and her annoyed tone. Remembering that her English was limited, he answered politely. "I'm starting a dairy farm over by Sand Creek, and I'd like to ask Mr. Jenson a few questions and maybe purchase some cows from him."

He watched her expression as she thought through his words and considered his request. Apparently she decided it was a worthy one, for she motioned to the barn. "He's in there," she said, and she went back into the house.

"Thank you, ma'am," Rex called after her. "Come on, Eddie." And he started across the yard to the barn.

Off to the side of the house he noticed Irena in the vegetable garden. She was crouched down pulling at beans and putting them in a bowl at her feet. Eddie noticed her too and ran over to her calling, "Miss Aarestad! Miss Aarestad!"

Irena turned so swiftly, she knocked the bowl and green beans flew everywhere.

"Oh! I'm sorry!" Eddie stopped in his tracks and clapped his hands over his mouth, but Irena only laughed.

"Eddie! How nice to see you again!" She smiled happily at the young boy, and it seemed only natural that she respond by hugging the boy when he threw his arms around her. She was unaware of the three sets of eyes that watched in amazement. Rex stopped his stride, at first to scold Eddie for startling Irena, and then because he was startled himself at the change in the girl when she smiled and laughed with Eddie. Eddie took her hand and led her to Rex.

"Good afternoon, *Mrs. Jenson*. It's a pleasure to see you again."

Rex watched in amusement as Irena looked around. Why, she didn't realize he was talking to her! Rex remembered his sister saying once that it was difficult to get used to being a Mrs. once she was married.

Finally, Irena answered, "Good afternoon, Mr. Newly."

"I wasn't aware when we met yesterday that it was your wedding day. May I offer my best wishes?"

"Thank you."

Rex was too polite to ask any questions, but several ran through his mind, like why she was spending her honeymoon picking green beans or why her mother-in-law was living in the same house as the newlyweds or why Irena had gotten married the moment she stepped off the stage in Grandville. Instead, he made a comment that, much to his delight, put the smile back on Irena's face.

"I believe I told you that there is only one other person I know of who has an accent quite like yours and that is my mother. Did you tell me, Mrs. Jenson, that you are from England?"

"Yes, Mr. Newly. I lived the past seven years in London and before that—"

"Let me guess," Rex cut in, "Norway?"

She nodded and smiled again.

"You are going to have to meet my mother one day, Mrs. Jenson, and talk with her about England. She grew up there, and I know she would enjoy visiting with you."

Irena nodded and smiled once again, but the smile disappeared when Nels approached with a scowl on his face. Rex noticed that Irena looked anywhere but at her husband, and he wondered why.

"It was nice to see you again, Mr. Newly. Please excuse me," she said, and she headed back to the garden.

Rex put his hat back on and held out a hand to Nels, but before he could speak, Eddie popped up between the two men.

"Can I help her pick up the beans, Uncle Rex? It was my fault they spilled."

"Sure, Eddie, that would be nice." Rex looked again at Nels and finally shook his hand. "Good afternoon, Mr. Jenson, I'm Rex Newly. Heard you were the man to see for advice on dairy farming."

Their voices faded as the two men walked back to the barn, and Irena found that she had been eavesdropping. She smiled at Eddie. "Did I hear that your father is going to start a dairy farm?"

Eddie looked up from the beans he was tossing back in the bowl along with a mixture of grass, weeds, and dirt that clung to his hands, and replied, "Not my father, my Uncle Rex." He motioned to the two men in the barn.

"Your uncle?"

"Uncle Rex and my pa are brothers, but Uncle Rex lives in Sand Creek with my Grandpa and Grandma Newly, and we live in Grandville."

Irena nodded that she understood and listened with interest as Eddie chattered on about his other aunts and uncles and cousins. Not that she would be able to keep it straight, she thought. It seemed quite complicated.

"You pick beans fast."

"What?"

Eddie pointed at the beans Irena was putting in her bowl. "You pick faster than my mama even."

"Thank you. I like to do things quickly. You're pretty fast at this yourself."

The little boy's face showed he was pleased by the compliment. "But everyone is always telling me to slow down," he admitted.

"I think we have enough now; Mrs. Jenson just wanted a bowl full. Shall we go to the house for a cold drink?"

Apparently that was just what the boy was hoping she would say, for he jumped up and ran ahead of Irena to the house. Mrs. Jenson heard him pound up the porch steps and stuck her head out the door.

"Wash up!" she commanded.

Irena was pleased to hear amusement in the older woman's voice. *She really loves children,* she thought, and from that moment she began to hope that she could really make a home for herself here.

Mrs. Jenson brought milk and cookies out on the porch, and the two women listened to Eddie tell about his dad's horses while they snapped the beans. Eddie was just finishing his third cookie and gulping down the last of his milk when the men approached.

"We're ready to go, Eddie." Rex turned and shook hands with Nels. "Nels, thank you for the helpful information. I'll see you in about a month when I come to pick up those calves." He tipped his hat at the ladies and moved to leave then swung back again.

"Oh, Mrs. Jenson, I almost forgot."

Both women looked at him.

Rex grinned but turned to Irena first. "My sister-in-law Jade asked me to tell you that she's looking forward to meeting you at your wedding party on Sunday after church, and"—he turned to Nels' mother—"to remind you both that the ladies of the town will take care of the food and everything." He stopped at the puzzlement on their faces. "You did know about the party, didn't you? I mean, Jade said she spoke to..." He stopped again as he saw the scowl on Nels's face.

Nels shuffled his feet when the two women turned to him. "I forgot to mention it, I guess."

Mrs. Jenson fired some words in Norwegian to her son, and Irena looked uncomfortably at Rex while the mother and son conversed in their native tongue. Irena was listening to the exchange, but she smiled apologetically at Rex.

Mrs. Jenson spoke to Rex, and Irena could see that her stiff back was held even straighter than usual. "Thank you, Mr. Newly. Please tell your"—she stumbled over the words—"sister-in-law we will be there. It is a kind thing. We will see you then."

"Oh, I won't be there," Rex informed them. "I'm sorry to miss it, but I leave for Sand Creek tomorrow. I'll see you all in about a month, though. Good day."

Irena watched as Rex helped Eddie up onto the horse's back, and then he swung up behind him. She waved in answer to Eddie's shouted "good-bye!" and let her eyes follow the two of them. She didn't know how to deal with all the emotions she was feeling at Rex Newly's announcement of a party for her and Nels.

She was far too bashful to face a town full of people, and she certainly didn't feel a need to celebrate her marriage. Rex wouldn't be there. He was the only person she knew besides Eddie and Swede. How could she face all those people? She became aware of the Jensons' voices beside her.

"You should have told us about this, Nels," Mrs. Jenson scolded her son. "It is a good thing the people are doing for you, and it will help your business in town to grow too."

"I just forgot about it."

"I must get started on a new dress for Irena right away. Irena, come with me."

Irena moved to the door to follow Mrs. Jenson, but she paused to watch as Nels strode angrily back to the barn. He kicked into the ground with his foot before he disappeared through the doorway.

"That's an arranged marriage if I ever saw one."

"What's an 'ranged marriage'?" Eddie asked as the horse walked along the road back to town.

Rex was unnerved by the question since he didn't know that he had spoken out loud and at the same time aware that he should not have. He searched for a proper response to his young nephew.

"An *arranged* marriage is when someone arranges for two people to get married. Maybe the two people don't even know each other first."

"You mean Miss Aarestad and Mr. Jenson?"

Rex took a deep breath. "I really don't know anything about them, Eddie, so I should not have said anything. Let's talk about something else, okay?"

Rex absently listened to Eddie tell about a rabbit he was feeding in the woods by his house while he continued to think about the Jensons. Irena didn't seem very happy, and Nels acted like he wished she didn't exist. Not exactly the start of a happy relationship. Rex shook his head. He hoped they could work things out.

Irena stood very still while Mrs. Jenson made the final examination of her newly sewn outfit. She still could not believe how swiftly the last four days had gone by, and now here it was Sunday morning, and she was more nervous about the coming events of the day than she had been about coming to America.

Her new dress was beautiful, stylish, and fit her perfectly. She carefully smoothed the fabric, convinced she had never seen anything lovelier in her life. She certainly had never worn anything as fine before, and the thought of doing anything to damage it made her wish she could change back into her plain, rough, gray dress again. She marveled that Mrs. Jenson dared cut into the exquisite piece of material.

"I think this color blue is just right for you, Irena. It is almost a robin's egg blue, I would say; wouldn't you? It brings out your lovely blue eyes."

Irena's cheeks tinted pink at the compliment, and Mrs. Jenson actually smiled at her.

"Yes, I think that blue is just right, and it certainly shows off your white shirtwaist under the jacket."

Irena looked at the white cuffs that peeked out at the ends of the sleeves of her blue jacket and nodded her agreement. "It is so beautiful, Mrs. Jenson. You are truly skilled with a needle."

The older woman beamed with pride at the praise. The front door banged, and they heard Nels call, "Wagon's ready."

Irena's face paled at the thought of leaving for town. On one hand she was excited about seeing Swede and attending church for the first time. On the other, she was dreading the thought of being the center of attention and having everyone see what a phony marriage theirs was.

Irena's lips tightened. It had been almost a week now since she became Nels's wife, and though they shared a bed, her husband had not touched her or looked at her or spoken to her. She could only imagine what he thought about her. Now a whole town full of people was going to celebrate and congratulate this marriage. How could she endure it?

"We're coming, Nels. You go ahead, Irena. I need to get my shawl." Mrs. Jenson gave Irena a slight push towards the kitchen.

Irena stepped from the parlor through the sitting room and into the kitchen and stopped suddenly as she saw Nels. He was looking out the window, but she could see his profile, and for once there was no scowl on his face. But what stopped her was what he was wearing. She had only seen him in his rough farm work clothes, but today he had on a fine suit that altered his appearance dramatically. *Why, he's handsome!* she thought and immediately blushed.

Nels turned when he heard someone enter the room and he found himself staring at the sight of Irena in her new clothes. He had to force himself to look away. She looked so different! *Her eyes are blue,* he thought and then wondered why he noticed that right away. If anyone would have asked him at that moment what color her dress was, he wouldn't have known.

He continued to stare out the window as he recalled how Irena had looked in the garden that day Rex Newly stopped by. She had laughed with that little boy, and it was the first time Nels had heard her laugh. She had the kind of laugh that made others want to smile when they heard it. When she smiled, she was transformed.

He glanced back and saw her head was down. He couldn't believe his ears when he heard himself speak.

"You look nice," were his words. Then he left the house.

Chapter 14

Grandville

Church was unlike anything Irena had ever imagined. Pastor Malcolm Tucker, the man who performed their wedding ceremony, spoke about God and love and faith and trust, and Irena drank in every word.

When she had first sat down, she did not think she was going to be able to concentrate. Mrs. Jenson entered the row of benches first, and Nels had motioned for Irena to follow, which left Nels sitting right beside her. Strange as it seemed to her, this was the closest she had ever been to him, even in their bed. Even on the wagon seat, Mrs. Jenson continued to sit between them, and Irena imagined it was because the older woman didn't want to fall off. Then another couple joined their row, moving them all closer together, and Irena found that she had to sit very still in order not to brush against Nels's arm.

On top of that, she had the nervousness of being at the wedding celebration on her mind, and Swede had waved at her, and she could tell he was pleased as he admired her new finery, which made her self-conscious of her clothing once again, so much so that when Pastor Malcolm began preaching, she barely heard what he was saying. But gradually the words got through to her, and she found that she was hungry for God's Word.

"God has made each one of us for a reason," the pastor spoke sincerely. "We are all special to him and have been specially designed. He's given each of us a job to do and collectively I can say that we are all given the job of bringing glory to our Lord and of spreading the gospel of salvation to the lost. But individually, we all have different tasks as well. God gives us gifts or talents that are uniquely ours, and he wants us to use our talents for him."

By the time the service ended, Irena's thoughts were racing. She was intrigued by what she heard. God had given her special talents, but what were they? And how could she use them for him? She made mental note of the verses Pastor Malcolm read so she could look them up again. And next time she would bring Swede's Bible. So many people had their Bibles with them.

Irena felt Mrs. Jenson give her a nudge, and she saw that Nels was standing and waiting for them. She had been so lost in her thoughts that she had not seen that the service was over. Not given to blurting out her thoughts, Irena was silent as they made their way to the door, but when they reached Pastor Malcolm, she was ready to voice her thoughts to him.

"Thank you, sir. Other than hearing the salvation message, that was the most wonderful thing I have ever heard."

It took the young pastor only a moment to hear the sincerity in Irena's words. He took her hand. "I'm glad God's Word spoke to your heart today, Mrs. Jenson."

Behind them, Nels paused in thought, and Pastor Malcolm waited for his attention before offering to shake his hand. A backward glance told Irena that her husband was puzzled at the exchange she had with the pastor.

Pastor Malcolm had announced the wedding celebration following the service and invited all to attend, so when the Jensons exited the church, they were met by Tyler and Jade Newly to be escorted to the hotel. Eddie ran immediately to Irena and took her hand.

"We're having a big party for you," he announced proudly as though he had planned it all himself.

Someday, Irena thought later, she would have to tell Eddie how grateful she was for him that day. With childlike exuberance, he led her from person to person, introducing her and jabbering on about this one and that. At one point Tyler tried to rescue her from his son's *help*, but she persuaded him to let Eddie remain by her side.

Later when Tyler returned to the hotel kitchen without Eddie, he explained to his puzzled wife, "I think young Mrs. Jenson would be terrified if I took Eddie away from her."

Jade peeked through the swinging doors at the group in the dining room. Eddie was still holding onto Irena's hand as she smiled and talked with Mallory Trent. "I don't understand, Ty. She seems to be having a good time—oh!" Jade put her hand to her mouth.

Eddie dropped Irena's hand and ran to greet a friend just as Mallory moved on. For a few moments Irena was left on her own, and she clasped her hands in front of her and looked down, afraid to meet anyone's eyes.

"What's the matter?" Tyler asked Jade as he peered over her shoulder.

They watched as Irena kept her eyes down. After a few moments she glanced up and looked around uncomfortably. Jade had just started to walk over and save Irena when she saw the newlyweds lock eyes across the room. Jade watched with joy as Nels grinned bashfully and ducked his head as if embarrassed at being caught staring at her.

"Did you see that?" Jade pushed Tyler back into the kitchen and smiled gleefully at him.

Tyler grinned back. "I'm not surprised. He hasn't taken his eyes off her the whole time. Aren't you just a bit ashamed, Mrs. Newly? Spying on a newlywed couple like that!"

Jade tapped her chin with her finger. "Well, if that's the way it is, why does she need Eddie?"

As the Newlys finished their conversation in the kitchen, Irena stole another glance at Nels, but he was talking to a man and had turned slightly so that she couldn't see his face. *What just happened?* Had Nels actually smiled at her? She was so stunned that at first she didn't realize that someone was speaking to her. *Who is this beautiful red-haired lady again? Oh yes, Eddie's mother.*

"Mrs. Jenson, if you and your husband will start the line, I think we're ready. We'll just wait for Pastor Malcolm to quiet everyone and give thanks for the food."

"Thank you, Mrs. Newly."

"Oh, please call me Jade."

"I'm Irena."

Jade smiled. "I hope we haven't overwhelmed you with all the new names and faces, Irena. We're really happy you are here and hope you and your mother-in-law will join our ladies' sewing group and Bible study time."

At the mention of a Bible study, Irena's interest perked up, but she only smiled and nodded at Jade.

"This dress is so lovely on you, Irena."

"Thank you. Mrs. Jenson just finished it last night."

Jade looked more closely. "Such fine work! She's very talented."

Irena rubbed her hands together and dared ask, "Do I need to know how to sew to come to the Bible study?"

"No, of course not, but we'll be glad to help you learn if you like. You're welcome to just come to visit and to study with us."

Irena nodded again and wondered if the Jensons would agree to let her come.

The meal was wonderful, and Irena hoped that she would be able to learn to cook like the ladies of Grandville. And there were presents for the newlyweds too—nothing grand, but much appreciated items like linens and quilts and preserves. Irena said thank you so many times that her mouth felt stiff, but her smile remained genuine.

As Nels put their things away in the wagon, Lucy Riley invited Irena and Mrs. Jenson into her home connected to the hotel to see Molly, who had been napping.

Lucy led her guests into her parlor then she excused herself to get the baby, and Irena walked around the room, admiring the furnishings and handwork. Suddenly she stopped in front of a mirror and stared.

"Oh my!"

"What is it, Irena?" Mrs. Jenson asked.

"It's beautiful! I had no idea…I mean…I didn't know it looked so…" Her voice trailed off. How could she explain to her mother-in-law that for the first time she had just seen herself as a woman, not as a child? She actually looked…pretty.

Mrs. Jenson seemed more than pleased with Irena's reaction. "I'm sorry that I did not show you the mirror in my room, Irena. I am glad that you are pleased with the dress."

After their short visit with Lucy, Irena had a few moments with Swede, and then they headed back to the farm. Her mind was full of the events of the day, and she was almost sorry to see it end.

"I have been thinking," Mrs. Jenson's words broke into Irena's thoughts. "Nels, what if you taught Irena to drive the wagon and she could bring the milk into town every day and free you up to do your work?"

Nels seemed to consider this request while Irena sat in amazed silence. "She'd need someone to help her unload."

Mrs. Jenson dismissed the problem with a wave of her hand. "Mr. Tunelle could do that at the store."

Nels nodded. "We'll start tomorrow, then. Irena can ride to town with me, and on the way back she can try her hand with the wagon."

Mrs. Jenson sat back with a satisfied smile, but Irena stared straight ahead and wondered why the thought of tomorrow frightened her even more than this day had.

Chapter 15

Sand Creek

Rex folded his arms across his chest and leaned against the counter while he waited for Bud to get his mail. He nearly jumped when he felt a tap on his shoulder, and he turned swiftly, but it wasn't Bud who greeted him but rather Bernadette Nolan, grinning at him with a mischievous look in her eye.

"Where have you been hiding yourself, Rex? I haven't seen you for a whole week now."

"Hi, Bernadette." Rex resumed his relaxed position against the counter while he watched Bernadette cross her arms. She tilted her head one way and then the other as she examined him.

"Looks like you've been up to no good."

He raised his eyebrows. "What makes you say that?"

"You have that satisfied 'cat got the mouse' kind of look about you. What *have* you been up to?" Now her tone was serious.

Rex grinned, enjoying his news. "Well, other than buying my own property and starting a dairy herd, you mean?" He was rewarded with the astonished look on her face.

For just a moment she was speechless, a rare occurrence for any Nolan woman, then the questions began.

"Really, Rex? Why, that's wonderful! Is that why you've been gone? Are you building a house this year? What do your folks think?"

"Whoa, Bernadette! Slow down!" Rex took his mail and smiled his thanks at Bud as he escorted Bernadette out to the walkway. "So many questions you have!" he teased her. "It might take a while to answer them all. How about I come by your place Friday night and tell you all about it then?"

Bernadette's mouth formed a surprised O when she understood what a Friday night visit meant. "Friday… Friday would be just fine."

Rex grinned again and tipped his hat to her. "Until Friday, then, Miss Nolan." His eyes lingered on hers for a few moments before he moved to his horse.

Rex turned back and waved to Bernadette as he rode out of town. She was still standing where he had left her, and she lifted her hand to him. He rode on but looked back one more time and couldn't help chuckling when he saw Bernadette spinning in a circle before running for home.

Chapter 16

Grandville

Irena sat very still on the wagon ride into town. Nels was quiet too. Nothing unusual there. The morning started just as all the others had so far. After Nels left the bedroom, Irena was up and doing household chores even before Mrs. Jenson was out of her room. Then she helped with breakfast preparations and cleaned up and was waiting when Nels came to announce that he and the wagon were ready to leave.

Nels had not talked any more than he usually did, but *something* was different. Irena could feel it. She ran her hand over the skirt of the new dress Mrs. Jenson had just finished altering for her. The dress was actually one that belonged to Mrs. Jenson, but the woman had stayed up late making alterations on it so it would fit Irena.

Apparently Mrs. Jenson was not about to let her daughter-in-law appear in public in her scullery maid, serviceable gray ever again. Even now she was busy cutting out another dress from the fabric Nels brought home only days ago.

Irena pulled her hands back into her lap and tried to concentrate on how Nels handled the horse. The suggestion that she drive the wagon had at first scared her, but she was so used to following orders that she had given no thought to refusing. Besides, she wanted to help Nels and his mother. She wanted to do her part in this family. She found that she had time on her hands, something she couldn't remember ever having in her short life.

"Daisy is a good horse; she'll do what you want. You just have to make sure she understands what you want." Nels gave Irena a quick, sideways glance while he spoke, and she gathered her thoughts together to listen. His glances her way had been frequent, and she was more than a little uncomfortable with the unexpected attention.

"It's good that Daisy appears to like you. She's usually not friendly with strangers."

Irena nodded slightly. "I seem to get along better with animals than I do with people." She nearly jumped on the seat when she heard Nels chuckle.

"I think Eddie Newly would disagree with that statement. He wouldn't leave your side yesterday at the party."

Irena smiled. "I was grateful for Eddie's attention." She paused. "I think children like me because I'm their size." Again Irena jumped when the man beside her laughed out loud. She was astonished at the change in Nels's behavior toward her.

Nels explained the new arrangement to Ralph Tunelle when they arrived at the store.

"No problem. I'll be sure to be around to unload the wagon for you, Mrs. Jenson, and Philippa will enjoy a daily visit and cup of coffee with you."

"Oh. I wouldn't want to disturb her work." Irena hastened to speak, but Philippa approached them at that moment, a wide smile on her face.

"Did I hear that you'll be coming in every day, Mrs. Jenson? How wonderful!" She squeezed Irena's arm and led her through to the front of the store while the men began unloading the milk cans from the wagon.

"Call me Irena, please."

Philippa smiled and led Irena behind the counter to the kitchen that was part of the Tunelle's living quarters attached to the store. In just a few moments Irena found herself seated at the table with a cup of coffee in front of her. Philippa also set a plate of cookies in front of her then seated herself.

"This is going to work out so well! I'll take my morning coffee with you, and we'll get to know each other. And I promise not to keep you too long. I know you'll need to get home again."

Irena returned the smile and thanked her hostess. She was uncertain what to say, not knowing if Nels would approve of her visiting daily with Philippa Tunelle. After all, the Jensons sold their milk products to the Tunelles' store. She listened politely to Philippa's chatter while she kept an eye on the doorway for any sign of Nels. A bell tinkled, indicating that a customer entered the store, and Philippa stood to go.

"No, you can stay. I shouldn't be long." She motioned for Irena to remain seated, but Irena shook her head.

"Thank you, Mrs. Tunelle, but I must see if Mr. Jenson is ready to leave. You have been most kind."

"It's Philippa, and I'll see you tomorrow, then, all right?"

Irena nodded and moved to the back of the store as Philippa pleasantly greeted the couple waiting at the counter.

Irena handled Daisy on the ride home with Nels's guidance. The trip was uneventful, and Irena felt she could handle the job, but before they reached the farm, she knew that she had to approach Nels about Philippa's suggestion.

"Mr. Jenson?"

Nels turned to her at once, surprised that she had something to say. She was so quiet.

"Mrs. Tunelle asked that we have a visit each day when I deliver the milk. Would that be all right with you?"

Nels took a moment before answering, and Irena worried that her request had been too bold. She was about to apologize when Nels spoke.

"Irena." He took the reins from her and pulled Daisy to a stop then turned to look at her. Irena found that her heart was pounding, and she wished she had never spoken. "You do not need to ask my permission to visit with a friend. If you plan to stay in town for several hours, I may wish you to tell me just so that I know you're safe and haven't had an accident with the wagon, but you're not a servant in my house. You're my wife."

He paused. "I'm sorry I didn't treat you with the respect a wife deserves when you first arrived."

Irena had been staring at Nels, dazed by his words, but she averted her eyes when he took her hand in his own. She was confused by the change in Nels and unsure of what was expected of her next.

The contact of their hands was brief. Nels must have sensed Irena's discomfort, because he let go of her hand and cleared his throat. "I am sorry, Irena." He handed the reins back to her again, but she hesitated.

"What is it?"

Irena forced herself to look at Nels but could not maintain eye contact. "I do not mind work, Mr. Jenson. I am used to it, and I wish to help in any way I can. I believe as Pastor Tucker said that God has a plan for my life." She darted a sideways glance at the man beside her and saw that she had his attention. "I believe it was God's plan for me to come here. You see, I accepted Jesus as my savior on the way here when my friend Swede showed me how from the Bible."

She noticed Nels's brow pucker as though he were puzzled by her words, but she drew a deep breath and boldly continued. "Do you have Jesus as your savior too, Mr. Jenson?"

Nels shrugged his shoulders and with a shake of his head replied, "Of course, I believe in God. I have all my life. The best any of us can do is live a good life, Irena. That's all God can expect of us." He cleared his throat. "When we have children, we'll take them to church and teach them about God too." He smiled at her reddening face. "And I think a wife should call her husband by his name, don't you?"

IRENA'S BOND OF MATRIMONY | 131

Nels's words were in Irena's mind the rest of the day. Fortunately, Mrs. Jenson was so busy with her sewing that she did not notice Irena's distracted demeanor. Nels's answer about his belief in God had not satisfied her completely. She wasn't sure why.

She was so new at her own beliefs that she couldn't say for sure if her husband was saved or not. And his comment about their children! Irena's face reddened again just thinking about it. Her nervousness seemed to increase with each passing minute as she watched the clock announce the time to go to bed.

Every night Irena lay in bed waiting until Nels's breathing told her he was asleep before she could relax and fall asleep herself. After today's conversation, she was uneasy about the approaching night. Was Nels ready now to truly accept that she was his wife? Was *she* ready?

Irena said good night to Mrs. Jenson at the usual time after asking if there was anything else she could do for her. Mrs. Jenson barely looked up from her work as she said good night. Irena prepared for bed in the usual way and then sat to read from her Bible, as was becoming her custom.

Usually she had plenty of time to read and then blow out the light and slip beneath the covers before Nels even came in the house from the barn. Tonight, however, she heard a footstep on the stairs shortly after she had begun reading.

With a sharp gasp, Irena slammed the book shut and nearly knocked the lamp over in her haste to blow at the flame inside. Pungent smoke filled the room as

Irena scrambled to find her way beneath the covers. It took several tries, and after she was tucked in up to her neck with her back to the door, she discovered that she wasn't even beneath the top sheet. As much as she wanted to pull it free from under her and right the tangled blankets, she remained perfectly still and anxiously listened as Nels entered the room.

It seemed to Irena that Nels stood in the doorway of the dark room for an eternity before he sat down on his side of the bed. She heard him release his breath in a quiet sigh as he began removing his clothing. She knew he knew she was awake, and she felt slightly ridiculous in the charade but was unwilling to be the one to expose it. Nels stood to pull the blankets down so that he could get into bed but found them resistant to his pull. Irena let out a little shriek as Nels tugged again, and this time he tugged hard enough that it flipped her right over the side of the bed onto the floor, pulling half the bedding with her.

"Irena, are you all right?" She felt Nels arms reaching for her and heard concern and puzzlement in his question. She couldn't help it; she started to laugh.

"Irena?"

Irena continued laughing while she tried to explain. "I was on the sheet when you pulled it, and I rolled right off the bed!"

Laughing with her now, Nels slid down to the floor and took his wife into his arms. Irena's laughter stopped abruptly. Her eyes had adjusted to the dark room enough that she could now see Nels, and she saw his head bending toward hers as his arms tightened around her.

She stiffened, and he paused as if waiting to see if she would pull away, but Irena remained still while Nels gently brushed her lips with his own. She was surprised at how pleasant it felt. She was surprised and—relieved.

Mrs. Jenson's call to them from downstairs startled them both. "Is something wrong? I heard a crash."

Irena started laughing again, and Nels pulled her head into his shoulder to muffle the sound, making her laugh harder.

"Everything's fine, Mother. I tripped on the corner of the bed is all," Nels called back. Irena felt his chest shaking as he tried to stifle his own laughter.

"Oh, for goodness' sake. *Uffda!*" they heard the woman mutter.

Nels and Irena sat on the floor with blankets wrapped around them and held on to each other until their mirth subsided. The ice now broken, Irena felt Nels turn her to face him. When he kissed her again, she responded. His arm tightened around her, but when Irena made to move away, Nels released her. They stared at each other in the dim room until Nels smiled.

"It's okay, Irena," he whispered. "We have a lifetime to get to know each other."

He kissed the top of her head and helped her to her feet. "Good night."

Irena watched Nels move to his side of the bed and pull the blankets back in place. She slipped back into the bed when he did and lay as still as possible until she heard his even breathing. Only then did she turn on her side, but sleep eluded her for a long time.

Chapter 17

Sand Creek

Rex ran a finger around his collar, trying to loosen it a bit. He sat in the Nolan's parlor with Bernadette, feeling as uncomfortable and nervous as an unbroken horse feeling his first saddle. He never expected his Friday night call would be as terrifying as this.

Bernadette seemed fine. In fact, she seemed perfectly at ease, poised, and beautiful. Rex marveled at her calm. When he suggested coming by this Friday evening, he hadn't really given their meeting another thought. He had never had trouble being around Bernadette before.

Even greeting Bernadette's parents on his arrival had been unsettling. Jonas winked at him, and Bridget's eyes sparkled with a knowing look. Rex stumbled over his "good evening" to them.

And Bernadette wasn't helping. She sat beside him on the sofa making small talk. She was all smiles and sweetness, polite and demure, but with a glint in her eye that Rex had never seen there before. Or had it always been there, and he was just now seeing it? At any rate, it made him uncomfortable and warm and *why is this shirt so tight around the neck anyway?*

Bernadette smiled sweetly as Rex tugged at his collar again. She reached for the cup and saucer in front of her. "Would you like more coffee, Rex? Another cookie, perhaps? I baked these earlier today, by the way."

"No, no thank you. They are delicious. Well, maybe another." He took a molasses cookie from the plate she held out to him, took a bite, and stared at the floor while he chewed. Bernadette made a comment about the weather, the third such comment that evening, and he nodded as if in agreement with whatever it was she had just said. *What is wrong with me?*

"Would you like to go for a walk since we agree that the weather is suitable for one?" Bernadette asked.

Rex felt a lifeline had been thrown to him. "Yes, a walk would be good." He rose and offered to carry the food tray to the kitchen for her. The dishes rattled precariously as he followed her out of the formal parlor into the more familiar comfort of the kitchen.

"We're going out for a walk, Mother," Bernadette called into the store beyond the kitchen to where her parents were doing some bookwork. Jonas and Bridget waved them away with big smiles on their faces.

Bernadette preceded Rex out the door and then took his arm while they started down the boardwalk together. Rex was uncomfortably aware of the looks from the people they met and greeted as they passed through the busiest area of the small town of Sand Creek.

Why do there have to be so many people out on a Friday evening? He couldn't help complaining to himself.

Rex led Bernadette away from the boardwalk, behind the buildings, and onto a less traveled back path surrounded by trees, grass, and moonlight.

"Could you maybe slow down a bit, Rex? I'm getting winded trying to keep up with the pace you've set for our moonlight stroll."

Rex realized immediately that he had been unconsciously pulling Bernadette's arm in his haste to get away from all the staring eyes. "I'm sorry, Bernadette." He slowed and grinned at her, feeling normal for the first time that evening. "I don't know what got into me."

"It's different when it's *courting*, isn't it?" There. She had said it.

"I guess you're right." Rex was a little surprised at Bernadette's bold comment. They walked at a more leisurely pace. "I don't think I could ever get used to sitting in a parlor!" he blurted out, and they both laughed.

"Then let's not." Bernadette hugged Rex's arm. "Let's just court the way we want to."

So we really are courting. Rex had started the move in that direction, but suddenly things were moving ahead of him, and he felt he was being pulled along. *Is this what you want for us, Lord?* Bernadette's words pulled his attention back to her.

"I've been waiting a long time for you to get up the nerve to come calling on me, Rex. I've already turned down two other fellows. Did you know that?"

"No, I didn't. Who?"

But Bernadette just smiled. "Why don't you tell me about this land you bought and this dairy herd you mentioned?"

"Okay." He began to explain his plans and was surprised at Bernadette's genuine interest. She didn't interrupt and was uncharacteristically quiet while he outlined some of his ideas and how he felt the Lord was leading him.

The evening ended with some general conversation, and before he knew it, Rex was promising to come again for Sunday dinner after church. He rode home with his mind filled with Bernadette, reliving the moments they shared that evening. He was beginning to see a plan for his future.

Chapter 18

Jenson Farm

Irena could not believe the change in Nels. Overnight he seemed to go from a quiet, withdrawn, broody man to a talkative, smiling, joking, and even loving husband. Mrs. Jenson nearly dropped the bowl of oatmeal she was carrying to the table when Nels entered the kitchen with a cherry "good morning" and winked at Irena. Irena's blush was all the proof the older woman needed, and she hid a satisfied smile while she finished the breakfast preparations.

Later, when Irena finished the clean-up and the other chores she usually did after breakfast, she heard Nels call to her, and she reached for her shawl and headed outside to find the wagon and Daisy all ready for her trip into town with the fresh milk and dairy supplies. Nels stood by the wagon and smiled while he watched his wife approach him. The morning sunlight made her squint, and though the brightness behind Nels hid his features, Irena knew his eyes were on her.

"Are you sure you trust me with the wagon?" Irena asked the question partly because she herself wasn't sure about it and partly because she was embarrassed and shy with the attention she was receiving.

"You won't have any trouble; just remember what I showed you. Are you sure you want to do this? Because I can if you don't."

"No, I want to help," Irena quickly assured Nels as he made the offer.

"Okay, then up you go." Nels pulled her into his arms and waited for her nod of permission before giving her a brief kiss; then he helped her atop the wagon seat. Irena felt all flustered and shy again. It was one thing to be kissed in the dark and quite another in the light of day. Nels just grinned at her timidity, and now he shaded his eyes as he looked up at her.

"Should—should I ask your mother if she needs anything from town?"

"No, I don't need anything today, Irena. Have a good trip."

Both Nels and Irena turned to find Mrs. Jenson on the porch, her arms folded in front of her and a big smile on her face. Nels turned back to see Irena's blush, and his eyes twinkled at her as he whispered, "Hurry back," for her ears only.

Irena gave him a shy smile then she flicked the reins and started Daisy on her way. She could hear Nels whistle as he headed back to the barn.

Is this love?

Irena pondered over the question as she drove the wagon carefully down the road to town. She wasn't sure she was qualified to answer, not really knowing what love was. All she knew was that she was happier than she had ever been in her young life. Other than occasional hugs from the Torkelson children, Irena hadn't been shown affection since she had been a child. And knowing Nels cared for her made her aware of the craving for love and affection that she had kept hidden inside all these years. Or was it knowing that Jesus Christ loved her that had opened her eyes to her own needs?

Irena thanked her heavenly Father as she drove along, and she even felt tears in her eyes, which for some reason made her want to laugh. Irena had become a new person.

Three days later she wondered if she would ever be able to change. Irena was thoroughly enjoying her trips to town. Not only was she being a big help to Nels, but also she was finding a good friend in Philippa Tunelle. Without fail, Philippa had coffee and a snack ready to share with Irena while Ralph unloaded the dairy supplies. Sometimes they were interrupted by a customer, but mostly they had time to visit, and Irena was learning what it meant to have a close friend for the first time in her life.

As she slowly started coming out of her shell and began to initiate conversation instead of always waiting to simply answer when spoken to, Irena started to believe that she had changed, that no longer was she a scullery maid, a servant, but was changing into a woman with thoughts and ideas that could be expressed and shared.

At least that's how she had been feeling until today. Irena was back from town and was unhitching the wagon when Nels approached. She needed to ask him a question today, and she suddenly felt again as though she were a little girl making a request to her aunt or worse, a servant again, begging for Cook's attention. She swallowed and kept her eyes lowered as Nels took over the care of Daisy. Nels spoke amiably while he attended to the horse.

"This has worked out so well for us, Irena, that you can drive the wagon for me. I can't believe how much I've gotten caught up on this week already." He began brushing the horse. "Of course, with harvest coming soon, it will get busier than ever for me. It is good I have a wife now to help, eh?" He paused, and Irena saw him look over at her. Her silence was not unnoticed.

"Is there something wrong, Irena?" Nels hung up the brush and moved around the horse to stand near his wife. He tilted her chin up so that he could look into her eyes.

"I have some things to ask you, but—" She paused then blurted out, "but I'm afraid to ask."

She could see that Nels almost smiled at this blunt statement but stopped himself.

"You don't need to be afraid to ask me anything, Irena. You are my wife and I, as your husband, will be glad to help you solve your problems. Now what is it? What are you afraid to ask?"

"I owe my friend Swede some money, and he is leaving for Dakota next week." She swallowed again. "You have already paid a lot of money for me to come here, and I used all my earnings as scullery maid plus working on the ship for my passage, but even so, Swede had to pay for part of my trip, and I need to pay him back. He says it is not necessary, but I promised him." Irena drew in a deep breath after this long speech, but she wasn't finished and held up a hand for Nels to wait when he started to reply.

"I have learned that there is a job at the hotel available, cleaning rooms and helping in the kitchen—things I am good at. If you would give me permission, I could work there after my delivery at the store and come back home after the supper meal is cleaned up. If you could lend me some money now to pay Swede, I could work until you are paid back." Irena's shoulders dropped as she exhaled in relief that she had said everything she needed to say.

Nels was silent and Irena waited, willing to be completely subservient to his wishes. She ran the plan through her mind once again, wondering if she had thought it through well enough and if she had presented it clearly enough. She nodded slightly. Yes, it seemed the only way, unless there was too much work here on the farm for Nels to allow her to be gone all day, but so far Irena hadn't found enough to do. With Mrs. Jenson taking care of the cooking, Irena's chores were few and easily done. Yes, it was a good plan.

"No."

Irena's head jerked up to look at Nels. She opened her mouth to speak and was promptly kissed then enveloped in her husband's arms. She heard him speaking, but the words were muffled because he held her so tightly. She pulled back a little.

"What?"

Nels grinned down at her. "I said I will gladly pay your debts, Irena. Dagne Torkelson was a greedy woman, and she kept back money that should have gone to you, but I will not have you suffer for it. If anything, I should be paying back your spent earnings as well."

Irena couldn't believe it. "But, it isn't right."

Nels slipped his arm around her waist and led her into the sunlight outside while he put Daisy in the corral beside the barn. "It is right for a husband to take care of his wife," Nels said simply. "But I do appreciate your offer. America has been good to us, Irena. We have enough money to take care of debts. The only thing I didn't have here was time to keep up with my work and a beautiful wife to keep me company. You are the answer to both those problems. Also, I don't want you working in town; I want you where I can see you." He winked at her teasingly.

Irena was dazed at this generosity. And having him court her as he had been doing since the night they first kissed was all new to her as well. She knew he was waiting for her to feel comfortable with him as her husband, and she realized at that moment that she was in love with Nels and wanted nothing more than to be his wife.

When night descended again and they were alone in their room, Nels reached for Irena and kissed her good night as had become his custom. Usually he then rolled over and went to sleep, but tonight Irena kissed him back and put her arms around him. It was only natural when their embrace became intimate. Irena no longer felt that Nels was a stranger to her. She accepted him as her husband and responded, timidly at first, but with increasing pleasure at being his wife, truly, at last.

It was hard for Irena to say good-bye to Swede. He met her after her delivery at Tunelle's Store and took her to the hotel for coffee and a short visit before the stage left.

"I've earned enough working for the Riley's to get to my son's place, and I've already wired him about when to expect me. I must say that America has grown on me, Irena. I don't think I could ever go back to the streets of London again. It seems America has done all right by you as well." The older man questioned Irena with his eyes.

"Yes." Irena nodded happily. "Mr. Jenson truly cares for me, and I'm treated well and fed well. I shall grow fat and lazy if I'm not careful."

"Praise the Lord, child. God answers prayer." Swede wiped at his nose with a handkerchief, and Irena saw how hard this parting was for him too.

"I'm going to miss you," she said truthfully. "I would never have gotten here on my own, but God sent you to help me. Thank you so much for all you've taught me and for giving me your Bible." She had carefully planned what she was going to say, but it was difficult to remember when she felt so sad at seeing her friend leave. Perhaps she'd never see him again.

Swede must have had the same thought. "If I don't see you here on this earth again, Irena, you can at least be sure that I'll be seeing you in the hereafter. I have been blessed to know you."

"Oh, Swede!" Irena choked on her tears, but she swallowed and made herself continue. "My husband wants you to have this." She slid an envelope across the table. "It is repayment of the money I owe you, and he says to tell you thank you for getting me here safely." Irena smiled a wobbly smile.

Swede appreciated the offer but was adamant in his refusal. "No, Irena, thank you, child, and thank Nels Jenson for me, but if anything, I owe you a debt of gratitude for giving an old man courage to start out on an adventure!"

"Now, Swede, you must take this!"

But he refused and slid the envelope back to her and placed her hand over it.

"Consider it a wedding gift."

She slid it back. "I consider the gift of your Bible a wedding gift. Swede, you need this money."

Swede laughed. "This reminds me of dealing with you at the meat counter in London. No, I don't need the money. I have more than enough for my needs. I want you to return this to your husband with my blessing." And he slid it back again.

Irena giggled, and Swede grinned in delight at her.

There were a few more tears when Swede finally departed on the stage, but as he waved from the coach window, Irena felt as if she were saying good-bye to her father. How she thanked the Lord for sending him to her when she needed him!

Chapter 19

Jenson Farm

Irena was used to hard work, but days were slipping by her when she felt that she hadn't done enough with her time. She felt indebted to the Jensons, not in a monetary sense, but in a sense of gratitude. She wanted to repay these kind people for all they were doing for her, but how? She had cleaned and re-cleaned so many times that Mrs. Jenson had told her she must stop or she would wear out the woodwork.

She was learning to sew, but Mrs. Jenson enjoyed her handwork so much that Irena hated to keep her from it to watch over her tutoring. She now helped with the cooking and was pleased with her efforts so far. But cleaning, gardening, and laundry just weren't enough to fill her days. She decided to help Nels.

Her opportunity came that evening when Nels was in the barn to do the milking. Supper was simmering on the stove, a pot of beef stew, and fresh bread was ready.

Irena had made her first pie earlier that day, and she admired its golden brown crust as she surveyed the menu for the evening's meal. Everything was ready including the dishes on the table, so she hurried up to her room and changed into her gray dress and headed out to the barn. Nels looked up curiously when she came in.

"Is something wrong, Irena?"

"No. I came to learn how to milk the cows," she stated matter-of-factly.

Nels laughed. "Now, why would you want to learn that?"

"I want to help."

Nels was quiet for a moment after hearing the serious tone of his wife's request. "Irena, you don't have to repay me. You don't owe me anything, and you're not my servant." He said the words gently, trying to convince her once and for all.

After she had returned the money intended for Swede, Irena had decided then that she should earn money to repay the Jensons for her travel money. Nels had nearly given up trying to explain to her again that she owed them nothing, but it appeared Irena was still determined to work off what she considered her debts. At least, that is what Nels thought she was doing.

Irena surprised them both by placing her hand on Nels's arm. He turned to look at her. "I want to help because…because you are so good to me, and because I care for you."

Slowly a smile crossed Nels's face. "I care for you too." The smile turned to a teasing grin. "And right now you look very fetching in that dress."

Irena gasped as Nels pulled her down into the hay with him. "Nels!" She shrieked and tried to scramble away, but he caught her and held on.

"What? Not *Mr. Jenson?*"

Her laughter was silenced with a kiss.

"I really do want to learn to milk," she whispered after several moments had gone by, and Nels laughed heartily at her determination.

"All right then, you shall. But I can see right now that you're going to be more of a distraction than a help."

Irena only smiled at him as she pulled some hay out of his hair.

Nels's prediction was only partly true. While Irena was aware that he found her presence a distraction at times, she, in her quick and efficient manner, was accomplishing the work of two people. They both found themselves looking forward to milking time and having each other's company while they completed the chore together. Nels put his foot down on her cleaning out the manure or carrying heavy pails. There were some things men should do for women, he told her. But she was quick to hand him a shovel or a rake as he needed.

Some days she followed him out and helped with the fencing. Again, he wouldn't allow her to do anything too hard, and he had to admit how much easier his work was because she seemed to anticipate his needs and had each tool or supply right at hand when he reached for it.

Irena was happy. Her days were satisfyingly full now with work inside the house with Mrs. Jenson and work outside with Nels. She was talking more and laughing more. She was learning more about her husband every day and loved to hear him tell about his childhood in Norway and about his trip to America with his parents.

One night as they held each other in bed, Irena told Nels that Philippa invited her and Mrs. Jenson to the Bible study and sewing circle the next Tuesday. Nels knew how eager she was to go, so he was surprised when she said, "But I don't want to leave you with all the work that day."

"Whoa, Irena! Do you hear what you're saying? You've been such a good help to me that I'm getting way ahead on my chores. I never expected to get this much fencing done so soon. Why, I may have to take a day or two off myself," he teased her. "Besides, you've been wanting to go to this ladies' thing, haven't you?"

Irena nodded against his shoulder. "There's so much about the Bible and God that I want to learn. Swede was a good teacher, and I love church on Sunday, but I don't understand so many things that I read myself. I'm hoping these ladies will be able to help me."

"It's not that hard, Irena. You live a good life and you go to heaven. You live a sinful life and you go to hell."

Irena was silent for a moment, and she felt Nels begin to relax beside her. She couldn't let him fall asleep yet.

"But, Nels, the Bible says that none of us are good, that we're all sinful."

Nels propped up on one elbow to better see Irena's face in the moonlight. "Well, then your good outweighs your bad, I guess. You do need to try to live a good life; I'm sure about that much."

"No, you don't," Irena insisted. "I mean, not to get saved, you don't. Swede explained it to me like this. If we could get to heaven by being good, how would we know when we've been good enough? We couldn't. We get saved by faith in the sacrifice Jesus Christ made for our sins on the cross."

"Well, I believe that." Nels sounded puzzled, so Irena continued.

"But you're adding your *goodness* to your faith, Nels. If your salvation depended on something you could do yourself, then Jesus would not have had to die for you. Heaven is a gift and gifts are received, not earned."

They were both silent then, and Nels continued to watch Irena's expression as she beseeched him with her eyes.

"This is important to you, isn't it?"

"Very," she whispered. "My life had no meaning to me until I accepted Jesus. I didn't even know that heaven and hell existed or that people argued about how to get to heaven, but do you remember what Pastor Malcolm said on Sunday about the different religions in the world? He said they all have one thing in common. They add good works to faith. They try to please God into letting them go to heaven. All God wants is for us to accept his Son's payment for our sins. 'For by grace are ye saved through faith; and that not of yourselves: it is the gift of God: Not of works, lest any man should boast.'"

Irena paused again then said, "I probably don't explain it very well, Nels, because I have only been saved such a short time, but it is so important to me.

I don't want to say anything wrong. Would you mind if we talked to Pastor Malcolm sometime? I know he could explain it better."

Nels nodded slowly. "What you say makes sense, Irena, and the funny thing is that I know those verses you just told me, but I never really thought about them before. I just learned them because I had to when I was a boy." He lay back down and sighed. "We'll talk more tomorrow, okay?"

"Okay," Irena replied, and they said their good nights. Irena turned onto her side with a silent prayer for Nels, and Nels turned onto his side with thoughts, verses, and questions going round and round in his head.

They talked the next day and the next. Nels asked Irena questions often beginning with "What if?" Irena did her best to answer and ended up quoting the same few verses she knew by heart over and over and apologizing to Nels for not knowing more. He didn't seem to mind, and sometimes Irena wondered if he was asking questions just to keep her talking, as he sometimes did, or if he was truly interested.

Friday morning came, and Nels announced to the women at the breakfast table, "I think I'll ride into town with you this morning, Irena. I need a few things. Anything we can get for you, Mother?"

Mrs. Jenson pointed to a list she had started. "I keep a list ready for Irena. I guess there are a few things on there, but if you're going, there's really no need for Irena to go. She may be tired of making the trip every day."

They both looked at Irena, and she almost laughed at the imploring expression on her husband's face, begging her to come with him, but she only said, "No, I'm not tired of it. I'd like to go."

They had barely gotten out of the yard when Nels laughed. "I'm so glad you didn't take Mother's suggestion, or I would have had to beg you to come with me in front of her."

Irena smiled. "What are you up to?"

"Well." Nels glanced at her. "I've been thinking a lot about God and heaven and things we've been discussing, and I thought today might be a good time to call on Pastor Malcolm. On Sunday Mother with be with us."

Irena squeezed his arm in excitement. "That's a perfect idea, Nels. You've made me very happy."

"I love you, Irena."

Irena could tell that Nels was bashful about saying the words but also that he was sincere. She stared at the passing scenery as if in a trance, hardly noticing the wild flowers along the road or the fluttering leaves on the trees. She felt the warm sun on her back and breathed deeply of the perfumed air. She smiled. "I love you too, Nels."

Nels had tried to wait patiently for her reply, knowing that she thought things through before she spoke, but his breath let out in a *whoosh* and then he yelled and waved his hat in the air and scared poor Daisy into a trot.

"Nels! The milk cans!" Irena scolded.

He calmed the horse and slipped his arm around his wife and pulled her close to his side. "I'm glad God brought you to me, Irena."

Pastor Malcolm Tucker welcomed the Jensons into his home while his wife, Hermine, set about preparing coffee for their unexpected guests. Irena was pleased to see children pop their heads in the doorway for a look at the company and then they disappeared again. Hermine shooed them all outside and apologized to Irena and Nels.

"They're not at all a bother, Mrs. Tucker." Nels laughed. Then he turned to Pastor Malcolm. "Irena and I have a few questions we'd like to discuss with you if you have some time."

"Of course." The man nodded, and Hermine rose and excused herself.

"You don't have to leave, Mrs. Tucker." Nels stopped her. "Unless you wish to."

Hermine glanced at her husband for his approval then sat down again. "A pastor's wife never wants to intrude on private conversations," she explained.

"No, it's nothing private. We just have some questions about salvation." He noticed that the Tuckers didn't seem surprised or shocked by this statement, so with relief he continued. "You see, as a boy I accepted Christ as my savior and I believed that he died for my sins and rose again. But I also believe that a person has to be a good person and do good things or God won't allow him into heaven." He looked over at Irena and smiled. "Irena tells me that the Bible says God doesn't measure our goodness or weigh the good versus the bad in our lives to see if we're worthy of his salvation. I'm confused."

Pastor Malcolm could recognize a searching soul, and he saw it in Nels Jenson. Slowly and carefully he went through the plan of salvation with Nels and Irena. "When you said you accepted Christ as your savior, Nels, did you understand what that meant?" He watched as Nels thought about the question and shrugged. Then he continued. "A savior does the saving. Christ did all the work for us, Nels. It could only be the perfect, sinless Son of God who could die for our sins. We deserve to die, but he came to earth and became our substitute."

Nels nodded in agreement.

"Why couldn't we pay for our own sins, Nels?"

"I guess because we aren't perfect like God?"

"Right. II Corinthians 5:21 tells us, 'For he hath made him to be sin for us, who knew no sin; that we might be made the righteousness of God in him.' And in Romans 4:5 it says, 'But to him that worketh not, but believeth on him that justifieth the ungodly, his faith is counted for righteousness.' You see, God doesn't want us to work for heaven; he wants to give it to us as a gift. It tells us that in Ephesians 2:8-9."

As Pastor Malcolm read the verses, Nels squeezed Irena's hand, remembering that she had quoted these same verses over and over to him.

"After we accept Christ's gift and become his child, it is our privilege *then* to work for him and serve him. Many people get the believer's walk mixed up with salvation. Listen to verse ten, 'For we are his workmanship, created in Christ Jesus unto good works, which God hath before ordained that we should walk in them.' God wants us to 'walk worthy of the vocation he's called us' but, Nels, he doesn't ask us to work for salvation. Does that help make it clear?"

Nels's response was enthusiastic when he said, "Yes, yes, it does. I understand now, Irena. I think I was taught correctly when I was a boy, but somehow I began including good works in my mind."

Pastor Malcolm nodded. "I think that happens a lot. As parents we tell our children, 'You better be good now' or 'if you're not good, you won't get a treat' or 'God wants you to be a good little girl or boy' and those thoughts develop into being 'good' to please God for his acceptance too."

Nels agreed, but he had another question. "So did I get saved when I was a boy or did I just get saved now that I understand that salvation is a free gift?" He grinned at Irena's happy smile in response to his declaration.

"I would say now would be the best answer, Nels, and you can be assured from this moment on that you are saved. No more worrying if your sin and good works have balanced; you can rest on God's promise. I would like us to pray together. Would that be all right with you?"

Irena and Nels rode home with much to discuss. Irena had thought her happiness was complete before, but now her heart was overflowing. They went straight into the house to share the news with Nels's mother, who listened carefully. When Nels explained to her that he had thought he was going to heaven because he was trying to be good enough to be allowed in, she was very surprised.

"But I never taught you that, Nels. I know we have never discussed these things much; your father was not one to talk about such things outside of church, but I always thought you understood that Jesus was the only way to heaven."

"I had confused things in my own mind, Mother, and I was very disinterested in the Bible or church for many years. I only went to church because it was one of the good things I thought I was doing to win favor with God. Now I'm looking forward to learning more, and Pastor Malcolm has suggested that we start reading together here at home and to feel free to bring any questions we have to him. He may even start a men's Bible study like the ladies' study you women are going to have."

Mrs. Jenson was amazed at her son's enthusiasm but pleased as well. She saw the special looks between Nels and Irena and realized that they had overcome many barriers in the last few weeks. "I will enjoy being a part of reading the Bible with you, but if the two of you wish to do this alone, I will understand."

"Oh no, Mrs. Jenson," Irena hastened to say. "We would very much like to do this all together. The Bible Swede gave me is in English, though; will that be a problem?"

"I have a Bible too, in Norwegian," Mrs. Jenson announced.

"Then Irena can work on teaching you English at the same time. How about that?" Nels suggested and all three agreed.

"Well, then, there's work to be done and we better get started." Nels turned to the door but stopped and looked back at the women. "Have I ever thanked you, Mother, for sending for Irena?" And he left.

Irena and Mrs. Jenson looked at each other and Irena spoke first. "I thank you too, Mrs. Jenson, for sending for me. I never thought of refusing to come because I was used to doing what I was told to do, and Aunt Dagne told me I must come to America and marry Nels Jenson. But I never dreamed what joy I would find in my journey and the happiness I would find at my journey's end. I love your son."

Mrs. Jenson was overcome by Irena's speech, not expecting to hear her say so much, for she was used to being around Irena and not hearing her talk for hours.

She smiled kindly at her daughter-in-law. "Then I think it is time you started calling me *mother*, my daughter."

Chapter 20

Sand Creek

Rex drove the buggy at a leisurely pace. Today he was taking Bernadette on a picnic, and then he was planning on showing her his land. His mother had prepared the basket for the two of them and when he asked Bernadette after their Sunday dinner, she had been excited about the idea.

She looked very beautiful today, he thought, as he glanced her way. She smiled and continued talking to him about the scenery and the weather and—he hid a grin—she had been talking the entire trip. He really hadn't heard what she was saying, but he liked listening to her voice. She was easy to be around because he needn't worry about what he was going to say; he never got the chance.

Their courting had taken a different course since that uncomfortable evening in the Nolan's formal parlor. Bernadette suggested that they continue their visits outside where Rex was more at ease. But, she teased him, maybe he better consider the fact that winter would be coming in a few months. What was he going to do then?

Maybe I'll have to marry her before then, Rex thought. He cast a sideways glance at Bernadette, wondering if she could read his thoughts. She rewarded him with another dazzling smile, and Rex felt his heart race.

He helped her down from the wagon with his hands on her waist and marveled that for being a tall girl, she was so slender and light. Her green cotton dress made her green eyes brighter, and her copper hair curled around her bonnet in a fetching way. He suddenly found himself still holding her and gazing at her stupidly, and he hastily dropped his arms and stepped back.

"Ah, Rex," Bernadette pouted the words softly, and she lightly placed her hand back on his arm as she stepped toward him. "That was a perfect opportunity for a first kiss."

As if he couldn't stop himself, Rex bent his head towards her uplifted one and met her lips with his own. He didn't know how long he held her. He was shaken by the emotion that overwhelmed him and had to force himself to release her. He took a step back again.

"That was nice, Rex." Bernadette smiled sweetly at him, and he wondered how she could appear so calm while he felt like the ground was moving under him. She turned to inspect her surroundings. "So this is your land? Which side borders your parents and which borders the Trents?"

Rex took a deep breath, willing his heart to slow down. Maybe if he didn't look at her, he would be able to quit acting like a stupid fool. What happened to that easy relationship he had with her? Suddenly Bernadette Nolan seemed like an entirely different person. A woman. A desirable woman. He took another step backward.

"Uh…my folks' place is over that way"—he pointed—"and Uncle Evan and Aunt Ella's is on this side." He walked a short distance away from her in the tall grass. "Here's where I want the barn and corrals, and as you can see—" He pointed beyond. "I have room for hay and alfalfa fields." He placed his hands on his hips and gazed over the expanse. He nearly jumped when he felt Bernadette take his arm.

"And where will the house go?"

"Over here." He led her to the wooded area he had chosen. "See, there's the lake. The house would sit up here and have all this for a view." He waved his arm to indicate the lake, the trees, and the fields.

"It's beautiful, Rex, really beautiful! When will you begin?"

Rex led Bernadette down a deer path as they talked. "I'm going back to Grandville next week to see about some dairy cattle. There's a farmer there named—"

"No, I mean, when will you begin on the house?" Bernadette interrupted him.

"Uh, well, I haven't really decided. I can stay at my folks' place while I get things here established. I guess I was going to put off building the house for a while, but now…" Her eyes were having the strangest effect on him.

"Yes?"

"Now…I'll probably start it sooner," he finished lamely. The green orbs of her eyes seemed to be pulling him toward her.

"Rex Newly, are you asking me to marry you or not?"

"What?"

Rex halted abruptly. Even though Bernadette's eyes appeared innocent, there were two bright red circles on her cheeks, indicating that she knew she was being forward.

"Well, we *are* courting, and if you're going to ask me, it better be soon so we can get a house built before winter or else you're going to be stuck in my parents' parlor every Friday night, and you'll hate it!"

Rex simply stared at her after this outburst then he began to laugh.

"What's so funny?"

"Bernadette, life will never be boring with you!"

She waited with her hands on her hips while Rex laughed.

"So, are you asking me?"

Rex let himself into the kitchen after taking care of the horse and buggy. His mother was baking golden brown loaves of bread, and the aroma was making his mouth water even though he and Bernadette had just finished their picnic lunch.

"Hi, Rex. Back already? Here, have some warm bread and jam. I'll get you some coffee too." Sky took the basket from her son and went for the cups and coffee pot.

Rex sat at the table and watched his mother move smoothly from one place to the next as she set things before him. He waited until she was seated and passed the bread to her first before he helped himself. The butter melted into the thick slice as soon as he spread it on, then he topped it with strawberry preserves.

He knew his mother was watching him while she sipped her coffee. She was waiting for him to tell her about his day. She always seemed to know what he was going to do.

"I asked Bernadette to marry me."

Hot coffee scorched down Sky's throat as she took an unplanned gulp. "You what?" she choked out.

Rex jumped up to get his mother some water and waited until she drank some before taking his seat again. "Are you all right?"

She nodded.

Rex's eyes were on her face as he began to explain. "I was planning to talk to you and Pa first, and I wasn't even going to ask her for a while—maybe not even until next year, but…I don't know." He looked away, and Sky watched him carefully. "Today just seemed like the right time, and we decided that if I get started on the house right away, we could be married and move in before cold weather comes."

"I see." Sky's voice came out in a hoarse whisper.

"You and Pa like Bernadette, don't you?" Rex was puzzled by his mother's reaction.

Sky nodded then cleared her throat. "I'm just surprised that you decided so quickly. You usually take more time with important decisions."

Rex agreed slowly. "I know. It was really Bernadette who suggested it, and I think she's right. I could probably have things ready by October, and we could be married then. I'm afraid I won't be much help around here for a while." He paused. "I hadn't thought of that."

"Abel doesn't leave until September, and your father can manage until you get on your feet." Sky assured him. "You say Bernadette suggested this? What do you mean? Did she ask you to marry her?"

"No. She asked if I was going to ask her."

"Oh."

"And I was," Rex admitted hastily. "That's why I started courting her, but I hadn't planned on things moving this quickly."

Sky cleared her throat again and sipped cautiously at her coffee. "Then are you sure it's God's timing?"

Rex thought about his mother's question before answering. "I have no reason to think that it is not."

Somehow, that answer didn't satisfy either of them.

Chapter 21

Grandville

Irena was enjoying having her mother-in-law ride into town with her. They were both excited. Today, after the regular delivery, they were going to meet with the other ladies for their Bible study and sewing time. Irena felt almost regal in her new dress, the fourth one Mother Jenson had made for her already.

This one was a sunny yellow with fancy tucks and lace, and it fitted her small figure perfectly. She had exclaimed over it again and again until her mother-in-law had thrown up her hands and said, "Enough! Just enjoy your dress, and I am happy I could make it for you."

"At least you don't have to wonder what special talent God has given you, Mother," Irena told her the evening before when she tried the dress on for its final fitting and had modeled it for Nels and his mother.

"What do you mean, Irena?" the older woman asked.

"God has given you the gift of sewing," Irena stated matter-of-factly. "And as Pastor Malcolm said, he wants you to use your gifts for him. I wish I knew what my talent was."

"I know what it is," Nels said quietly so that his mother couldn't hear, and Irena shot him a scolding look.

"You help others," Mother Jenson said.

Irena turned to her.

"You are always helping me or Nels or children in town. Yes, I have seen you." She pointed at Irena. "You do nice things without even having people notice them like when you fix me hot tea while I am so busy sewing, and I do not even look up to say thank you."

Irena blushed at this praise but looked doubtful. "But that's not really a talent; anyone can do that."

"No, I think Mother is right, Irena. You have a very special gift, and you do use it for the Lord. Look how you helped me see that I needed only faith, not works, to be saved," Nels pointed out.

Irena smiled happily.

The Grandville ladies welcomed the Jenson women as they gathered around the tables in the hotel dining room. Irena was nervous, and she saw that her mother-in-law seemed stiff and unfriendly and realized that she was nervous too. It almost made Irena laugh to see that while she had been frightened by that look the first time she met Mrs. Jenson, the older woman had simply been hiding her own nervousness as well.

Irena smiled warmly at her mother-in-law and was rewarded with a small smile that relaxed the tight features on Mrs. Jenson's face. Then Irena turned to answer the greetings of the ladies one by one. Some names she had forgotten and needed to ask, but no one seemed to mind. Each time she turned and said, "And you know my mother-in-law, Mrs. Jenson."

After they had spoken to each one, they took the seats that were offered them, and Irena sank down in relief. Her trembling limbs were barely holding her up anymore and she wondered if anyone else ever suffered from shyness like she did. She soon forgot all that as Lucy Riley stood up to open their meeting with a word of prayer. Irena had never heard a woman pray out loud before, and she listened intently, not wanting to miss anything.

Next Mallory Trent stood to give the Bible study for the day. She explained to the newcomers that they took turns leading, and Irena's face must have revealed her fear because Mallory hastened to add, "…if anyone wants to. We don't force anyone to take the lead."

Mallory's study was on Proverbs 31, and Irena listened in fascination to the description of a virtuous woman. Shortly after Mallory began, Irena saw a young woman come out of the kitchen and quietly sit down. Irena's eyes followed her for a moment before focusing back on Mallory. Then recognition hit, and her eyes flew back to the woman. This was the woman Nels had been watching shake rugs when Irena arrived on the stage.

Irena's mouth suddenly went dry, and she clasped her hands tightly together. She was startled when Mrs. Jenson unobtrusively patted her hands, and when Irena looked at her, Mother Jenson gave a negative shake of her head.

Irena understood. She would not worry about the woman right now. She would concentrate on what Mallory was saying. But it was difficult. Soon Mallory opened the meeting to discussion, and a few ladies shared with the others something that God had shown them in their lives, or some asked questions and anyone could participate in answering. Irena was captivated by it all. Maybe someday she would be brave enough to speak out loud in front of all these ladies and tell them how Swede led her to the Lord on her trip to America. Someday, but not yet.

The ladies were working together on quilts to give to new brides or new babies or to welcome new families to their town. So for the next hour, pleasant conversation hummed as the ladies either worked on cutting fabric, piecing blocks together, or doing the final topstitching. Irena stayed close to Mother Jenson and followed directions carefully for the simple tasks she was given. Now that everyone was busy with projects, Irena couldn't help but watch that woman again. She had gone back into the kitchen, and now she was busy carrying trays out to the dining room that held cups and saucers and platters of cookies and cakes.

"We take turns every month bringing the snacks for the meeting," Jade Newly explained to the Jensons. "This month was Philippa and Cora's turn, so they did the baking. Lucy always provides the coffee and tea, and usually Mattie Morrison, who works here for Lucy, takes care of the serving, like she is today. But I'm afraid this will be the last meeting that Mattie will be with us for a while. She's decided to take a teaching job in Norris and will be leaving next week. Lucy and Buck have put up a *Help Wanted* notice, but so far they haven't replaced her. We'll miss her; she's been a good friend." Jade continued to converse with Mrs. Jenson, but Irena was silent in her thoughts.

She must be leaving because of me. Was she in love with Nels? Did he love her?

"Shall we ask the blessing before we have refreshments?" Irena's thoughts were interrupted again, and she knew that now was not the time for them. After Lucy prayed, the ladies went to the serving table and made their choices of the delicacies there and went back to sit down again. Mrs. Jenson and Irena followed them. Irena was pleased to see her mother-in-law stop to visit with Hermine Tucker, and Irena moved on ahead of her to the refreshment table.

She picked up a plate at the same time that Mattie Morrison set down another tray of cookies, and their eyes met. Irena quickly dropped her gaze then forced herself to look up again.

Neither woman spoke, and Irena felt she was being rude, so she held out her hand and said, "Hello, I'm Irena Aar—uh, Jenson." How foolish that she stumbled over her own name!

"Oh good!" Lucy spoke behind Irena. "You've met Mattie. Did she tell you that she's leaving me to go teach school? I don't know what I'll do without her. She keeps the hotel running so smoothly."

Mattie smiled politely at the praise, but when Lucy moved on, she said coldly to Irena, "Congratulations on your marriage, Mrs. Jenson. Excuse me, please."

IRENA'S BOND OF MATRIMONY | 171

Irena felt like someone had kicked her. Even though in her young life she had never had friends, she had never had enemies either. But here was a young woman who disliked her very much. She found that her hand was trembling, and she knew she would never be able to swallow any of the delicious goodies on the table. She moved away and walked almost in a trance to the other end of the room. She needed to get away.

The doorway to Lucy and Buck's living quarters opened, and Irena recognized the man who stepped out as Buck Riley. He seemed agitated as he looked around the room for help. He spotted Irena and motioned for her to come to him. Curious, she approached and as she did she heard a commotion coming from the doorway—crying babies and laughing children.

"It was my turn to help with the children today," Buck explained to her as he led her inside amidst the melee.

"By yourself?" Irena asked in disbelief when she saw how many children were running around the room.

"No, Grace Morrison is in there with the small babies. But look, Mrs. Jenson, I'm sorry to bother you, but I just found out my horses are out of the corral, and I have to go round them up before the stage gets here. Could you take over for me here? I'm sorry to ask you—"

"Of course I will! Go! It is my pleasure," she assured him. Just then Eddie Newly came from the other room and shouted Irena's name. She was suddenly the center of attention as the other children looked to see who Eddie was talking to. Buck made his escape after a quick thank you, and Irena found herself in charge of a room full of children.

Some time later the door opened, but Irena didn't hear it for she was in the middle of a story and had the full attention of her audience. She changed her voice to a tiny hush and crouched down on the floor as she spoke for a frightened lamb, and then her voice became a harsh growl for the wolf, and she rose up on her tiptoes and waved her arms.

Lucy Riley motioned for Mrs. Jenson to follow her inside the room, and they listened in awe as Irena completed her story. Every child there was lost in Irena's tale, and they clapped wildly when she was done and curtsied for them. Irena turned and saw the women behind her, and her face burned with embarrassment. Lucy quickly stepped forward and took her hands.

"Irena, that was wonderful! Why, I don't think I have ever seen the children so quiet and well behaved. Your storytelling was fantastic! What a talent you have!"

Irena was surprised at Lucy's words. "I took care of children when I was younger, and I had to find ways to entertain them," she explained.

"Well, I think you have a real gift!" Lucy praised her again, and Mrs. Jenson beamed with pride at her daughter-in-law. "But where's Buck? And why are you here? We couldn't find you and began to worry."

"Oh, I'm sorry." Irena explained the situation.

Grace came from the next room, holding one of the babies, and she said shyly to Irena, "Your story was so good! I got lost in it too. Even the babies all seemed to settle down once you started talking."

"I didn't know you were listening." Irena was embarrassed again. "I can only tell stories to children; adults frighten me!"

The ladies laughed.

"Thank you so much, Irena. I'll take over now so that you and Mrs. Jenson are free. I hope you enjoyed our Bible study and will join us again next month."

Irena waited for Mrs. Jenson's answer and was happy to agree with her that they would be sure to come again.

"He was not in love with her," Mrs. Jenson spoke after they had ridden in silence for a time. Irena turned to her, understanding right away that she referred to Mattie Morrison.

"She's angry with me."

The older woman sighed. "I saw that too. I am sorry, but she will get over it."

Irena thought for a moment. "But Nels did care for her. I saw them when I arrived on the coach. I'm still surprised that he married me anyway."

"He obeyed our wishes, and I believe he is glad now that he did." Mrs. Jenson smiled. "Mattie Morrison was attractive to him, but Nels did not love her," she repeated. "And now she will go and find that God has a different path for her life. A much better one than she thought."

Irena nodded thoughtfully. "I still feel sorry for her."

Chapter 22

Jenson Farm

"You missed a spot," Nels teased Irena.

"Where?" She looked carefully over the area on the house she had just painted.

"There," he said, and he dabbed paint on the back of her hand.

"Nels!"

He laughed and ducked as Irena's paintbrush flew around to him. He popped his head up and saw Irena's eyes were wide in astonishment and her hand was over her mouth. He swung around to find Rex Newly with white paint spattered over his face. Nels didn't know whose expression was more funny—Irena's or Rex's.

There was a moment of silence, then Irena tried to apologize. "I am so sorry!" But the words came out between giggles, and soon all three of them were laughing. Rex wiped his hand across his face and smeared the paint, which only made the other two laugh harder.

Nels handed him a rag and said, "You'll have to excuse my wife, Mr. Newly. She's dangerous with a paintbrush in her hands."

"Me?" Irena said in mock outrage.

Mrs. Jenson appeared around the corner and appraised the paint-spattered threesome while shaking her head at them. "If you can manage to clean yourselves up, I will let you come in for coffee," she informed them. As she turned to walk away, they heard her mutter, "Oh, for goodness' sake. *Uffda!*"

The three headed for the porch and the washstand and soap awaiting them. Rex followed behind the laughing couple and tried to hide his amazement at the change he saw in them. He was even more surprised when he saw Nels dip a towel in water and gently clean some paint off Irena's face. She seemed to glow with the attention.

Rex put his thoughts away as he listened to what Nels was saying.

"So what brings you out here today, Mr. Newly?"

"Rex." Rex scrubbed at his face before answering. "I told you I'd be around again in a month. I'm still interested in buying some of your cows, but I was wondering if I could wait until around October to get them. I've decided to put my house up first, and I won't have enough time to get things done if I have milking responsibilities to take care of too. I could pay you for them now, though, if you'd like, and I'd even pay you for taking care of them for me."

They went inside, and Irena stepped to the stove to help Mrs. Jenson in serving the coffee and cake she had ready.

Nels waited until everyone had been served, then he explained Rex's request to his mother before he answered Rex.

"I think I would rather that you pay me for the cows when you actually come for them. You don't have to worry that I will sell them to anyone else; you can even pick out which ones you want now. We had several new calves this spring, and I don't want to get too many cows or I will have too many to take care of, even with Irena's help."

He smiled at his wife before he turned back to Rex. "That way I can continue to sell the milk and not have to keep track of which milk came from your cows or my cows and complications like that." He grinned. "Besides, you might even change your mind between now and then."

Rex shook his head. "It's not likely. I'll be getting married in October, and I'll need to get my own milk and dairy business under way by then. But I will wait until later to buy the cows as you wish."

Nels and the women offered their congratulations to Rex on his news. Rex saw Irena smile and knew that she was pleased.

Rex again marveled at the change in Irena. He could see she was happy and that her husband was proud of her. He also noticed that Mrs. Jenson treated her with great fondness, an entirely different attitude than he had first seen in the older woman. He discovered that he had been worried about Irena since the day he saw her get off the coach and stand alone and frightened in the street.

The men finished their coffee and went off to the pasture to look over the cows together. Irena helped clear up from their refreshments then she went back out behind the house and resumed the painting that she and Nels started earlier in the week. The house now boasted a clean white exterior, and its appearance was greatly improved. Mrs. Jenson requested blue shutters and eaves, and as soon as Irena finished the back side of the house, she would begin on that project.

She thought about Mattie Morrison again as she worked. She and Nels talked about it that night after the ladies' Bible study, and Irena was relieved to know that Nels had truly never loved the woman.

"I was a bit rebellious at the idea of a mail-order bride, Irena. I knew a Norwegian wife was important to my father, but I wanted to choose my own wife, and I argued about it with him a lot. After he died, I felt terrible that we had argued, and I knew I would honor his wishes if for nothing else but to honor him. Even though I felt attracted to Mattie, I never intended to marry her."

Nels paused in his explanation, not wanting to hurt his wife's feelings but knowing that she would want his honesty.

"I didn't want to marry you either, Irena. I was so rude to you those first days! I'm sorry. Then I remembered that this marriage wasn't your fault and that you probably didn't like it any better than I did.

I wondered what it must have felt like to you. Then I began to watch you, and I saw that you were frightened but brave at the same time. And when I *really* looked at you, I saw you were beautiful, and I started falling in love with you."

Irena blushed at the memory of her husband's words as she stroked the paint onto the wood, finishing the second coat. She stepped back and admired her work before she began cleaning up the brushes, and she noticed that the men were on their way back to the house again. Apparently they had finished their survey of the herd.

Nels saw Rex's attention turn to Irena as they walked and he commented, "It is good that you will have a wife. I cannot tell you the difference it has made in my life to have Irena. I thank God every day for her."

"My nephew Eddie thinks the world of your wife too. He told me all about the story she told the children the day the ladies had their Bible study. It seems she captivated them. It's all he can talk about, and he tells the story over and over to anyone who will listen. He begged to ride over here today with me, but his mother and father were taking him to visit some cousins. You may have competition for your wife's affections," Rex teased.

Nels laughed. "Irena will be an excellent mother someday. We look forward to God blessing us with children." He looked thoughtful. "It is the wish of every man, right? We want sons to carry on our names and daughters to keep our hearts soft."

Rex nodded his agreement while he smiled at Nels's words. He wondered how Bernadette felt about children. She seemed to enjoy baby Leon, but he didn't know how she felt about having her own children. Shouldn't he know that?

Irena joined the men as they neared the house. Rex noticed that she was wearing the same gray dress she had arrived in, although now it was spattered with white paint. He wondered how well she was being taken care of and then asked himself why that should concern him. She seemed happy enough.

Nels held out his hand. "Our best wishes to you and your bride. Will we be seeing you again before October?"

Rex nodded. "Actually, you probably will. The ladies in Grandville are planning an anniversary party for many of the couples who live in Sand Creek. You may have heard them talking about it. I don't know the details yet, but I imagine I'll be involved somehow." He grinned. "When my sisters and sister-in-law get to planning, I always seem to get roped into doing something. Perhaps I can introduce Bernadette to you then. I know she would be pleased to meet you. And, Mrs. Jenson, my mother will surely want a visit with you."

The men shook hands, and Rex tipped his hat to Irena. Mrs. Jenson stepped out on the porch and Rex called out, "Thanks again for the coffee, Mrs. Jenson," before he mounted his horse and left. He looked back once and saw Nels with his arm around Irena, watching him, and they lifted their hands to wave. The image of them standing together stayed in his mind for a long time.

Tyler and Jade begged Rex to stay in Grandville longer.

"It is such a treat for us to have family come," Jade cajoled him. "And Eddie and Pamela need time to get to know their uncle better."

Rex laughed at her excuses to detain him. "The road runs both ways. When was the last time you two were in Sand Creek?"

Their guilty expressions gave them away.

"Besides," Rex continued, "all the family will be here soon for that anniversary party you're planning, right? How's that going, by the way?"

Tyler started laughing as Jade threw up her hands. "We're really stumped on an excuse to get everyone here," she admitted. "Now that you and Bernadette are engaged, maybe you could have your wedding here?" she suggested hopefully.

"Oh no you don't." Rex put up a warning hand. "October will be soon enough, considering all the work I've got to get done before then. You'll have to come up with something else and leave me out of it."

"Irena Jenson suggested that we each invite our own families for a visit individually and not try to organize a big event for an excuse." Jade mused.

"When did you talk to her about it?" Rex was curious.

"At our ladies' Bible study. You should see how hungry she is for God's Word, Rex. I don't know her story yet, because she is quite bashful, but I'd sure like to know more about her. She seems so genuinely honest and sincere." She frowned slightly. "She did seem a little upset after talking with Mattie Morrison, though."

The men waited for Jade to continue.

She explained. "Mattie thought Nels Jenson cared for her and was very distraught when she found he had married Irena."

Rex thought about Irena again and wondered if her life was really as happy as it appeared to be when he saw her the day before.

"Anyway," Jade spoke again, "I discussed Irena's suggestion with some of the other ladies, and I think that is how we'll handle it. You're going to have to help keep the party a secret while you're in Sand Creek, Rex," she cautioned.

"Just try to keep me out of it as much as possible, please. I have enough going on in my life right now."

"You will come, won't you?"

"I wouldn't miss it!" Rex assured his sister-in-law.

"We're really happy about you and Bernadette," Tyler told his brother, "though we're not all that surprised. She's been chasing you since grade school."

Rex shot Tyler a quick look. "I guess it takes me a while to see things for myself. Hey, thanks for the good price on the lumber too. I can hardly wait to get to work on the house."

"I wish I could spare the time to help you," Tyler admitted.

"No problem. Pa and Abel will help when they can, and Hank, Uncle Evan, and their boys will be over too. I suspect that Jonas Nolan will pitch in as well. We'll get it done."

Chapter 23

Sand Creek

Rex thought about Nels and Irena a lot as work progressed on his house. When he had first seen them, he never would have believed that the two of them would have become the loving couple he saw on his last visit. They seemed to share something special between them now. Then his thoughts turned to Bernadette. She was so beautiful, and he really did love her, but…

He struggled to put his finger on what that *but* was. She was still attractive and vivacious and excited about their engagement. Indeed, she told everyone she saw about it and was full of wedding plans and ideas that she constantly shared with him. They discussed the building plans for their house, and Bernadette seemed enthusiastic about helping with the design and planning the sizes of the rooms. Still…

There was that comment she made that "perhaps Rex would like to work in her father's store sometime."

He had thought she was kidding and had laughed and said "that would be the day when I would be stuck working indoors." She had been quiet for a moment before smiling and agreeing with him, but he could see she had been serious.

Then she had mentioned that they would be awfully far from town and wondered what she would do with herself all day. Rex thought of his own mother and how she seemed to always have things to do, but he remembered that Bernadette had lived in town all her life and was used to being around people and seeing customers in her father's store.

"I'll be making the daily milk run to your father, remember?" he told her. "You could come with me to town." That had seemed to cheer her up. Still, Rex was beginning to wonder if Bernadette was having second thoughts. But moving ahead quickly had been her idea, he reminded himself.

Suddenly Rex saw that he was not trusting the Lord with these details in his life. He was worrying instead of bringing his concerns to the Lord. He also acknowledged that being around Bernadette stirred his emotions, and he didn't always think clearly while under her *spell*.

He understood the danger in a physical attraction, and he tried to keep his distance and be a complete gentleman with his intended, but there were times when Bernadette put herself in his arms and lifted her face for a kiss, and he could not refuse. She was a very desirable woman.

Rex wiped the sweat from his forehead with his shirt sleeve. He and his dad and Abel had been working since after morning chores, and it was almost time for lunch. He saw the two of them head to the wagon and the water bottles, and he went to join them.

"Tyler and Mike picked out some choice lumber for you," commented Russ. "It helps to have family in the lumber business, doesn't it?"

Rex laughed dryly while he agreed with his father. "I admit they gave me a good deal, but I think Ty knew what he was doing when he asked that I bring back a trained pony for Eddie's next birthday."

Russ chuckled. "Well, training horses is our business, so it's only right that we make trades. Eddie is going to love it, but Jade will have her hands full keeping track of him."

The men asked the blessing then went to work on the lunch Sky prepared for them while they discussed the progress they had made.

"With the shell almost completed, we should be able to start on rafters and get a roof on soon," Russ commented. "Hank and the boys have offered their help when you're ready." He looked around Rex's property. "You've got a good piece of land here. Your mother is especially pleased that you and Bernadette will be close by. It's hard on her to have grandchildren as far away as Grandville and Norris and rarely get to see them."

"Hard on you too." Abel grinned at his father. "I guess you'll have to have lots of kids to make up for it, Rex," he teased. "Sure you don't want us to build your house bigger?"

Rex endured his brother's teasing with practiced patience. There was that question of children again, something he and Bernadette still needed to discuss.

"Anything wrong, Son?"

Rex shook off his pensive mood. "No, just thinking of all there still is to do, I guess."

"Think you'll be able to spare the time to go to Grandville in two weeks? Buck and Lucy invited us and the Rileys to celebrate Molly's first birthday with them. Dorcas and Cavan are coming too, and Lucy said that Simon and Emma will join us from Norris, so it should be a real family gathering."

So that's how they're getting the Newlys and Rileys to Grandville, thought Rex. *I wonder what the story will be for the others.*

"I'll try to make it," he said to his father. Abel's grinning face bobbed up behind his father's shoulder, and Rex had a hard time keeping a straight face, so he bent down to reach for the water bottle. *Abel's going to have a hard time keeping this party a secret.*

The three men turned together at the sound of an approaching buggy, and Rex squinted his eyes to see who it was. He recognized with pleasure that Bernadette was in the buggy then narrowed his gaze to make out the man beside her. It was no one he knew.

"Rex!" Bernadette called happily to him, and he rubbed his hands on his pant legs and wished he wasn't all sweaty and dirty, but it couldn't be helped. He stepped forward as the stranger reined in the horse beside him, and Rex moved to Bernadette's side to help her down. He noticed her nose wrinkle when she was close to him and was embarrassed that she had to see him like this, but she smiled at him anyway.

"I want you to meet Steven Rowan," Bernadette said excitedly and turned to the stranger approaching them. "Steven, this is my fiancé, Rex Newly, and his father, Mr. Newly, and his brother Abel."

The men all shook hands in turn and greeted the newcomer while they listened to Bernadette explain who he was.

"Steven is a salesman from Minneapolis," she said, and Rex could hear how excited that information alone made her. "He's here to show father some new things to put in his store. You just wouldn't believe all the products we could market to the people in this area. Why, Steven can even provide us with goods shipped from other countries."

Rex listened as Bernadette continued to explain all the wonderful things that the salesman could do for Sand Creek while he studied the man. Rex was somewhat surprised to see that he was being appraised as well. The salesman was well dressed, handsome, and self-assured. Rex felt like a farmer, and though that is what he was, somehow it felt inadequate.

"Miss Nolan is a better salesman than I am, I'm afraid." Steven Rowan smiled when Bernadette finished.

"Steven, I told you to call me Bernadette. We're very informal here in Sand Creek." She turned to Rex. "Steven wanted to see some of the countryside and the farms so he would have a better idea of the needs we have here for the next time he comes through. I offered to take him around, and I wanted him to see how our house is coming. Steven has some wonderful furniture in his catalogs, Rex. Maybe we could order some things for the house?"

Rex started to reply, but Bernadette was already taking Steven Rowan's arm and leading him to the building site. A stab of jealousy pierced Rex, and he clenched his fist, though his face revealed nothing. Russ and Abel didn't speak as they put away their lunch things and went back to their tools. Bernadette's laughter flitted to Rex's ears, and he debated about what to do next, but finally he made his way over to the couple and listened as Bernadette explained what the rooms were to her guest.

"That seems rather small for a kitchen," Russ heard the man's comment.

"Bernadette designed the kitchen herself," he informed him as he moved toward them.

"Maybe it is a little small, Rex." Bernadette looked over the space critically.

"Is this your dining room then?" Steven pointed to the next space.

"Yes," Bernadette said proudly. "And we have a parlor and a sitting room over there."

"And would this be the library?"

"That's our bedroom," Rex informed the salesman.

"Oh, Rex! Wouldn't a library be grand! Do you think we could add that to the plan?"

Rex stared at Bernadette. "We've already put up the walls, Bernadette. It's a little late to change things now."

"Now's the best time while you can still take things apart," Steven pointed out. He took Rex's silence for agreement and continued, "It would probably please your future wife if she had her own sewing room too. I know my mother always enjoyed hers."

"Oh, I hadn't thought of that!" Bernadette exclaimed. "Steven, you have the best ideas."

Rex stood still while the pair moved away to discuss something else. He knew his father was watching him, but he wasn't ready to make eye contact with anyone yet. He prayed silently until Bernadette and Steven headed back his way, and then he walked with them to the buggy. He wasn't even sure that Bernadette knew he was there until he reached for her hand to help her into the buggy.

"I'm sorry, Rex, but we have to go now."

"I'll see you Friday night, Bernadette." Rex squeezed her hand gently, and she looked at him questioningly.

"Oh, Friday night. Yes, I'll see you then." She waved to the other Newly men while Rex said good-bye to Steven Rowan and watched the buggy drive away. His heart felt heavy, and a sense of foreboding stayed with him.

Friday night Rex rode into town, clean and polished and ready to discuss a few issues with his bride-to-be. For one thing, he thought she should understand how he felt about her riding around the country with another man. For another, he'd like to know how she felt about children. And he had to explain to her that he could change the house plans if she really wanted him to, but it would take more time and more money to do so.

He found himself nervous about the night's visit and prayed for the right words so that he wouldn't cause trouble in their relationship. He wanted Bernadette to be happy, but he wanted her to understand his feelings and thoughts too.

It was a warm night, and the heat made his shirt stick to him as he rode into town. He hoped they could go for a walk, anyway, and not stay in the stuffy parlor.

Jonas Nolan answered Rex's knock, and it took only one look at the man's face for Rex to understand that Bernadette was gone. He had to admit that it had been in the back of his mind since her visit out to the house, but he had refused to believe it would really happen.

"Come in, son." Rex heard the sympathy in the older man's voice and steeled himself for what was ahead. They went to the kitchen, where Bridget sat with coffee ready. They had been waiting for him.

Bridget rose and went to Rex and hugged him but didn't say a word. Rex felt his eyes sting. These people were suffering because their daughter had just left, but here they were, concerned about his feelings. He took a deep breath and sat down with them.

"We tried to talk her out of it, of course," Bridget began, "but Bernadette is headstrong, and she fell head over heels for that Steven Rowan. They went to the preacher this morning. We went too." She hesitated as if afraid to explain their actions. "After all, she is our daughter, and it was her wedding day. She was a beautiful bride—" Bridget choked on the words, and

Rex felt something cold inside him despite the heat of the night.

Jonas continued while he patted his wife's hand. "They took the stage to Freesburg this afternoon, and they'll be on the train tomorrow to Minneapolis. I'm sorry, son. We were so happy that you and Bernadette were going to marry, and now this." Jonas shook his head. "We want her to be happy, and she insisted that Steven Rowan was who she wanted. She left a letter for you." He pointed to the envelope with Rex's name on it that had been sitting on the table. Rex hadn't even noticed it.

Bridget sniffed as she poured the coffee and set a cup in front of Rex. The three of them sat in silence, and Rex finally realized that the Nolans were waiting for him to say something. He would have to put aside his own emotions for a while and concentrate on how these dear friends were feeling.

He took a drink of the hot coffee, hardly tasting it at all. The heat in the room was making him feel damp inside his shirt, and he longed to get out of the house. He searched his mind for something to say and found himself beseeching the Lord for help. A peace stole over him slowly, something he hadn't felt in a while.

"I want Bernadette to be happy," he found himself saying to the Nolans. "If Steven Rowan is the man she wants, then she would not have been happy with me, and eventually I would not have been happy as well. Although I feel at a loss right now"—he glanced up at the couple—"I will trust that God will direct me and show me the next step to take. Please, when you talk to

Bernadette or write her, tell her that, and tell her that I only wish her the best."

Bridget smiled at Rex through her tears. "You are a good man, Rex Newly." Jonas stood as Rex rose to depart. Rex slipped the letter into his pocket and thanked Bridget for the coffee before he left. Jonas shook Rex's hand.

"Thanks for making this easier for us, Rex. We can't tell you how badly we feel."

Rex nodded to the man before mounting his horse and turning it away from the town. He felt an overwhelming urge to break into a gallop and just ride and ride, but he resisted and rode quietly along and let his heart commune with God.

Why did you let this happen, Lord? I thought you were leading Bernadette and me together. How could I have been wrong? I feel so stupid, like a fool! Now everyone will be talking about this and feeling sorry for me. I don't think I can take that, Lord.

Rex rode for a while and let his prayer echo through his mind again. He stopped his horse when he got to his land, and he swung down and walked to the house in the fading light. The skeleton of bare lumber seemed to mock him.

Lord, my pride is hurting. I'm worried about what people will think of me. I feel like a fool to think that Bernadette loved me.

Rex's boots echoed on the wooden floor as he walked up the steps and around the partitioned walls of his house. *How could I have been wrong, Lord? How will*

I ever know when you are leading me or if I'm just doing what I want to do?

A verse came to his mind as he sat down on the edge of the porch and let his legs swing free. It was somewhere in Romans, he thought: "that ye may prove what is that good, and acceptable, and perfect, will of God."

That ye may prove... Rex thought about that. Had he *proved*, was he sure about his marriage to Bernadette? He had to admit that there had been doubts growing in his mind. What was the first part of that verse?

Rex let the quiet of the night calm his heart and the breeze off the lake cool his body as he reached into his memory for the verses he had learned as a child.

He found himself saying the words out loud: "I beseech you therefore, brethren, by the mercies of God, that ye present your bodies a living sacrifice, holy, acceptable unto God, which is your reasonable service. And be not conformed to this world: but be ye transformed by the renewing of your mind, that ye may prove..."

The words spoke to his heart, and he realized that in the past few months he had let his infatuation with Bernadette slowly pull his mind away from God's Word. He had moved forward with his plans with little time spent in prayer and had made his decisions based more on his emotions than on knowing it was God's will for him.

Rex bowed his head humble before the Lord. "I have not been letting you transform me, Lord. I have not been renewing my mind with your Word. Thank you for bringing me to that realization and putting me back on the right track."

Rex felt as if a burden had been removed when he lifted his head. His heart still stung, and he would carry the wounds for a while, but he would heal. He praised God for that. He looked around at the unfinished structure.

"What next, Lord?" he asked simply.

Chapter 24

Grandville

Irena watched her hostess carefully. Something was not right with Philippa this morning, and Irena wasn't quite sure what it was that made her think so, but she was beginning to fear that it had something to do with the cookies she had baked and brought for a treat for their morning coffee together.

Philippa took a second small bite of the cookie and closed her eyes briefly before she slowly began to chew. Irena knew the exact moment when her friend was going to be sick, and she jumped up to grab the basin out of the sink for her. As Philippa retched, Irena reached for a towel then quickly went for a glass of water. Philippa's face was white as she took a small sip from the glass, and she sat back in her chair weakly and tried to protest as Irena set about to clean up after her.

Irena said some soothing words as she quietly and efficiently took care of things, thinking as she did so that Philippa hadn't been eating any of the refreshments she served at their coffee time for the last several days. It was only today because Irena had brought the treat that she recalled seeing Philippa eat. She nodded in understanding.

"I am so sorry, Irena," Philippa apologized as she watched her friend return to her seat. "I don't know what's the matter with me. I haven't been able to eat for the last several days, and I thought I was getting over it, but...I'm so embarrassed."

Irena smiled. "Have you been extra tired as well?" she asked.

"Yes, terribly!" Philippa complained. "In fact, yesterday Ralph had to mind the store so I could take a little nap. Why, has someone else been ill that you know of?"

Irena's smile widened. "These are the symptoms my aunt had when she was expecting her babies," she said simply and watched carefully for Philippa's reaction. She wasn't disappointed.

"What? Oh no, Irena, it couldn't be. Ralph and I have been married four years!" Philippa studied Irena's knowing face. "Do you think so? Oh, my goodness!"

Irena laughed. "Or it could be that you don't like my cookies."

Philippa put a hand to her tummy as she giggled with Irena. "Could it really be? Ralph and I used to pray about having children, but as the years passed, we gave up hope." She sat up a little straighter, and Irena could see her mind was working. "It is possible," she said as she counted on her fingers, and Irena watched the hope spring into her eyes. "But I have to be sure before I say anything to Ralph. I don't want to get his hopes up if it's not true. Could you do something for me, Irena?"

"Anything."

"Could you watch the store while I go see Dr. Arnett? I'm sure I won't be too long. Please, Irena?"

Irena quelled the touch of nervousness this request gave her and quickly assured her friend, "Of course, go. I will write down everything I do."

"Thank you, Irena!"

Philippa hurried out of the kitchen so fast that Irena couldn't help but laugh as she finished cleaning up their coffee dishes. She wasn't sure if she should stay in the Tunelle's kitchen or go into the store to wait for a customer, but the decision was made for her when she heard the bell ring, signaling that a customer had entered through the doorway.

Irena smoothed her green skirt, another of Mother Jenson's creations, and patted her braids nervously before she stepped through the doorway and moved behind the counter. To her relief, it was Lucy Riley who was looking at some items, and in her arms was Molly.

"Oh, hello, Irena. How are you today?" Lucy asked in her pleasant manner.

"I'm fine. And you, and Molly?"

The women chatted for a few moments before Lucy asked if Philippa was around.

"She needed to go on an errand and asked if I could watch the store for a short time," Irena explained. Then she confided, "I really don't know anything about watching a store."

Lucy laughed at Irena's serious expression. "You seem to be doing just fine. I'm looking for some lace to make some decorations for the anniversary party. Oh, you know about that, right?"

"Yes, Jade and I spoke of it at the Bible study, and your brother Rex mentioned it too when he spoke to Nels about some cattle."

"Oh, that's right. Did you know that we're using your suggestion and each family is inviting their folks to come at the same time for different reasons? Ours are coming because I told them we'll be celebrating Molly's first birthday, which we will, but they don't know that we'll be celebrating their anniversary too."

"What about the others?" Irena asked.

Lucy grinned. "It has been so much fun coming up with reasons to invite everyone, but mostly grandchildren's birthdays will do it. Bernie Riggs is asking Clyde and Bertha to come because he wants to show Clyde the blacksmith shop. Clyde taught Bernie everything about being a smithy," Lucy explained. "And the Nessels and Spencers are coming because, as it happens, they are both purchasing lumber from Tyler and Michael, so that worked out. Buck has asked the Nolans to come as our guests so we can get advice on running the hotel better.

"One big problem we have is Philippa's parents," she continued. "Mrs. Gray has never come here and sees no reason to. I don't know what excuse Philippa will come up with to get her mother here."

Irena had to hide a smile. There may be one soon.

"May I hold Molly while you look around?" she asked.

"She's getting heavy," Lucy warned. She handed the baby over and admired the ease with which Irena held her. "Babies and children love you, don't they?"

Irena blushed at the comment.

Fortunately, no other customers came in, although once Ralph walked through and was surprised to see Irena instead of Philippa behind the counter.

"She had a small errand to run," Irena repeated the explanation and was relieved when Ralph accepted that news without further questions. Nearly an hour later, Philippa hurried back through the door. Her face was glowing, and her eyes were sparkling in excitement.

"It's true!" She clasped both Irena's hands in her own. "About April, Dr. Arnett thinks. I'm so excited! How shall I tell Ralph?" She didn't wait for Irena to reply but rambled on. "Maybe I'll plan a special dinner tonight and surprise him with the news afterward, or maybe I should wrap up some baby items from the store and have him open them. What do you think?"

Ralph walked into the store at that moment to see his wife, and Philippa blurted out, "We're going to have a baby!"

Irena had to cover her mouth to keep from laughing out loud at Philippa's outburst. She was satisfied to see the shock on Ralph's face, and she heard his bewildered questions and Philippa's excited answers as she slipped past them and out to her waiting wagon. Nels and Mother Jenson would be wondering what happened to her. She was sure she would hear more details from

Philippa at their next visit together. Meanwhile, she thanked the Lord for the Tunelle's wonderful news.

Irena admired the newly painted house with its blue shutters as she drove the wagon into the yard. As she had suspected, Mother Jenson appeared at the doorway with relief evident in her eyes, and Nels walked to her from the barn with an anxious look on his face rapidly disappearing as he saw that she was all right. How good it felt to have people care about her!

Nels pulled her into his arms briefly after he helped her from the wagon. "I was worried," he whispered.

"I'm sorry," she said, with a grateful smile for his concern. She waited until Mother Jenson approached before she gave them both her explanation for being late. They were pleased with the news and laughed heartily at Irena's description of how Philippa told Ralph.

"Four years!" Nels exclaimed. "That is a long time to wait for children. Is that normal?" His question was directed at his mother, but Irena was the one who answered him.

"Not really. My aunt had children right away, and with us it has taken only a few months."

She waited, maintaining an innocent look on her face while she enjoyed the dumbfounded looks on theirs. Nels remained speechless, but Mother Jenson broke her promise to speak only in English and fired questions at Irena in her native tongue.

"Are you sure, Irena? How long have you known? How are you feeling? Nels, maybe she shouldn't be driving the wagon, and she certainly doesn't need to be out helping you with the chores any longer or painting houses. Goodness, Irena! What if you had fallen from the ladder? Come inside. You need a cup of tea."

Irena listened with only half an ear to this tirade as she watched her husband's reaction. Nels's look of wonder turned to joy then to pride then to love as he stared at his wife. She stepped toward him as soon as he made the move toward her, and she found herself being turned around and around in the air.

"Nels Jenson! Stop that this instant!" His mother scolded. She took Irena's arm and led her to the house. Nels left the care of the wagon and horse and followed. Irena noticed that the grin never left his face.

"Why didn't you say something sooner, child?" Mother Jenson questioned.

"I wanted to be sure. I didn't want anyone to be disappointed if something happened, and I didn't want to be treated differently. I can still do work, you know. The doctor always told my aunt that it was good for her baby if she kept active."

"Well, you *will* be treated differently if I have anything to say about it," announced Mother Jenson. "This is my first grandchild, and I expect you to take very good care of him." She moved around the kitchen, preparing things for tea when she suddenly sat down and burst into tears.

"Mother, what is it?" Nels patted his mother's arm in concern.

"I'm so happy!" she wailed, and Irena and Nels laughed in relief.

"Yes, Irena has made us all very happy today." And Nels bent to kiss his wife.

Chapter 25

Sand Creek

Rex was confused by his feelings. At times he felt that a burden had been removed from his shoulders and he was happy in a relieved sort of way. And at other times he felt that he was recovering from deep wounds and that he had to work hard to get through each day. His parents had been anchors for him during this turbulent time. How he thanked God for their guidance! Not once did he hear an "I told you so" or any other recrimination from them. He knew they were praying for him, and that was the biggest help they could be right now.

Rex felt that he was experiencing the "peace of God that passeth all understanding." Their pastor spoke on that passage in Philippians 4 just this past Sunday, and the timing couldn't have been more perfect to Rex. Already the people of Sand Creek were aware of Bernadette's broken engagement and hasty marriage to the traveling salesman. Rex endured sympathetic looks and heard whispered comments wherever he went. But the pastor's words had been a healing balm to his soul.

"God tells us not to be anxious, not to worry, and not to fret or stew about what today or tomorrow may bring, but rather on a daily, nay—a moment-by-moment basis to bring our requests to him. And let's not forget to be thankful no matter what his answer may be. When we do that, the peace of God will keep our hearts and our minds through Christ Jesus. The world doesn't understand how we can be at peace, other believers may not understand, *we* may not even understand because God's Word says it "passeth all understanding." But, nevertheless, it is there. Peace in the midst of whatever circumstances we find ourselves. This is God's promise to us."

So Rex got through each day. He kept working on the house and now without a time schedule to pressure him, he found the work enjoyable and relaxing—an outlet physically. He was pleased with the progress he was making, and he took pride in doing careful, detailed work. Occasionally Bernadette's face would flash in his mind, and he'd remind himself that this was no longer for her. Then he'd ask the Lord to give him patience and that if it was his will that Rex never marry, he would be content with that as well.

"I have some news from town," Sky announced to her family one evening at the supper table. Russ, Rex, and Abel all waited for her to continue.

"Violet received a letter from Philippa, and you'll never believe it, Philippa and Ralph are expecting a baby! Violet is telling everyone in Sand Creek the news—even people she normally won't talk to, like me." Sky laughed. The rift between Violet and Sky dated back twenty-five years ago, and though Sky tried to befriend Violet, her efforts had always been rebuffed. "So she and Taylor are going to Grandville to help Philippa out for a few weeks. I guess Philippa has been ill with morning sickness. Maybe this is just what Violet needs to get her to think seriously about the Lord. Grandchildren can do that."

"So, will they be there the same time we will be next week?" asked Russ.

Rex heard a note of suspicion in his father's voice.

"I'm not sure when they're leaving," Sky said, "but I wouldn't be surprised. Violet sounded like she was ready to leave today!"

Later, when Rex helped his father with the evening chores, Russ commented, "It seems that quite a few families are headed to Grandville next week. You know anything about that, Rex?"

"Who's going?" Rex sidestepped the question.

"You should probably ask, 'Who isn't going?'" his father said dryly. "I notice you didn't answer the question."

Abel chuckled from a few stalls away.

"You know something about this, Son?" Russ called to him.

"Not that I care to say," was the amused reply.

Russ looked at Rex again, but Rex kept a careful guard on his expression.

"I see." Russ went back to work, and Rex breathed a sigh of relief. "But I'll find out," Russ warned, and Abel chuckled again while Rex just smiled to himself.

Chapter 26

Grandville

"Grandma! Look at me ride!" Eddie called to Sky as he clung to the back of his new pony, a gift from his parents and his uncle Rex. Russ and Sky waved to their grandson, and Russ laughed as Jade covered her eyes, barely able to watch her son for fear of seeing him fall.

"Be careful! Hang on!"

Eddie's face beamed with pride and joy as he walked the pony in a circle, guided by Rex.

"How did you survive watching your children learn to ride?" Jade asked Sky.

Sky laughed in sympathy with her daughter-in-law. "I knew they had the best teacher on earth," she replied," and I also learned that broken bones heal." She took Jade by the arm and led her back to the house. "It's best not to watch. Now suppose we leave the men to the teaching and you and I have a little chat about what's really going on in Grandville besides a birthday party for Molly."

At Jade's bewildered expression, Sky laughed. "You don't really think we believe that's the only reason we're here, do you? Nearly everyone in Sand Creek has an excuse to be in Grandville at the same time. Now, spill the beans. What's going on?"

"Who else is here?" Jade asked innocently, but Sky just shook her finger at her.

"You aren't fooling me, Jadyne Newly! You know very well that Evan and Ella are staying with Mike and Mallory." Sky counted off the people on her fingers. "Taylor and Violet Gray are at Ralph and Philippa's. The hotel is filled, what with Hank and Randi and the boys there, not to mention the Nessels and the Spencers, who just *happen* to be able to get their lumber orders filled now. Then there are the Nolans, supposedly giving Buck and Lucy help with advice on running their hotel, as if they need it. The Riggs are at Bernie and Pearl's, and so are Clyde and Belle Moore. And there are more coming. Now, what's going on?" Sky planted her hands on her hips, and her tone brooked no argument although there was humor in her voice as well.

As Jade searched for a reply, Tyler and Russ walked in and hearing Sky's last words, Tyler grinned wickedly at his wife's discomfort.

"I think I've solved the mystery." Russ put his arm around Sky and asked her, "What do all those people you just mentioned have in common?"

Sky's brow wrinkled in thought. "They're all from Sand Creek or nearby."

"Uh huh."

"And they're all our friends."

"Uh huh."

Sky searched her husband's face then glanced at Tyler, who was grinning at Jade. She looked at Jade and found her face anxious. Slowly Sky said, "They all got married the same time we did, didn't they?"

"Oh no!" Jade exclaimed, and Tyler burst out laughing.

"Yep." Russ turned and grinned at Rex and Abel who were just joining them. "Told you I'd figure it out."

"Always the detective, huh, Pa?"

"But it's supposed to be a surprise!"

"Oh my!" Sky stared at Jade. "You mean we're here for an anniversary party, not Molly's birthday?"

"Both, actually."

Jade looked so crestfallen at the surprise being discovered that everyone had to laugh. Shaking her head, she joined in.

"At least we got you here *before* you figured it out," she said smugly.

Grandville was bustling with people when the Jensons rode into town for the Sunday service. The back of their wagon was filled with food and packages for the big party that they would deliver to the hotel before heading to the church. Mrs. Jenson had been busy sewing pillows to put in the gift baskets that each anniversary couple was to receive, and Irena had spent several days baking treats to go in them as well.

She was proud to be able to contribute even though none of the families were related to her. The ladies of Grandville were like family to her now and that was enough. Nels helped unload the items and added them to the growing pile in the hotel kitchen.

"I'll come help as soon as Pastor Malcolm finishes the sermon," Irena told Lucy. Some of the ladies would work in the kitchen all morning and miss the morning service, but Irena couldn't bring herself to do that. She could hardly wait each week for Sunday to come. She wouldn't miss it for anything!

As it was, she might have been of more use in the kitchen, thought Irena. The church was crowded with all the Sand Creek visitors, and Irena worried part of the time about all the work that needed to be done for the party afterward, but she calmed herself and concentrated on the last part of the message, drinking in every word.

Pastor Malcolm had chosen the topic of marriage for his sermon in view of the upcoming anniversary celebration. His chosen passage was Ephesians 5, and Irena noted with interest that the word *reverence* meant respect. A wife should have respect for her husband.

Irena looked up at Nels beside her. Yes, she respected this man. He felt her gaze and turned to her. Their loving look was witnessed by a few people, Rex Newly being one of them. Again, Rex noted what a change he saw in this couple. For a moment he felt emptiness in his own life, but only for a moment. As was becoming his habit, he turned to the Lord and let God's peace fill his heart.

Irena and Nels stole out of the church just after Pastor Malcolm announced the twenty-fifth anniversary celebration that would take place immediately following the singing of the last hymn. He was asking for the couples to stand as he called out their names, and Irena paused when she heard Russ and Sky Newly's name. She was interested in Sky since Rex had told her that his mother had lived in England, and she was curious to know who she was in case she got a chance to speak with her later.

Irena was impressed with the strong resemblance Rex had to his father, and as she saw Sky's blonde hair and noticeably blue eyes, she immediately recognized where Lucy's attractive looks came from. Then Nels led her out the door and they hurried to the hotel.

"Now remember, you promised not to overdo."

"Yes, Nels. I will respect your wishes," Irena said honestly. "If there is something too heavy, I will get help."

In moments tasks were assigned to the new helpers, and Irena found herself facing the multitude of items that were to be assembled into attractive gift baskets for the anniversary couples.

"But I—" she tried to explain to Mallory who had given her an assignment that she had no idea how to do, when she saw Mother Jenson begin to wash the dishes that had started to pile up in the process of putting together the meal. She hastened to her mother-in-law.

"Mother, I need help." She led Mrs. Jenson to the gift baskets and explained in Norwegian so that the woman clearly understood, "You are so much more creative than I am. You do my job and I'll do yours. Okay?" And before the surprised woman could answer, Irena made her way to the wash basin and, tying on the apron she brought with her, went right to work.

Irena had been at her job for a while when she was finally relieved and told to go eat with Nels. She protested, but the woman, a stranger to her, said, "After you've eaten, come back and switch places with me. Go on."

Irena dried her hands as she walked over to Mrs. Jenson. The gift baskets were beautifully arranged. "Oh, Mother! They are so lovely that no one will want to take them apart!" exclaimed Irena. "I am so glad you did this instead of me. Oh, look at the ribbon and the bows you've made!"

"Do you think they will like it?" Mrs. Jenson seemed unsure.

At that moment Jade walked in and heard Mrs. Jenson's question. She gazed in amazement at the artfully arranged baskets. "How did you ever—? Why, I never imagined they would look so attractive. Mrs. Jenson, you are so talented."

The older woman beamed under the praise.

"Now, you two have been in here enough." Jade led them both out of the kitchen into the busy dining room. "I sent Rex for Nels and I want you to fill your plates and eat and visit for the rest of the day. Thank you so much for all your help." She moved off quickly to attend to something in the kitchen, and the women saw Nels and Rex approach them.

"There you are. Rex insists that I stop mixing ice cream long enough to come eat with my two favorite women. Mrs. Jenson and Irena smiled their pleasure at Nels's comment, and Irena smiled at Rex.

"You said you would introduce us to your bride the next time we saw..." Her voice trailed off as she saw Nels's warning look.

"I'm sorry, Mrs. Jenson, but I won't be able to do that," Rex told her politely, but Irena noticed a flicker of something in his eyes. "I won't be getting married after all." He seemed about to say more, but they heard someone call his name, and he excused himself.

"I'm sorry, Nels," Irena said. "I shouldn't have asked."

"You didn't know, Irena. Don't let it worry you. He told me that she married another man."

"Oh."

"He seems to be doing well, though," Nels commented.

Irena watched Rex across the room. He did seem to be doing well, she thought, as she saw him laugh at something the man beside him said.

They filled their plates and joined the others at tables set up outside. Fortunately, it was a beautiful September day. Irena ate the delicious food as she watched and listened to the many people around her. Occasionally Nels would say something to her or he'd visit with the man beside him, but mostly Irena enjoyed being quiet. She marveled that she was here among so many friendly faces. Even the people she did not know smiled at her and greeted her pleasantly. She was amazed at how much her life had changed.

Irena saw that Lucy and Jade were pleased with the success of their party. She didn't believe that everyone was surprised. Once the people started arriving in Grandville, the secret leaked out, but by that time they were all here and happy to have an event to celebrate together.

The mail-order bride story fascinated Irena. She could relate to these women who traveled to unknown futures and unknown husbands. When Jade, Mallory, and Lucy told her the story of the Grandville marriages, Irena had been even more shocked. She had no idea that women right here in America also found themselves in situations like hers.

It was time for the gift basket presentation, and Irena felt Mother Jenson fidget beside her, nervous about people seeing her work, but she needn't have worried. There were exclamations of delight as soon as they were carried to each table.

Buck Riley called for attention and announced the many people who had contributed to the items in the baskets, and then he said, "And each basket was arranged and decorated by our own Mrs. Jenson. Mrs. Jenson, will you please stand?"

Everyone applauded while Ingeborg Jenson blushed with pleasure. "Such foolishness," she said to Irena in Norwegian, but Irena could see her mother-in-law was enjoying the attention. Several ladies came to speak with her soon after, so Irena excused herself and went back to take another turn at washing the dishes. The same woman was there, and she gratefully gave the task over to Irena.

Tying her apron back on, Irena noticed that the water needed to be changed before she could wash any more dishes. She checked that there was more hot water available on the stove then looked at the dirty basin again. She tested its weight.

No, Nels would not want me to lift that, she thought, and she wanted very much to please her husband by honoring his wishes. Besides, she had promised him. Just then Rex entered the kitchen.

"There you are, Mrs. Jenson." He was followed by the woman Irena recognized as Sky Newly. "I wanted you to meet my mother. Mother, this is Irena Jenson, the woman I told you was from England. Irena Jenson, this is my mother, Sky Newly."

"How do you do?" Irena said politely.

Sky's blue eyes sparkled. "I'm very pleased to meet you, Irena. Rex tells me that you haven't always lived in England?"

"No, I lived the first twelve years of my life in Norway." She was taken aback when Sky suddenly responded with a delighted laugh.

"Forgive me, dear, but it has been a long time since I've heard that accent, and Rex knew that I would enjoy listening to you speak. Have you got time to sit and visit for a while?" She noticed Irena's pensive face. "Perhaps later?"

"Yes, please," Irena was relieved. "I promised to help here first."

"May I give you a hand?"

But Irena quickly said, "No, you are the guest of honor."

"Later then, Irena. It was nice to meet you." Sky left with a smile.

"Thank you, Mrs. Jenson, you've made her happy." Rex looked at the pile of dishes stacked near her. "Can I give you a hand with those?"

"Not with the washing," Irena said quickly, "but could you empty the dirty water for me? I promised Nels I wouldn't lift anything too heavy." She clapped her hand over her mouth when she realized that she had said more than she intended to.

Rex wasn't too quick to catch on. "Why is it that you can't lift—?" he started to ask then stopped when the answer occurred to him. "Are congratulations in order?" he asked in a whisper.

"Yes, thank you, but—"

"But you haven't told anyone yet?"

She nodded.

"Then it will be our secret," he whispered, and Irena giggled. He carried the water out for her and even refilled the basin with the water in the pot on the stove. "Anything else I can do for you?"

"No, but thank you so much and…and I'm sorry about…about your bride." She stumbled, trying to find the right words.

"Thank you. It's okay. I was pretty hurt at first about Bernadette, but God has taught me a lot. One thing I've learned is that sometimes God uses bad things in our lives to draw us closer to him. Do you know the verse in Romans 8:28?"

She shook her head, but her eyes were alive with interest like he had seen in them during the church service. "It says, 'And we know that all things work together for good to them that love God, to them who are the called according to his purpose.' God is working out the events in my life for good. All I have to do is trust him and let him direct me in the path before me. That doesn't mean that I won't suffer pain or that I'll never be unhappy, but whatever I go through, he'll go through it with me. And the end result is that I will be more conformed to his image, to be more like him."

Irena was silent for a moment, and Rex wondered if he had said something she didn't like, but then he understood that when she spoke, she had first taken those few moments to think over his words.

"There are so many things that I am learning about walking with God. Thank you for telling me that. I will look that verse up and memorize it."

She smiled radiantly at Rex, and he said, "You're welcome," as he backed out of the kitchen.

Irena was relieved before she needed to empty the washbasin again. She dried off her hands and removed her apron and patted at her braids. She wanted to talk with Mrs. Newly again, but she was bashful about joining her. When she stepped out into the dining room, she was hailed almost immediately by Philippa.

"There you are, Irena! I've been looking for you everywhere. Come, I want you to meet my parents."

Philippa led Irena to a handsome couple. The woman resembled Philippa, but instead of having Philippa's cheerful countenance, she wore a disdainful expression on her face. Her eyes never warmed as Philippa made the introductions.

"How do you do, Mrs. Gray?" Irena said softly.

Violet's eyes flickered with interest. "Are you a foreigner?"

"Mother!" Philippa's tone was full of caution.

"I am Norwegian, if that's what you mean, but I lived the last seven years of my life in England," Irena replied. She understood Violet's attitude immediately, which surprised her because it was the first that she had encountered in America. Violet was looking at her in much the same way that the Cavendish family had.

"Why were you in England?" Violet pressed her.

Irena's eyes never left Violet's face as she replied without hesitation, "I was a scullery maid."

A slight smile crossed Violet's face at this admission, as if she had just won a victory of some kind.

"Really, Philippa," she began, "if you can't do better for yourself than this…"

Violet's voice faded as Irena was led away. She looked at the person holding her by the arm and saw Russ Newly, Rex's father, smile down at her. "My wife was hoping you could chat with her for a while. She tells me you have a lot in common. I'm Russ Newly, by the way, and you're Irena Jenson, if I'm not mistaken."

Irena nodded and walked with Russ in silence. When she saw Sky's surprised expression upon their arrival at her table, she knew that Sky hadn't sent Russ to get her for a visit; he had seen she needed rescuing from Violet Gray and had come on his own. She smiled her thanks at him, and by his answering grin, she knew he understood.

After seeing that she was settled, Russ offered to get the ladies coffee.

"No, tea, please," Sky requested.

"Ah, of course. Tea for the English ladies," he teased and headed off.

Sky smiled warmly at Irena. "That's a beautiful outfit you are wearing. The color goes so well with your complexion and eyes."

Irena relaxed a little. "Mother Jenson made this when I first arrived. I had only two dresses, and they were only suitable for my position as scullery maid," she informed Sky and waited for her reaction.

"Your mother-in-law does exquisite work. I am so enjoying hearing you speak, Irena. It has been so long. What would you like to talk about? How about you tell me a little about Norway," she suggested.

Irena felt herself relax a little more. "I don't remember a lot," she said. "I was seven when my parents died, and I lived with my aunt and uncle until I was twelve. On the ship to England I looked back at Norway and thought it was the most beautiful place on earth. I remembered thinking the same thing about America when I watched the endless land go by the train window."

Sky nodded. "It was the same for me when I traveled so far by train. Then I traveled by wagon train." She laughed. "Be thankful you didn't have to do that, Irena." She paused and tilted her head at the younger woman. "We have something else in common, dear. I lost both my parents too. My father died before I was born, but fortunately I had my mother until I was grown. After she died, I came to America and found my twin brother. That's him over there—Evan Trent." Sky pointed to a man talking to Michael and Mallory.

Russ brought them tea and they visited awhile longer. Irena had never enjoyed herself so much. When she caught Nels looking for her, she excused herself saying, "We must go now and do the evening milking."

"Of course. I've enjoyed talking to you, Irena. I hope we can visit again soon." Irena couldn't have been more surprised when Sky gave her a hug.

The Jensons had a lot to talk about on the ride home. Irena listened to Nels and Mother Jenson tell about the people they met and who had said what and so forth. They noticed her quietness, and Mrs. Jenson said, "The little one is making you tired. Maybe you worked too hard today, Irena."

"No, I was careful, and I didn't lift anything," she informed her husband proudly. "It was a fun day, wasn't it?"

"Yes, it was. Several ladies asked me to show them how I tied the bows and…" Mother Jenson continued telling about the day while Irena laid her head on Nels's shoulder. Life was good. God was so good to her.

Chapter 27

Grandville

Irena missed her daily coffee time with Philippa. She still drove the wagon to the store daily, although it had taken some convincing before Nels or his mother would agree. Irena wasn't the type to argue, so it was the doctor who informed the Jensons that she would be fine. They all agreed that she should stop the daily trek when her pregnancy got further along.

The coffee breaks had stopped simply because Violet Gray was still staying with Philippa and Ralph. When Irena arrived with the wagon, she heard Violet's voice from the Tunelle's kitchen and decided that a normal visit with Philippa was not going to be possible. Philippa seemed determined to carry on despite her mother's presence, but Irena politely refused, knowing the tension it would create.

"I'm sorry, Irena." Philippa's understanding was more than Irena had hoped for. "You are still my friend, and I don't care what my mother thinks, but I won't subject you to her sharp tongue. It's bad enough for Ralph." Philippa winced as she heard her mother's complaining voice in the background. "I think we've convinced her that I'm all right now and that she can go home until the last month or so before the baby comes. I don't know if she'll ever go home after that." She sighed. "We'll cross that bridge…"

Nels wouldn't allow Irena to help with the chores in the barn any longer either, and Irena was beginning to feel restless without enough to do. She had cleaned and cleaned until everything was spotless.

Mother Jenson was sympathetic to Irena's plight and told her, "It's a 'nesting' instinct that expectant mothers have. You want to prepare for your baby's arrival. Here, I have an idea. I'll teach you to knit, and you can start sewing baby things as well. You will be very busy."

So Irena's days began to take on a pattern. After breakfast chores and clean up, she would drive the wagon to town. Occasionally she did a little shopping, and once in a while she was invited to the hotel for a visit with Lucy when things weren't too busy there. When she got back to the farm, she would brush down Daisy—one chore Nels allowed her to do. Then she would work with Mother Jenson on lunch and supper preparations and if there was no laundry, she would work on her sewing and knitting.

Irena kept her Bible close by and tried to memorize verses as she worked. She had memorized Romans 8:28-29 as she had told Rex she would, and she had also memorized most of Ephesians 5 because the pastor's message had meant so much to her. She and Mother Jenson often discussed Bible topics as they worked.

She missed being with Nels during the day, so she made it a point to walk out to the fields in the evening and help him herd the cows to the barn, although they rarely needed herding; they were eager to be milked each night and came on their own. Then she stayed and visited with him as he did the milking. She thought he was being overprotective of her, but she also enjoyed the care and concern and didn't want to do anything to displease him. Irena watched as Nels lifted the heavy milk cans into the stock tank to keep them cool.

Nels kept a block of ice in the water and replaced it whenever it melted from the supply in the ice house where it was stored in sawdust. She understood why he didn't want her to do that kind of heavy lifting, but she still thought there were many small tasks that she could help with, yet she let him have his way.

The three of them—Mother Jenson, Nels, and Irena—often sat together after supper and would read a passage of Scripture. Mother Jenson's English was improving rapidly, and they formed a bond together in their quest for God's wisdom. Irena kept a notebook of questions they had, and Pastor Malcolm did his best each Sunday after the service to answer their questions. They had been invited to the Tucker's home for Sunday dinner once, and Mrs. Jenson had returned the invitation, and they had the Tuckers out at the farm. The Tuckers' children had loved the open country and the animals, and Irena could easily see how her children would enjoy being raised here.

Swede wrote to Irena, and she hastened home from her trip into town to share the letter with Nels and Mother Jenson.

"He says that Dakota is even more beautiful and untamed than Minnesota," she read. "His son and daughter-in-law had their first baby, a boy, so Swede is a grandfather now!" She read on,

> I have my own house already. It is small with only one bedroom, but it is a great plenty. I am walking distance from the main house, so I take my evening meal with the family. I cook my own breakfast and lunch. Every day I help in the fields and the barn. People have heard that I am a butcher, so they hire me to butcher for them. I may even open a shop in town. The Lord has blessed me greatly. I thank him daily for sending you to me that day, Irena, and I thank you for giving me the courage to come here. I hope you are doing well also. I continue to keep you in my prayers as I would a daughter. Give my regards to the Jensons. Swede.

Irena folded the letter. "I am so happy for him. He thought he would never be able to see his grandchildren and now he is living right next to his son's family. Won't he be surprised when I tell him about our baby!"

∞

Fall was blowing in, and there was a chill in the air and dark clouds pressed down on the earth. Irena's disposition was sunny despite the gloomy weather, and she smiled warmly at Nels when he came stomping into the house from the morning's chores. She handed him a hot cup of coffee as she took his coat and hung it on the peg by the door.

"I don't like the idea of you out in this weather, Irena. I think I'll take the wagon in this morning."

"A little rain and wind won't hurt me. I'm not made of sugar. I won't melt." She teased him.

Nels pulled her into his arms while he set the hot cup down. "Still, I think I would feel better if I went today."

"If you wish, except, maybe I should come along. Mother has a list with some particular things she wanted me to look for like buttons and lace." She laughed at his scowl.

"Can't those things wait?" he asked.

Mother Jenson entered the kitchen and smiled at the embracing couple. "Cold, are you?"

Nels grinned. "I'm going to take the wagon today, Mother, so Irena doesn't have to go out in this weather." They heard a low rumble. "See, it's already starting to thunder."

Irena laughed at his "I told you so" expression.

"Well, I need things from town today, and you're not the one to shop for me," Mother Jenson spoke to her son. "I'll go with you."

"No, Mother. The weather is windy and rain is about to start. Can't you get these things tomorrow?"

Irena was amused at the tug-of-war between mother and son. Nels was not only over protective of her but of his mother as well. But Mrs. Jenson was strong-willed and not used to obeying orders from her son.

"As if some rain and wind will harm me," she scorned. "Irena, the bread needs to be baked in about an hour," she reminded her. "Let's eat breakfast and get started before it gets worse."

Nels shrugged in defeat, and Irena almost felt sorry for him. They ate their breakfast quickly and prepared to leave. Irena rushed to find a hat and scarf for Nels, but he surprised her by producing a rain slicker. He even had one for his mother to use that had belonged to his father, but Mother Jenson scoffed.

"I'm not putting that heavy thing on. I have an umbrella. Mind the bread, Irena, and you could put together a pie for supper if you have a mind to. Hot pie sounds good on a day like this, and we have plenty of apples." She smiled affectionately at Irena. "Your baking is coming along very well."

"I've had a good teacher," Irena reminded her. "Stay warm and be safe." She accepted the quick hug and kiss that Nels gave her, and she watched from the window as they drove away. She smiled at how Mother Jenson's umbrella was almost taken by the wind, but the older woman hung onto it with determination, and she definitely seemed to have the upper hand.

Irena listened to the rumbling outside as she cleaned up from breakfast. She began work on the pie as soon as she could and was rolling the crust when the first flash of lightning struck. The light blinded her for a moment, and then seconds later the boom of thunder almost deafened her. The kitchen grew dark, and Irena looked out the window in concern. The trees were bent by the force of the wind.

Then she heard the beginnings of raindrops peppering the west windows, and in moments, sheets of rain struck the house. The yard out front was instantly turned into a small lake.

Irena checked the time and wondered if the wagon had made it to town before this onslaught. It should have, she reasoned. Nels and his mother would probably wait in Grandville during the worst of the weather and come back as soon as there was a break.

Protect them, Lord, she prayed as she worked. She lit a lamp in the dark house and continued with her baking. The bread was filling the house with its aroma, and as soon as it came out of the oven, the pie was ready to go in.

She felt safe and warm in the midst of the storm. She poured a cup of coffee from the pot that was still hot on the stove and helped herself to some of the warm bread. Her appetite was increasing, and small snacks throughout the day seemed to suit her better than Mother Jenson's three large meals.

Lightning and thunder and rain continued, and Irena became restless with only knitting and sewing to do. She decided to bake some molasses cookies to fill her time, and she set to work mixing the ingredients and forming the balls of dough. After dipping each ball into sugar, she placed them on baking pans and popped them in the oven. Soon the house was filled with ginger, molasses, and cinnamon aromas mixed with those of the apple pie and the fresh bread. Irena breathed deeply. Underlying the intoxicating smells was the freshness of the rain.

The hours ticked by slowly on the clock, and Irena tried not to notice. Lunch time came and went. Irena had everything ready for making sandwiches as soon as the wagon pulled in the yard. She waited and waited, but the Jensons did not return for lunch.

They must have eaten in town while they waited out the storm, she decided. She went to the list that they kept posted in the kitchen and began a new one for the next trip to town. They were low on cinnamon.

Her knitting needles flew as she added stitch after stitch to the growing blanket on her lap. It was the second blanket she had made for the baby. She glanced down at the tiny clothes piled in the basket. Between her efforts and Mother Jenson's sewing skills, the new baby would not lack for clothing. Suddenly Irena stopped knitting and put her hand on her tummy. *Was that...?* Yes, there it was again. It was just a flutter, a small movement, but it was there, and it was real. Irena hugged herself and thanked the Lord for the life inside of her.

Suppertime came, and Irena watched anxiously out the window. Her prayers had grown more fervent with each passing minute, and she began to fear that something was terribly wrong. The rain was still coming down but more gently now. Only the wind gusts made it seem severe.

The cows were already in the barn. They had taken shelter there during most of the storm. Irena knew that milking time was late, and she debated as she looked out the window and then decided that she better take care of the evening chores. Nels would understand.

She pulled on her work boots and grabbed the large slicker that had belonged to Nels's father. Outside, the wind nearly blew her off her feet. She put her head into it and made her way to the barn. She had to light a lantern in the gloomy building, but the animals' bodies made for some warmth from the chill outside.

The cows were used to Irena, and she set to work milking each one, thankful that she had learned how. There was some mooing and obvious complaining from them at her tardiness, but she only half heard them; she was listening for the approach of the wagon. It took much longer to complete the task by herself, and she was worn out when it was over. She carried the partially full pails one by one and emptied them into a larger one that she had placed in the stock tank. She wouldn't carry full pails like Nels did, so it took many more trips.

The wind was still howling, and Irena stepped over fallen branches as she made her way back to the house with the lantern burning in its window. The welcome warmth and delicious aroma from the soup on the stove enveloped her as soon as she stepped inside. Hastily she washed and went to the window to peer out again. It was very black out now, and she doubted that Nels would even be able to see the road.

He must be as worried about me as I am about him, Irena thought. Again she brought her concerns to the Lord. "Let him know that I'm safe, warm, dry, and comfortable, Lord. Tell him the animals have been taken care of. Protect him and Mother too." She said the words out loud, and they sounded strange to her in the empty house.

Irena ate a small portion of the soup and kept the pot warm as long as she could before deciding to pull it off the stove and letting it cool. Finally she got a blanket from her bed and sat curled up by the kitchen table and read from her Bible. She fell asleep several times, and each time she awoke, she went to the window and looked out into the night.

The rain stopped some time before the morning sky turned from black to gray then to a golden yellow. Irena stirred and looked around her as the sun's rays made their way into the kitchen. She blew out the lantern and moved to the window automatically. The yard was a muddy lake with debris and branches and tree limbs scattered all around it. She checked the time and knew the cows were waiting for their morning milking.

They must have spent the night at the hotel, she thought. *That would have been what Nels would want for his mother. If it was just him, he would have come home in the storm to check on me.*

She splashed through the mud in her boots on the way to the outhouse. On the way to the barn she looked down the road as far as she could see, but it was empty.

The cows seemed just as impatient this morning and bellowed at her to hurry so that they could go out and feed on the wet grass. She went through the chores as quickly as she could without causing any undue stress on herself. She had her promise to Nels to think about, and the little life inside her reminded her of his presence as well.

Irena was just finishing washing up her breakfast dishes when she heard the wagon. She cried out in relief and ran to the door, flinging it open with a crash as she rushed out onto the porch.

But it wasn't Nels and Mother Jenson.

Irena stopped and stared as Tyler and Jade Newly and Pastor and Hermine Tucker got down from the buggy and made their way through the puddles to the house. The sympathetic looks on their faces told her the news before they spoke, and in her heart she knew she had been expecting this.

Jade reached for Irena as soon as she climbed the steps. She pulled the small young woman into her arms and held her tightly. Irena felt like a wooden statue and couldn't seem to move. Tyler opened the door, and Jade led Irena inside. They could see the lamp, the Bible, and the blanket—evidence of her night-long vigil.

Hermine went to the stove and checked that the coffee pot was full and hot. She looked for cups and poured while the others took chairs around the table. Pastor Malcolm reached for Irena's cold hand and softly began.

"We found the wagon this morning, Irena. When you didn't come to town yesterday at your normal time, Philippa and Ralph became alarmed. But with the awful storm, we all assumed that Nels had decided not to let you make the delivery. This morning a man came into town and said he found a wagon along the road, tipped on its side and two people dead, a man and a woman. When we went out, we found Nels and his mother. We can only assume that lightening frightened the horse and it bolted and—we may never know for sure how it happened. We came to you as soon as we could."

Irena shivered, and Jade slid the blanket over her shoulders. In the silence that followed as the others let her take in the news, Irena relived the moments of the day before when she said good-bye to Nels. She again felt his quick kiss and hug and saw the warmth in his smile. She heard the admonishment in his voice when he told her to be careful. She heard Mother Jenson's reminder about the bread. She saw them wave to her from the wagon seat.

Her staring eyes slowly focused on Pastor Malcolm, and she heard his words play over and over in her mind: "…two people dead…a man and a woman…we found Nels and his mother."

Her eyes closed and big, silent tears splashed from them onto the back of her hand and the pastor's. Jade's arm tightened around her, and Irena allowed herself to be pulled into an embrace. Her sobs were silent, but the others could see her body shake with them. Tears fell from Jade's eyes as she looked at Tyler over Irena's head. He squeezed his wife's shoulder, knowing that she was thinking how she would feel if she lost him.

It was several minutes before the people in the room realized that Irena had fallen asleep in Jade's arms.

Tyler whispered, "I'll go check on the animals," and quietly left the house. Hermine moved silently around the kitchen, gathering Irena's fresh-baked goods, the soup, and other perishables. They were not going to leave her to spend another night alone, and they would take anything with them that could spoil.

Next, Hermine moved to the other rooms and went upstairs to pack some things for Irena. Irena would stay with the Tuckers until she knew what she wanted to do next. Hermine paused by the sewing basket and gently picked up the tiny garment on top. Her sharp gasp made her husband and Jade turn to her as she stepped into the kitchen and held the garment for them to see.

A baby.

Not only had Irena lost a husband and a mother-in-law, the only family she had, she was left to raise a baby on her own. Fresh tears pooled in Jade's eyes, and Pastor Malcolm had to wipe at his own. He reached for the things his wife had gathered and began loading them in the back of the buggy.

Tyler came back into the kitchen and spoke quietly to the others. "The milking's all done and she's cleaned out the barn. I found the fresh milk cooling in the stock tank, and I've added a block of ice to it from the ice house."

Irena began to stir, and Tyler saw Jade wince. Her arms had gone numb holding the sleeping woman.

Irena looked around to see the others watching her. "It wasn't a dream, was it." She stated more than asked.

Hermine knelt by her side. "I have some things packed for you; we're taking you to stay with us for a while. I have all the food too so that nothing will spoil. Is there anything else you can think of that you need along?"

Irena couldn't seem to think clearly, but she reached for her Bible on the table and handed it to Hermine. She was relieved that she wouldn't be left alone. She couldn't endure being all alone right now.

"What about the cows?" she asked. "I did the milking, but someone has to be here to—"

"I'll take care of things here," Tyler assured her. "And I'll get the milk you put in the tank into town as soon as I can. Don't worry."

Irena nodded in relief, and she allowed the ladies to help her out to the buggy. They drove away in silence, and Irena looked at the bright white house with its blue shutters dripping from the rain in the morning sunlight and wondered if she would ever live there again. She doubted that she could.

Chapter 28

Grandville

Children were once again Irena's salvation. The first few days at the Tuckers, Irena could only sleep. Hermine prodded her to eat by reminding her of the baby, and Irena would obediently swallow a few mouthfuls.

The funeral was the hardest thing she had ever been through in her life. Someone provided her with a black dress, a little ill-fitting, but it didn't matter to her. The others were well meaning and tried to convince her not to look at the dead bodies of her husband and her mother-in-law. It was better to remember them the way they were, they told her, but she had to see them.

It broke the heart of every person watching when Irena gently stroked her husband's face. He wore the only suit he owned, the one he wore to their wedding party when she had first realized that she was married to a handsome man. Mother Jenson lay peacefully in her Sunday best, and Irena patted her hands and told her good-bye for the last time.

She hardly heard Pastor Malcolm's words. She asked him later if he would write them down so she could read them one day. He assured her that he would. His concern for Irena was great and his prayers constant. She had already had so much heartache in her young life. He struggled himself to understand God's purpose while he tried to comfort her.

Rex Newly was at the funeral. Word came to Sand Creek by telegram, and Sky insisted on being at Irena's side through the funeral; and though Irena clung to her at times, at other times she hardly seemed aware of Sky's presence. Now that news of the baby was out, they were all concerned about Irena's mental and physical condition.

But it was the children who began the healing process in the young widow. Eddie Newly sat and talked to Irena non-stop when Jade brought him and Pamela to the Tuckers to see Irena and to update her on the farm and the animals. It seemed to help her to know that things were being taken care of.

Irena appreciated Eddie's chatter. He had the forgivable innocence of a child in his questions, and he could get away with asking Irena things that the adults were afraid to bring up.

"Why did God take your husband and Mrs. Jenson to heaven, Irena? Why didn't he take you too or me? I can't wait to go! Did you know that in heaven it is always day time? They never have dark there. Do you think God likes dogs, Irena? I want my dog to go to heaven with me."

Irena didn't always answer Eddie's questions, and once when Jade tried to shush him, she said, "No, I like to hear what he says."

The Tuckers' three small boys welcomed Irena into their household cautiously. They weren't sure why this sad woman was at their table or why she slept all the time and they had to be quiet, but the oldest one—Paul—remembered the story she had told at the ladies' Bible study a long time ago, and one day he got brave enough to ask her to tell it again.

Irena was startled.

"Please, Mrs. Jenson? I tried to tell it to Mark and Jesse, but I can't remember what the wolf said to the lamb when the wolf wouldn't let him pass. Did he say—" and Paul made a growl in his voice—"'not unless you bring me some black wool'? Or was it 'not unless you bring me some wood'? I don't know."

Irena stared blankly at the three little boys and tried to recall the story. "He asked for wood first, then for food, then for wool," she told them.

Paul tried to tell his brothers the story in front of Irena, but he kept getting mixed up, so Irena injected some help every now and then, and before she knew it, she was telling the whole thing herself. Hermine listened from the next room and thanked the Lord. Irena was beginning to heal.

Each day was a struggle for Irena, but she gradually became aware of life going on around her. The Tuckers' home had become a haven for her, but she knew she couldn't stay with them indefinitely. She began to wonder what would become of the farm and the animals, and she remembered that Rex Newly wanted to buy some of Nels's cows.

She knew the Jensons had an account with Tunelle's store, but she didn't know if they had money or owed money there. She had never asked. If it hadn't been for the baby reminding her day by day of his presence, Irena wouldn't have worried so much about money. But she had someone to take care of besides herself now, and she thought it was time to find out where she and her child stood.

She brought up the subject after breakfast the following day.

"Pastor Malcolm, do you know who I could talk to, to find out if I have any money? I don't know if I owe people money or anything. Also, Rex Newly had an agreement with Nels to buy some cows. I should see about that. And I need to find somewhere to live and a job. And—"

"Hold on, Irena, slow down." Pastor Malcolm told her. "Let's take one thing at a time. I knew you'd have questions soon, so I've been making inquiries for you."

"Really?"

"I don't mean to overstep my bounds," Pastor Malcolm hastened to assure her. "I only want to help, Irena. How about if we help Hermine clear up here and then we make a list of things you need to know?"

Irena nodded and as she picked up some dishes she said, "You do not over step. I don't know what I would have done without both of you. I don't know why

God did this." She stopped and stared at the table. "I keep asking myself, 'Did I do something to make God punish me?'" Tears ran down her cheeks, and the pastor and Hermine gently guided her to a chair and took the dishes from her hands.

"We can't give you a reason why things happen, Irena. I've asked myself that question countless times. But, no, I don't believe these things are God's punishment. We live in a cursed world and death is part of that curse. I know that God loves you—you are his child. I know that he cares for you more than you can imagine and that he'll remain faithful by your side through every trial life has to offer."

Irena listened to the pastor's words, and he could see her need for answers.

"I know that he loves Nels and Mrs. Jenson too, and he has taken them home. Can you imagine the joy they are experiencing being in the presence of the Lord, their God? The Bible tells us in Psalms 116:15, 'Precious in the sight of the Lord is the death of his saints.'" Pastor Malcolm smiled at Irena's tear-stained face. "Don't be angry at God, Irena. Trust him to know what's best."

"I'm not angry at God."

Pastor Malcolm was taken aback. "You're not?"

Irena shook her head. "God has been so good to me by giving me a happy life and a wonderful family. It hurts so much to lose it all, but I still have God and I'll see them again, and I have a child." Irena placed her hand on her abdomen. "I know I will struggle with sadness and loneliness, but think how much worse I would feel if I didn't know God was taking care of my Nels and Mother Jenson."

The pastor sat back in amazement. "It takes some people a lifetime to figure that out, Irena."

"I feel like I have lived more than a lifetime," Irena told him, and a wobbly smile followed her words.

After the breakfast things were cleared, they made their list and Pastor Malcolm suggested that they go see Palmer Granville at the bank for information on the Jenson's finances.

Irena was keenly aware of the sympathetic looks directed her way as she walked with the pastor to the bank. She reminded herself that these people truly cared about her, and it reassured her to know she was not alone.

Palmer greeted them graciously and led the way to his office. After seating them and expressing his condolences to Irena, he asked, "What can I do for you?"

Pastor Malcolm spoke, "Irena wishes to know about her husband's finances. She needs to know if there is a mortgage on their house or if the Jensons had an account with the bank. I'm afraid she knows very little."

Palmer listened to the pastor but shook his head before the man had even finished speaking. "I checked already when I heard the news because often the surviving family members need to get their finances in order, but the Jensons have had no dealings with the bank. They've proved up on their homestead, so it should be theirs free and clear, but they never borrowed money from the bank to build, and they've never deposited any money into an account. I'm sorry I can't help you."

Irena seemed concerned, so Palmer continued, "The good news, Mrs. Jenson, is that apparently you have no debt. The house and land and all the belongings are yours to keep or to sell as you wish. I would suggest, though, that you look for a place where your husband may have hidden his money. If people don't put their money in the bank, they usually hide it somewhere in their homes. I can make inquiries for you at the Norris and Sand Creek banks, but I doubt the Jensons traveled that far to do any banking business."

He waited while Irena digested this information.

"I don't think I could live there again," she said quietly, more to Pastor Malcolm than to the banker.

Palmer spoke again, "May I make a suggestion, Mrs. Jenson?"

"Irena."

He smiled. "Irena, if you wish to sell, I may have a buyer for you. Tyler's sister, Emma, and her husband, Simon Chappell, live in Norris, but they asked me to watch for something here for them. They want to live closer to the family. Since they have just a small farm now, they are looking for something bigger."

The room was quiet for a few moments, then Pastor Malcolm said, "We'll let you pray about that for a few days, Irena. There's no hurry to decide just yet."

Irena nodded with relief. They thanked Palmer and started back for the parsonage, but Irena decided to stop at the store and see about the Jensons' accounts there first. "You go on," she told the pastor. "I'll be fine here. I'll visit with Philippa for a while."

The pastor took this as a good sign and left Irena at the Tunelle's Store.

Irena felt strange entering the store from the front. She and Nels always used the back entrance after the wagon had been unloaded. She wondered if Tyler was delivering the milk still, and she was suddenly aware that he really didn't have the time to be taking care of her job and his own as well.

Irena's heart sank when she saw Violet Gray standing beside Philippa at the counter, and she started to turn away, but Philippa saw her.

"Irena!" Philippa ran to Irena with open arms and hugged her tightly. "Come in, we'll have coffee. It's so good to see you!" She led Irena past the counter to the kitchen beyond. "Mother, would you please take care of the store while Irena and I have a visit?"

Irena heard Violet answer, "Yes, of course," and was relieved that Philippa's mother wouldn't be joining them.

Philippa moved quickly to heat the coffee so she could sit and visit with her friend. Irena noticed that Philippa's figure was filling out, and she glanced down and noticed for the first time her own slightly rounded form. Suddenly it occurred to her that she didn't know how much time had passed since the accident.

"What day is this, Philippa?"

Philippa seemed surprised by the question. "It's Wednesday."

"I mean—the date—what date is it?"

Philippa thought a moment. "It's the fifteenth, I believe. Yes, the fifteenth."

Irena felt relief. Then she became suspicious again and though she felt foolish, she asked, "What month?"

Now Philippa looked at her in concern. "It's October, Irena."

"October!"

Philippa leaned over to take Irena's hand. "You've been away from us for a long time."

Irena couldn't believe her ears. Days and weeks had gone by without her noticing. Had she been ill, in a coma, what? She looked at Philippa. "I didn't know," was all she could say.

Philippa patted her hand and poured the coffee. "And now I find out that you are expecting a baby too. You must have known the day you told me I was."

Irena nodded. "Are you feeling better?"

"Much, much better," Philippa said with relief. "And you?"

"I never was sick," Irena said almost apologetically.

The women smiled and Philippa said softly, "I'm so sorry, Irena. How are you doing?"

It felt good to talk to Philippa again. They cried together, they even laughed some. Irena thanked God for her friend and she told her so.

They turned when Violet came through the doorway and looked at them in disbelief. Obviously she had been eavesdropping. "How can you thank God for anything after what he's done to you?" she asked Irena in outrage. "What kind of a God do you people believe in?"

"Mother!" Philippa stood to her feet.

Irena looked at the angry woman in front of her and said calmly, "My God is so powerful that he created you and me and everything in this world by simply speaking the words. My God is so full of love for me that he offered his only Son's life as a payment for my sins. My God is so forgiving that he accepts me into his family because I believe in him. My God is so caring that he holds me in his hand when I'm hurting and he comforts me there. I can be thankful for a God like that because he's my Father and I'm his child. Don't *you* know this God?"

"No!" Violet blurted out the word. She turned to leave but then sank into a chair beside Irena. Irena recoiled, wishing the woman would just go. Then Irena and Philippa watched in amazement as tears welled up in Violet's eyes. "No, I don't," she said more softly. "But, but I wish I did."

Philippa gasped and sat down with a loud *thump*.

"I wish I had the confidence you have," Violet continued, looking at Irena, "and I wish I didn't always feel alone."

In that moment, Irena was able to look past the woman's haughtiness and see someone who was hurting, just like she had been. Philippa rose to go to her mother, but Violet waved her away. "I've heard about God for twenty-five years from practically every person in Sand Creek or here. Can *you* explain it to me?" She pointed at Irena.

"What do you want to know?" Irena saw the hunger behind Violet's haughtiness.

"How do you do it? How do you get *saved*? I want to know for sure I'll go to heaven if something should happen to me like happened to your—"

"Mother!" Philippa stopped her mother with a command, and Violet saw Irena wince.

"I'm sorry."

Irena prayed for calmness and clarity as she looked Violet Gray in the eye. "Do you believe you are a sinner?"

Only a slight hesitation, then, "Yes," Violet admitted.

"Do you understand that God sent his Son Jesus to die for your sins? He was perfect and without sin and willingly took *your* punishment."

Violet watched Irena carefully. "I know that Jesus died on the cross; everyone knows that, but I didn't know he did it in my place."

Irena nodded. "He did. He died for the sins of the whole world, and that includes you and me."

Violet didn't say anything but continued to watch Irena closely.

"But the good news is that he couldn't stay dead. He rose from the grave, and he offers this life to us if we believe what he did for us. Just accept it by faith." Irena took a deep breath before she continued. "My husband Nels believed all this, but for a long time he thought he had to add his good works to his faith to please God into letting him into heaven. Several months ago he realized that God offers us heaven as a gift and we only need to accept his Son's sacrifice for us—we can't work for it. I'm happy to tell you that Nels and his mother are in heaven with the Lord and that I will see them again. Do you want to accept this gift?" she asked Violet.

Violet hesitated then nodded. "I've always believed these facts, but I didn't understand that Jesus had to die because of *me*. I want the gift of God too. Oh,

Philippa!" Violet gladly received the tearful hug her daughter flung on her.

The women prayed together, and Violet Gray told the God of heaven that she accepted Jesus, his Son, as her savior. Irena was exhausted, and it must have showed because Philippa insisted on Ralph walking her back to the parsonage. While she went to find him, Violet thanked Irena.

"When I heard how you and Philippa talked and laughed and cried and thanked God together despite your recent tragedy, I knew you had something in your life I needed." Violet smiled and Irena was immediately aware that there was a change in the woman. "I can hardly wait to tell Sky Newly!" she suddenly exclaimed.

It wasn't Ralph, but Rex Newly who Philippa brought back to the kitchen. "Rex will bring you back, if that's all right, Irena."

"Of course." Irena was confused that Rex was in Grandville, and then she remembered that it was October, and he wanted to buy some cows. She was so tired after her talk with Violet that she couldn't seem to think straight.

"You want to buy some cows," she startled Rex by saying as they left the store and started down the boardwalk.

"Yes, but I'm in no hurry. When you get to feeling better we can talk about it. Meantime the cows are doing well, and I'm getting the milk to town every day for you."

Irena stopped. "*You* are? I thought Tyler was."

"I took over the job about a month ago," Rex informed her.

"A month!" Irena stared at Rex. "That's right; it's October. Aren't you getting married in October? You should buy the cows soon."

Rex was more than concerned about Irena as he led her up the steps to the parsonage. Hermine took one look at the weary widow and said, "She needs to sleep. Help me get her up the stairs, please."

Together they led Irena up the steps while she still babbled about cows and milking. Hermine dismissed Rex with a thank you, and she tucked Irena under the covers before joining him in the sitting room.

"She's out already," she told him.

"Has she been like this the whole time?"

"No. She's only now started talking—at least to us. She's been telling stories to the children for a couple of weeks now. The doctor says she's been in shock and that eventually she should be fine again."

Rex nodded thoughtfully. "She just led Violet Gray to the Lord." He grinned at Hermine's expression. "I don't know the details because Philippa told me rather quickly, but she also said that Irena didn't know it was October already."

Hermine shook her head. "Keep praying for her, Rex. She has a long way to go yet."

Chapter 29

Grandville

It took about another week for Irena to get her thoughts clear enough to make some decisions. She went to see Buck and Lucy Riley before she moved ahead with her plans to talk to Palmer Granville again. This time she went to the bank alone and was welcomed warmly by Palmer into his office.

"How can I help you today, Mrs. Jenson?"

"Irena," she reminded him.

He nodded.

"I would like to sell the house and property to the Chappells if they would like to buy it," she informed him. "And I would like to ask you to handle it for me, and I will pay the bank for that, if that is correct?"

"I can do that for you, Irena. I'm sure we can arrange a fair price for both parties."

Irena agreed. "Then I would like to keep the money in your bank. I would like most of it to go into an account for my child, but I will need to use some to live on when I'm not able to work when the baby comes. I am going to live at the hotel and work for the Rileys," she informed him.

Palmer drummed his fingers on his desk while he thought. "Irena, you do realize that there will be a good amount of money from the sale, don't you? You probably won't need to work for quite some time."

"That money will go to Nels's child."

"I think Nels would want you to be taken care of too, Irena," the bank manager insisted gently.

But Irena shook her head.

"As you wish," Palmer capitulated.

"Rex Newly wants to buy some of the cows," Irena continued. "So I need to talk to him before I can tell you how many I will sell with the farm. Could they buy it soon, do you think? Because Rex has been taking care of the animals, and I'm afraid he has had to leave his own work to do so. He should be paid for that too," she added.

"I can see to it that he is compensated, if you wish," Palmer offered while he made some notes, "although I doubt that he will accept."

"Why?"

"He just wants to help, Irena. We all do, so if you need anything else, please don't be afraid to ask."

"Thank you." Irena was thoughtful as she left the bank. Her next stop was the store. Violet had gone home two days earlier, eager to share her news with her husband, and though her visit had been a trial for Ralph and Philippa, they were now sorry to see her go.

"Good morning, Philippa!" Irena said as she walked to the counter.

"Irena! Come in for coffee," Philippa offered, but Irena declined.

"Not today; I have too much to do. Philippa, I need to know how our account is at the store. Do I owe you money?"

"Goodness, no!" Philippa laughed then she saw Irena's serious expression. "Look here." She opened the account book. "We add what we owe you each time you deliver the milk, and we only subtract when you buy something. You have a large sum built up. You can either use the money to buy items from the store or we can give you the cash," she told her.

Irena breathed a sigh of relief. "I was afraid I owed you money and you were not telling me," she admitted. "Nels took good care of things," she added with a mixture of pride and sadness. "I will keep it on account. Did you hear that I will be living at the hotel and working for the Rileys?"

"Oh! Why, you'll be close by then," Philippa said after a short hesitation. Then she dared ask, "Are you sure about not living in your home?"

Irena shook her head sadly. "I can't live there. There are too many memories and quite honestly, too much work for a woman alone. I've asked Jade to go with me this afternoon to pack my belongings. Pray for me; I'm afraid it will be a difficult task. Buck has offered to let me store some things at the hotel."

"We could find room here, too, if you need it," Philippa offered. "I *will* be praying for you."

Jenson Farm

Tyler and Jade picked up Irena in town after dropping off Eddie and Pamela with Lucy.

"Rex is already there," Tyler informed Irena. "He's been taking care of the place and makes sure no one has been snooping around. He was even sleeping in the barn before this cold spell. The last few nights he's been at the hotel."

Irena listened to this news in disbelief. "But he shouldn't be spending so much time here. He has his own place to take care of."

"His house is finished enough to protect it for the winter, and he and my dad and some neighbors helped him get the barn up. I don't think he put fences up yet, but since Simon and Emma are buying your place, I think he may just leave the cows with Simon until the spring. Don't worry, Irena, he's here because he wants to help you. He's not just waiting for the cows."

They saw smoke coming from the chimney of the house when they rode into the yard. Irena struggled with her emotions as she saw the pretty white house and recalled the fun she and Nels had painting it. She would never get through this day if she crumbled now, she told herself. Rex crossed the yard to greet them, and they all waited for Irena to start up the steps, but she fell back. She felt their eyes on her and finally forced herself forward. Rex's hand moved to her elbow as he walked with her up the steps. She was grateful for his help.

Everything looked just as they had left it that morning. Irena swallowed and turned to the others. Her voice sounded strange to her ears.

"Mr. Granville said that since Nels didn't have a bank account that he might have hidden money in the house. I need your help to look for that hiding place as we pack things up."

"How about if Tyler and I start with the kitchen?" Jade suggested.

Irena nodded. "I'll work on Mother Jenson's room. I'm planning to leave some of the furniture, but I'll need the baby's cradle and the rocking chair from upstairs." She indicated the stairway, and Rex nodded that he understood.

Irena reverently folded each of her mother-in-law's dresses and laid them in the trunk at the foot of the bed. The quilts and other sewing projects she would keep to use now, but she put away the few pieces of jewelry she found to keep for her child. There were a few books in Norwegian and some letters that Irena would read later.

The sewing things were next. She boxed up everything to take with her. Mother Jenson would have wanted her to keep sewing and knitting, and if the child was a girl, it was her responsibility to pass on the knowledge she had learned.

There were some pictures and pillows in the parlor that Irena boxed, and then she faced the stairs leading to her and Nels's bedroom.

It was an effort for Irena to climb each step. She glanced in the small baby's room and saw that Rex had cleared it out already. Taking a deep breath, she entered the bedroom.

It all came back to her at once. Irena could feel again how she felt those first few nights when Nels wouldn't speak to her or look at her. She remembered her fright finding him in bed with her; then she recalled that first night when they had laughed together on the floor. Memories swam over her, and she had to sit on the edge of the bed to steady her shaking body.

"Are you all right?" Rex stood in the doorway and took in her white face and tightly closed eyes. He could *see* her pain. "Is there anything I can do?"

Irena slowly opened her eyes, and the memories began to dim. "Don't—don't leave me alone," she whispered.

Rex nodded and waited as she began to fold Nels's clothes. He saw the tears slide down her cheeks, but he was helpless to comfort her. When that task was complete, Irena quickly gathered the remaining items of her own then stripped the bed and folded the bedding.

They carried everything downstairs and found that Tyler and Jade were finished with the kitchen items.

"What would you like done with the tools in the barn?" Rex asked.

Irena's shoulders sagged. "I don't know."

"I'll take care of them," Rex offered, and she nodded in relief.

"Here, sit down for a while," Jade instructed. She brought out the lunch basket she had prepared and put some food in front of Irena. "I'll get you some coffee too."

Soon the others joined her, and they visited quietly while they ate. The rest was just what Irena needed, and she went back to work with the others soon afterward.

It was Tyler who found the money box.

Irena stopped sweeping when Tyler held out the gray metal box before her. "There was a loose floor board near the fireplace. When I pried it up…" He waved his hand to indicate the box much as a magician would display his magic tricks. Irena smiled at his effort to make things light, and she set the broom aside. Tyler placed the box on the table then motioned for Jade to join him out on the porch.

"No, you don't have to leave."

Tyler and Jade hesitated at Irena's words. Their faces clearly showed that they didn't wish to intrude into her private affairs.

"Please. I have no secrets, and I may need some advice, especially if there's nothing in here." She laughed lightly, and Rex, who was just entering the house, looked at her in surprise.

"Tyler found what we think is the money box," Jade informed him.

"Oh, I can wait outside." He started to back away, but Irena protested.

"Nonsense. Sit down and look through these. She handed him some folded papers then pulled an envelope out of the box and peeked into it. "I think this is the money. Maybe you would count it," she asked Tyler and passed it to him.

"How beautiful!" Jade exclaimed, and they all looked at the brooch Irena pulled out next.

"Here's another one and two rings and—" She pulled open a small pouch, and several—what appeared to be gems—fell from it. Irena was stunned. "Where did these things come from?"

Rex held out one of the papers he had been studying. "I'm not a lawyer, but this looks like a will." He scanned the document briefly. "It says something here about an inheritance from Ingeborg Johnsdotter Hellergaard."

"That would have been a relative of Mother Jenson's." Irena stared at the items on the table. "I wondered where they got the money to come to America, but I assumed it was just from selling their home in Norway."

Rex shuffled through the papers in his hands. "It partly was." He held out a paper to her. "I think this shows each piece of jewelry they sold and what they got for it in United States dollars. Mrs. Jenson's relative must have been quite wealthy."

Irena looked over the list in amazement. "That would explain why there are no debts to pay and how they were able to send for me and…" She stopped, but she was remembering the fabric for her new dresses, the paint for the house, the equipment for the barn—Nels and his mother never seemed well-to-do, but they were very comfortable compared to many struggling farmers and ranchers around them.

"There's over a thousand in cash here," Tyler informed her, but she was deep in thought and barely heard him. Jade's words got her attention, though.

"That's wonderful, Irena! You won't have to work at the hotel after all. With what you have here"—she indicated the money and jewelry—"and selling the farm, you and the baby will be pretty well set."

But Irena was shaking her head before Jade finished speaking. "These things and the money belong to Nels's child. It will all go into the bank."

Jade was about to protest, but Tyler stopped her. They watched as Irena returned the jewels to the pouch and placed them back in the metal container.

"You may want to look over these papers on your own, especially since most of them are in Norwegian. If you have any questions, I'm sure Palmer would be happy to help you with them."

Irena nodded her thanks at Rex. She handed the box to Tyler to put in the wagon with the other things, but she didn't see the concern on the faces of her friends as she picked up the broom to resume sweeping.

The ride back to town was made in silence. Irena was exhausted physically and emotionally. She requested that Tyler drop her off at the bank.

"I'll meet you at the hotel to help with the unloading. I want to get settled in as soon as possible and begin working tomorrow if Lucy and Buck are ready for me." She missed the exchanged glances between Tyler and Jade and didn't notice Tyler's restraining hand on Jade's arm.

They watched Irena step into the bank before Tyler spoke. "She's made up her mind about the money, Jade. Nothing you or I say is going to change that."

"But it's not right!" Jade protested. "I can't believe that Nels wouldn't have wanted her to use that money *now* for *herself*. She shouldn't have to work and live at the hotel, especially while she's expecting the baby. It's not right!" she repeated.

"I agree with you, but we have no influence on her decision. Perhaps Pastor Malcolm could have a talk with her or"—he snapped his fingers—"or maybe we could write to Swede and he could persuade her. Or maybe she'd listen to my mother."

Jade smiled at her husband. "I thought it was none of our concern."

"No, I said *we* couldn't change her mind. I didn't say that would prevent us from asking someone else to try."

The unloading went quickly since everything had been organized as they packed up. Buck and Tyler stored most of the items that Irena pointed out to them away in the building behind the hotel, and the rest was taken to a room on the first floor, which would become Irena's new home.

"Don't even think about starting work for a few days," Lucy said kindly as she handed Irena her key and led the weary woman to her door. "Take some time to settle in and get rested, and we'll go over your duties when you're feeling up to it."

Irena barely managed to say good night, and moments later when she pulled the blankets over her and closed her sleepy eyes, she remembered that she hadn't thanked Jade and Tyler properly either. Or Rex, for that matter, who was still out at the farm.

The next morning Buck entered the kitchen and stopped abruptly at the sight of Irena on her hands and knees scrubbing the floor. A quick scan of the room confirmed that Irena had been hard at work for a couple of hours.

"Irena!"

Irena turned and, seeing Buck, got quickly to her feet. "Good morning! I've started the coffee, and I thought I'd begin in here until you give me a schedule to follow. I hope that's all right."

Buck's first reaction was to tell her, "No, it's *not* all right," but he stopped himself in time and gently admonished her, "You were supposed to rest up for a few days before you started work."

Lucy entered the kitchen at that moment, and Buck shot her a quick look that silenced the outburst she was ready to make. Irena's back was to them as she hastened to pour coffee for them. She carried the two cups to the table and stood next to it as if awaiting her instructions for the day. Then she watched curiously as Lucy went to get a third cup and poured coffee in it. She set the cup on the table and motioned for Irena to sit down with them. Irena hesitated a moment then sat.

Leisurely Lucy explained Irena's duties while Buck listened and watched for Irena's reaction. He noticed that she didn't touch her coffee as she listened carefully to Lucy's instructions, and he could tell she was going to protest before Lucy had even finished.

"I know you are trying to make things easy for me, and I appreciate that, but right now I need things to do, not time to just sit and think."

"You need to be thinking of the baby—" Lucy began, but Buck signaled for her to stop.

"Cora will be in soon and can show you what help she'll need with preparing meals. Lucy and I are around if you have any questions."

Buck smiled at Irena and got up. "Thanks for the coffee, Irena." He began to lead Lucy from the kitchen, but he turned back and said, "Oh, one more thing. Cora always calls me to help with any heavy lifting. I expect you to do the same, all right?"

He waited for her nod, then he and Lucy went back to their home.

"She's going to overwork herself." Lucy shook her head. "What can we do, Buck?"

"I think we need to let her work for now, honey. It seems to be what she needs. Later we'll have to convince her to take it easier, but for now—well, let's just give her some time, okay?"

Lucy walked into her husband's embrace. "It could have been you," she spoke softly against his chest. His arms tightened around her.

"I know."

Chapter 30

Sand Creek

Sky heard Russ call out to someone in the yard, and she went to the kitchen window to see who it was. She couldn't have been more surprised when she saw Violet Gray descend from the buggy. She watched, transfixed, as Russ assisted Violet and was even more astonished when she saw Violet smile at him.

Sky realized that Violet was headed toward the house, so she patted her hair and smoothed her skirt. Violet had never visited the Newly ranch before. Something terrible must have happened. No, she shook her head, Violet had smiled at Russ.

Sky's lips tightened. In her past experiences with Violet, a smile usually meant that Violet was enjoying something that would not make Sky happy. She steeled herself for whatever unpleasantness Violet had brought with her.

The knock on the door brought Sky's wayward thoughts back to the present, and she took a deep breath before she moved to answer it.

"Good afternoon, Violet. What brings you way out here?" Sky spoke pleasantly, but she was on guard.

"Sky."

Violet's tone was so odd that Sky looked at her sharply.

"Please, come in."

But Violet couldn't. Having come this far, she struggled to make the next move.

"What is it, Violet?"

Something between a laugh and sob escaped the woman's lips, and Sky stared at her. "I told myself I wouldn't cry!" Violet burst out as she entered the house.

Worried now, Sky led her guest to a chair. "What is it, Violet? Has something happened to Taylor?"

At Violet's negative shake of her head, Sky continued. "To Philippa, then? To Ralph? To the baby?"

Another choked exclamation came from the woman, then she blurted, "I came to apologize to you!"

Sky dropped to a chair.

Violet smiled at the astonished woman. "Twenty-five years of being hateful, nasty, and cruel to you, Sky Newly. Twenty-five years! Can you forgive me?"

Sky's dumbfounded expression clearly revealed that this was not what she had expected to hear. Beginning on the bride train that brought them to Sand Creek years ago, Violet had despised Sky, Randi, and some of the other mail-order brides. Sky knew it was partly because she had stood up against Violet's manipulative ways and refused to allow her to eat their supper until she had helped with the chores, but that was only one incident. Violet had stirred up trouble for Sky whenever she got the chance from then on.

Violet took a deep breath. "I finally did it, Sky." She beamed as she leaned toward Sky. "I finally accepted Christ as my savior. Twenty-five years of fighting it, but it took one young woman's tragedy to make me open my eyes to what you've been trying to tell me all these years."

"You mean Irena?"

Violet nodded. "I overheard her and Philippa talking. She was saying how thankful she was to God for Philippa's friendship, and I just had to know how she could feel grateful to God for anything after what she'd been through and…"

The story took over an hour to tell. The women shared tears and laughter as the barriers between them melted away and a bond began to form. Russ joined them, curious to know Violet's reason for the visit and wondering if Sky needed *rescuing* from her. His joy was as great as his wife's. Long had they prayed for Violet's salvation.

Chapter 31

Jenson Farm

Rex carried another load from the wagon into the house and waited for his sister's instructions on where to put it. The twins, Troy and Trudy, were running around exploring their new home and getting in the way of the adults who were trying to unpack.

Simon called to Emma, who was working in the downstairs bedroom. "That's the last of it out of the wagon. Do you need help in here or should I start putting things away in the barn?"

Emma joined her husband and brother in the kitchen. Her blonde hair was mussed, and her cheeks were red from exertion, mostly from keeping up with the children than from the unloading.

"No, I'm fine in here. Goodness, everything was so clean; I only had to deal with a little dust, so I can start putting things away already." She turned to her husband. "The house is perfect, Simon, but I can't help feeling badly about how we were able to get it."

"I know. It almost feels wrong to be blessed by someone else's tragedy."

Rex looked at the couple thoughtfully. He heard Troy and Trudy giggling together about something in the sitting room, and he smiled. "I think Irena will be grateful that this house will be filled again with love and laughter." He nodded. "She would want it this way. Come on, Simon, I'll show you around the barn."

Grandville

Irena rubbed at the spot on her back that was protesting her efforts to scrub the floor. She glanced around to see if Lucy was within sight. If she was, Irena was sure to get another scolding for working too hard. Irena sighed. As well meaning as Lucy was, she just didn't understand the necessity—the absolute necessity—of Irena filling her days with labor.

After a full day of scrubbing floors, washing laundry, cooking and serving and cleaning up the dishes, Irena could collapse into bed at night and sleep. She found that the harder she worked, the less likely she was to dream. It was her dreams that tortured her.

Although not always. Sometimes she would find, just before waking, that she could relive moments with Nels and remember the warmth and love of her husband. She wished she could stay wrapped in the protective cocoon of her memories, but consciousness would steal it away and reality would sink its bitter teeth into her mind once again when she awoke.

She prayed and knew others were praying for her. She still wasn't angry with God, just as she had told Pastor Malcolm, but she did have questions. Swede had taught her so many wonderful things about God's love for her and his protective care of her, but he had also made it clear that becoming God's child didn't mean that she would never have problems again. It did mean, however, that she had someone to go through the problems with her. And knowing that was the only way to keep bitterness from getting a hold on her.

Another thought that sustained her was knowing that Nels and Mother Jenson were in heaven and knowing that they were so much better off there. Irena thought of her own parents and wondered if it were possible that they had been saved. It was something she would only know once she too went to be with the Lord.

Irena stood to her feet and surveyed the scrubbed floor with a critical eye. Satisfied, she backed into the hallway, carrying the bucket of dirty water with her. A noise down the hall drew her attention, and she turned to see Miss Pike, the town's schoolteacher, leaving her room. For a brief moment, Irena wished she could step back into the room to avoid drawing the schoolteacher's attention, but she told herself she was behaving cowardly.

"Oh, Mrs. Jenson, I'm glad I caught you before I left for the day."

Irena watched Deborah Pike approach her and waited while the schoolteacher swept a condescending look over her attire; when scrubbing floors or washing laundry, Irena always wore her old scullery maid dress and apron. The serviceable gray dress had been let out at its seams to accommodate Irena's expanding figure, and rather than risk doing damage to any of the fine dresses that her mother-in-law had made her, Irena had taken some of Mother Jenson's everyday dresses, and with Lucy's help, altered them for her own use. Lucy also lent Irena some of the things she wore while expecting Molly.

Miss Pike came to Grandville from St. Paul in answer to the advertisement for a teacher. She was of medium height with non-descript brown hair and plain features. Her clothes were stylish, but having laundered them, Irena suspected that they were second-hand dresses made over for the young woman. She carried herself with an air of authority, something one might expect in a schoolteacher, but Irena had discovered that snobbery lie carefully veiled just under the surface of the woman's polite demeanor. She was also aware that the townspeople of Grandville were ignorant of this second side to their teacher's nature.

"Good morning, Miss Pike." Irena curtsied without thinking, realizing how easy it was for her to resume her scullery maid role. The woman was no older than Irena, yet Irena felt subservient in her presence because that's exactly how Deborah Pike expected her to behave. Irena knew that if Buck and Lucy or her other friends in Grandville knew of the teacher's treatment of her, they would do something to stop it. Everyone was overprotective of Irena, and as much as she appreciated that, she didn't want to add another of her trials to their concerns.

Miss Pike tugged on her gloves as she gave Irena her orders. "After you've made up my room today, Mrs. Jenson, I'd like you to press the outfit I've laid out on the bed and blacken my shoes. I have a dinner invitation this evening, so I expect everything to be ready by five o'clock. Is that understood?"

"Yes, ma'am."

They both turned as Lucy came to the top of the stairs and, seeing them, headed their way with a warm smile lighting her face.

"Good morning, ladies. I'm sorry to interrupt, but Palmer would like to have a word with you, Irena, if you have time."

"The banker?" Miss Pike asked with interest.

"Yes, have you met him yet, Miss Pike?"

"No."

"Well, come along with us and I'll be happy to introduce you." Lucy reached for the bucket in Irena's hand and linked arms with her as they headed for the stairway.

"Irena, this place is scrubbed clean enough. I think you should take the day off and rest or go do some visiting for a change."

Irena saw Miss Pike's sharp look. "I have a few things I'd like to finish first," she spoke to Lucy, "then maybe I'll go over and see how Philippa is doing."

Lucy was delighted. "Good! You have been working too hard, my friend. Take as much time as you like. Cora and I will handle things here."

Irena could sense the schoolteacher's disapproval of the familiarity between the hotel owner and the hired help, but Miss Pike kept her thoughts quiet. Palmer Granville was waiting in the hotel lobby and greeted the ladies with a smile.

"How do you do, Miss Pike?" he said after Lucy made the introductions. "I'm sorry I did not meet you earlier, but my wife and I have been in Chicago for a few weeks."

"Chicago? Really? How interesting!"

Palmer smiled politely then turned to Irena.

"Irena, I wonder if you could come by the bank sometime today to sign some papers, or if it's inconvenient for you, I could bring them by here."

Irena was aware of the schoolteacher's interest as she replied, "I am free this afternoon to come to the bank."

"Fine. I'll look forward to seeing you then." Palmer tipped his head at the ladies and left.

"Strange that the bank owner himself would deliver a message," Miss Pike said to Lucy. "He could have sent a messenger."

Lucy laughed. "Oh, you'll find that we all pretty much do our own work here in Grandville. If Palmer had been busy, he would have sent someone, but he likes to get out and see his customers too."

Irena felt the woman's perusal again, but she turned to Lucy and reached for the bucket. Lucy held it out of the way.

"No, I'm headed to the kitchen too." Lucy laughed. "Have a good day, Miss Pike."

"Good day, Mrs. Riley." Miss Pike gave Irena a brief nod and left.

Irena noticed that Lucy frowned at the schoolteacher's back as she walked away. It was obvious that Miss Pike had not included Irena in her good bye, and Irena hoped that Lucy wouldn't mention it. Instead, Lucy linked arms with her, and they walked to the kitchen together.

"You know as the winter approaches, we won't be as busy, so you should have a little more free time, Irena. I mean, you could have more time now too, if I could just get you to quit working so hard." She squeezed her friend's arm. "How are you really doing?"

Irena was silent, wondering how to reply, and Lucy stopped her to study her face.

"I...I have trouble sometimes believing it really happened, I guess," she admitted. "When I keep busy, I can forget for a while, then it all comes back again and it hurts just as much."

Irena saw that her words had made Lucy too emotional to speak, so she continued, "But I could never get through this without my Lord. Knowing how happy Nels and Mother Jenson are is a great comfort."

Lucy took a shaky breath. "We'll keep praying, Irena."

Later, after Irena finished the chores for Miss Pike, she changed clothes and put on a coat and gloves to ward off the fall chill and headed to the bank. Palmer greeted her warmly.

After they sat down, he began, "Simon and Emma have finished moving into the farm, Irena. It's a little unusual for the new owner to do so until the paperwork has been signed by both parties, but I knew how much you wanted Simon to take over the dairy business so that Rex could get back to his own work."

Irena nodded.

"Here's where you need to sign, but first take a moment to look over the figures. I believe you received a good price for the farm, and the Chappells are more than pleased with their purchase. Does everything appear satisfactory to you?"

Irena looked at the documents, and Palmer was surprised when she asked, "Should it be so much?"

"It's a fair price, Irena. The farm is well worth it."

Irena sat in silence, and Palmer allowed her the time to digest the information he had given her. He understood; the sale of the farm plus the money and jewelry she already had in the bank had just made her a wealthy woman.

Irena reached for the papers and signed them where Palmer indicated. Then she surprised him further when she reached into her handbag and pulled out a few bills.

"Could I keep this money separate from that money?"

"I don't understand. Do you want two accounts under your name?"

"One under my name, this one." She indicated the money she set on his desk. "And the rest in the baby's name, but I don't know what that name is yet."

Palmer hesitated. He had heard Irena's request for the money to go to her baby the last time she came to the bank and had tried to convince her then that Nels would have wanted her to use the money for her own needs as well. Apparently she hadn't changed her mind.

"It would be best if you kept both accounts in your name, Irena, and"—he held up a hand to forestall her protest—"and the reason is that until your baby is of age, you will have to handle the account for him or her. That means you can withdraw for expenses as the child grows or for investing in land or another house or a business, whatever you want. When the time is right, you can turn it over to the child; but my advice to you is that you manage it until then. I will be glad to help you in any way I can."

Irena nodded slowly. "All right, but can I still have my earnings in a separate account?"

"Of course."

Satisfied, Irena finished signing Palmer's papers and thanked him. She felt relief at having the money matters settled for now, although she was still felt uneasy over whether or not she had done the right thing by selling the Jenson farm. She brought it up to Philippa after they were settled at the kitchen table with their coffee and cookies.

"I was thinking of myself," she explained. "I knew I couldn't continue to live there. For one thing, I couldn't have handled the work alone, but more than that, I couldn't live there with the memories." She watched Philippa sip at her coffee and set the cup down. "But then I began to think that maybe Nels would have wanted his son to have the farm someday. I know how important owning land was to him."

Philippa listened to Irena's arguments. "You're right. You couldn't have stayed on there by yourself." She fiddled with her cup as she considered the other woman's words. "If you have a son, he *will* want his own land someday, but you can't know now *where* he would want it or what he would do with it. He may not want to be a farmer. Maybe he'll be a store owner like Ralph or a banker like Palmer. If you have a daughter, she most likely would live where her husband chooses."

Irena nodded at Philippa. "So you agree that it's better to hold the money, then, and let my child decide when he's old enough what to do with it, right?"

"Well..." Philippa stood and went to the stove for the coffeepot. As she refilled their cups, she asked, "Where are you planning to live while your child grows up, Irena? In the hotel?"

"I need to earn money for us to live on," Irena insisted.

Philippa sat down again, and suddenly she laughed. At Irena's puzzled expression, she explained, "I'm sorry. It's just that this reminds me of trying to convince someone that they don't have to work for their salvation."

Irena shook her head, indicating that she didn't understand.

"You know. Salvation is a free gift, there for the taking, yet people still insist on trying to earn it. Here Nels provided for you a way to take care of yourself as well as a way to raise your child, plus still have a healthy chunk to give him when he's grown, yet you refuse it and want to earn your own money to live on."

She waited to let the words sink in a moment. Irena stared at her. "But—"

"If Nels had left you debts to pay, Irena, would you have passed them on to his child? You and Nels were *married*, Irena. What was his becomes yours. Don't refuse his provision for you *and* the baby."

Irena stared thoughtfully at Philippa. "I have to think about this."

Philippa nodded. "Here is something else to think about. How about buying a small place here in town that you can call your own? You'd have no outside chores to worry about and you'd be close to the church and the store and *people*. Plus, you'd have a home to raise the baby in, not just a room in the hotel.

"And if you wanted to work, I'm sure Lucy would still want you, or you could work here when I need time off. Ralph's brother Ray prefers work at the sawmill to running the store, and Cora has always liked cooking at the hotel rather than being a shopkeeper, so it's just Ralph and me, and sometimes we'd like a break, especially now with our baby coming."

The bell over the door to the store rang, and Philippa sighed as she got heavily to her feet. "See what I mean?" She smiled. "Be right back."

Irena barely heard the voices in the other room as Philippa waited on her customer. She was deep in thought over what Philippa had just said. Her words made sense, and Irena wondered why she was having a hard time using Nels's money for herself. Was it pride? She closed her eyes.

Lord, I do not mean to be stubborn, but I'm confused about what to do. Please show me.

Chapter 32

Grandville

A welcoming warmth greeted her when she opened the door to the hotel. Irena shivered as she undid the buttons on her coat, which was actually Mother Jenson's coat remade to fit Irena's much smaller frame. As she made her way to her room, she saw Miss Pike come toward her from the lobby as if she had been waiting for Irena.

"Mrs. Jenson, I've changed my mind about which dress I'm going to wear tonight. It's turned out colder than I expected, so I set out a different outfit for you to press. Please see to it at once."

Irena hesitated. Miss Pike had clearly heard Lucy tell Irena to take the rest of the day off. Besides that, Irena knew that Buck and Lucy had agreed to board the town's teacher and feed her her meals, but she didn't think that included washing her laundry or pressing her clothes. In fact, she recalled seeing Lucy show Miss

Pike the laundry area and explain to her that she could take the irons to her room and heat them on the stove there to press her clothes.

Irena should have refused the first time the teacher had ordered her to do it, but that was just it. She had been *ordered*, and Irena had obeyed orders all her life.

Irena's hesitancy did not sit well with Miss Pike. "I haven't much time, Mrs. Jenson."

"Yes, ma'am."

Irena pondered her servile demeanor as she pressed the tucks and laces of Miss Pike's dress. She released the cooled iron on the stove and attached the handle to a hot one as she continued. She had always been a servant, she reasoned, at least until she married Nels. She paused. It was different to work and do things for someone you loved instead of doing it because you were told to do it. The baby moved inside her, and she smiled, but then she stopped again. Is this how she wanted her child raised? In an environment where others could order him about like they did her? If she continued to stay at the hotel, there would be more people like Miss Pike in her life who would treat her like a servant again.

Her brow was furrowed in thought as she brought the finished dress up to Miss Pike's room. The teacher answered her knock on the door and grabbed the dress from Irena's hand.

"It's about time!"

The door was shut in Irena's face, and Irena scowled. Then she shrugged. Being treated like a servant did not mean she was one. Yet…

Tyler Newly was in the lobby when Irena descended the staircase. "Irena Jenson, just the person I wanted to see." He approached her, and Irena saw the now-familiar sympathetic expression appear on his face, and she knew she couldn't deal with it just now.

"I'm fine, Tyler. That's what you were about to ask, wasn't it?"

He nodded in understanding. "And you've been asked it a lot, I'm guessing."

She smiled.

"It's just that everyone cares, Irena," he said softly.

"Thank you."

"Anyway…" He cleared his throat. "We're having some people over tonight for dinner, and Jade wants to know if you're up to joining us." He saw the instant reluctance in her eyes and tried coaxing her. "Rex is here for only one more night. He's leaving tomorrow since Simon has taken over for him at the farm. And we asked Simon and Emma and the twins to come too. They've been pretty busy getting settled, and Jade wanted to give Emma a night off from cooking. I know they'd like a chance to talk to you."

Irena stared at the floor. Talking about Nels's farm was the last thing she felt like doing, but Irena knew she had to face it someday. She hadn't really spoken with the Chappells yet, and she wondered what they were like. And she needed to thank Rex.

Yet, did she really want to talk about the farm and be reminded that Nels was gone and someone else was living in their home?

Tyler was waiting, so Irena knew she had to make a decision. "Do I have time to change?"

"Of course. I'll be right here when you're ready and—thank you, Irena."

She nodded and hurried to her room. Minutes later, Irena returned to the lobby.

She was buttoning her coat and did not see Deborah Pike right away, but when she looked up, she caught the shocked expression on the teacher's face. Clearly she was upset that Irena was joining them, but then, Irena was upset as well. She didn't realize this was the dinner Miss Pike was attending.

"Irena, I forgot to mention that Miss Pike is joining us this evening too." Tyler looked at the teacher. "Eddie is very excited to meet you, Miss Pike. I'm afraid you're going to have your hands full next year when he begins school. He can hardly wait. It's all he talks about... when he's not talking about horses, that is."

Neither woman spoke.

"You ladies do know each other, don't you? I mean, I just assumed—"

"Of course. Good evening, Miss Pike."

"Good evening, Mrs. Jenson."

Irena couldn't help it. The faintest of smiles revealed her amusement. She caught Tyler's eye on her but refused to meet his inquiring look.

The ride to the Newly home was brief, cold, and would have been silent if Tyler hadn't kept a running monologue going.

Irena regretted her decision to come. Had she known Miss Pike was one of the dinner guests, she would surely have turned Tyler down. She was apprehensive about the evening in the first place, and now with Miss Pike's disapproving eyes on her...

Irena broke off her turbulent thoughts. Her friends, her dear friends, had invited her into their home because they cared about her. She was not about to let a snobbish young woman ruin their evening together. Besides, the stunned look on the teacher's face had been pretty funny. Irena smiled.

Rex Newly stepped out of the shadows to meet the buggy as Tyler reined the horse to a stop.

"Hey, Ty. Thought I'd take care of the horse for you while you brought your guests into the house. Good evening, ladies. Mrs. Jenson, I'm glad to see you could make it."

"Nice to see you again, Mr. Newly."

Rex glanced at the second woman when Tyler made the introductions.

"How do you do, Mr. Newly?"

Irena heard interest in Miss Pike's greeting to Rex. *Oh, oh! Look out, Rex!*

"Miss Pike."

Rex stopped Irena as she started to follow Tyler and Miss Pike to the house. "I just wanted you to know, Mrs. Jenson, that everything has been fine at the farm."

Irena smiled, yet sadness crossed her features. "I don't know how to thank you for taking over like you did. Mr. Granville told me you refused payment, but I—"

"No, enough of that. Friends help each other. I'm glad I was available to help you."

Irena nodded, too choked to speak. She caught up to Tyler and the teacher, who were waiting by the door, and Miss Pike's face was lit with curiosity.

Jade was waiting to greet her husband and her guests as soon as they came through the door. "Eddie has been beside himself hoping that you would come, Irena. I'm afraid he may monopolize you all evening," she warned as she hugged her friend.

Jade turned her attention to the schoolteacher. "Miss Pike, how nice of you to join us this evening! We are so happy to finally have a teacher in Grandville. I know you don't have many students this year, but I'm pretty sure that by next year attendance will have doubled."

Jade chatted on while she took her guests' coats, and Irena let the warmth of the greeting calm her. She moved aside as Jade reached for Miss Pike's coat and noticed for the first time what the teacher was wearing. It was not the second dress that Irena had been commanded to press at the last minute after all but rather the first one that she had pressed that morning.

Irena looked over at Miss Pike and saw her smug look. *She's probably waiting for me to say something. Well, I won't.*

Jade led them into the large sitting room and introduced both women to Simon and Emma Chappell.

The couple politely greeted the schoolteacher first, but it was obvious that their attentions were focused on Irena. Miss Pike's lips tightened as she stepped back to allow them to move around her.

"Mrs. Jenson." Emma startled Irena by embracing her. "I am so glad you came tonight. I know this is all still so difficult for you, but we want you to know that we love the farm already and that we will take good care of it. It's obvious that time and care has already been put into it, and—"

"Thank you." Irena wanted to put a stop to Emma's praise of the farm. She did not realize that it would hurt so much to visualize someone else living there. She needed time to adjust, so she tried changing the subject.

"I remember you now from the anniversary party," she said to Emma. "You look so much like your mother."

"Thank you. I hear that a lot." Emma seemed to quickly understand that Irena wasn't ready to discuss the farm, and she went along with the new subject. "My mother mentioned how much she enjoyed visiting with you that day too, Mrs. Jenson. Your English accent is so much like hers."

"Please call me Irena." Irena breathed a sigh of relief. "Your mother is very kind. I enjoyed our visit as well."

"And we're Emma and Simon." Emma looked over at Miss Pike. "We're pretty informal here." She smiled at the woman, waiting for her reply.

"Yes."

If Emma was taken aback at the woman's tone, she did not let on. They all turned as Tyler ushered the young children into the room while holding his daughter Pamela in his arms.

"The children tell me it's their turn to greet our visitors." Simon reached for the twins to slow their entrance or they would have raced ahead. Irena smiled in delight at the two adorable children, but her attention was immediately required by Eddie, who stood before her with a big grin on his face.

"I knew you'd come! Mama and Papa said maybe not, but I knew it!" He reached out his arms, and Irena bent forward and let the boy squeeze her around the neck. Rex entered the sitting room and laughed.

"You'd better let Mrs. Jenson breathe there, Eddie!"

"Irena don't mind," Eddie declared to his uncle.

"*Doesn't* mind."

Eddie's interest was immediately on the teacher. "Huh?"

Miss Pike smiled primly at the boy while out of the corner of her eye she looked to see if Rex Newly noticed. "The proper way to reply is to say, 'Irena *doesn't* mind,' not 'Irena *don't* mind'."

"Well, she don't," Eddie assured her, and all the adults except for Miss Pike laughed. Jade apologized to the teacher.

"You see why Grandville is so happy to have you here, Miss Pike?"

Eddie turned his attention on the schoolteacher. "I get to go to the school next year," he informed her enthusiastically. "I can hardly wait! Will we have stories like Irena tells us?"

The teacher glanced uncertainly at Irena. "We'll read from books."

"But will you *tell* us stories? I don't…I doesn't…" Eddie tried to put his words together correctly. "I can't read yet."

There were chuckles as Miss Pike answered, "I will teach you to read."

But Eddie was still uncertain. "Irena don't…doesn't," he quickly corrected himself at the teacher's look, "need books. She can just tell a story without even reading it." He gave Irena an admiring look, and while Irena was acknowledging Eddie's praise with a smile, the teacher said, "Perhaps Mrs. Jenson doesn't know how to read."

Every eye turned to stare at the schoolteacher, who remained unmoved by the attention. "Some servants never get the opportunity," she explained.

"Servant!" Rex looked to see if the teacher was joking, and they all became uncomfortably aware that she was not.

Irena remained motionless, not knowing what to do in the tense moments that followed; then, unbelievably, she felt an irresistible urge to laugh. She cleared her throat, hoping to disguise it, but Tyler, who had been watching her, laughed outright.

"Why, I guess we're all considered servants, then, Miss Pike. I serve my lumber customers; Simon will serve his dairy customers, and even you, Miss Pike. You serve the needs of the community."

Other than the tightening of her lips, Miss Pike made no acknowledgment of Tyler's words.

"And, Eddie, not only can Irena read English, but she can also read Norwegian."

"Wow!" Eddie turned his admiration back on Irena.

Jade's voice was strained as she announced, "Dinner will be ready shortly, everyone. I've just got to check on things."

"I'll help," Tyler volunteered, and he handed Pamela to her uncle Rex.

After the couple left the sitting room, there was only a moment of silence before Emma engaged Miss

Pike in conversation. "I was a teacher in Sand Creek not long ago," she began, and Irena was relieved the teacher's attentions were off of her for a while.

Simon pulled the twins a little closer to Irena. "I don't think you've met Troy and Trudy yet, have you, Irena?"

"No." Irena smiled kindly as the children hid their faces against their father. They peeked out at her then hid again. Irena automatically made a face at them each time they peeked, and soon they were giggling at her. She enjoyed the laughter and relaxed as Eddie chatted to her about his new pony. She watched Simon with his children and felt a calm steal over her.

"I'm glad the twins will be raised on the farm. They will make it a happy place again." She spoke with sincerity.

Simon caught Rex's eye before he answered Irena. "Rex thought you would feel that way, Irena. I'm glad that you do, and I hope, someday, you'll feel able to come out for a visit."

Irena nodded but said no more. She prayed that, in time, that would be possible.

"She's rude and she's arrogant and she hurt Irena!"

"Shhh." Tyler held his wife close to his chest to silence her. They were in the kitchen, filling the serving bowls when Jade could contain her thoughts about Miss Pike no longer.

Tyler spoke against Jade's hair. "She's also our guest, and we will treat her with politeness no matter how rude she is. And don't forget, Eddie is all eyes and ears. We don't want him to hear us say anything bad about the teacher."

"Hmph! A woman like that is *not* teaching our son! I'd as soon take on the job myself as to let her try."

Tyler chuckled at his wife's temper. "I know." He sighed. "Let's just get through this evening and try not to let her hurt Irena anymore, okay? We'll tackle the problem of her teaching our children later."

Jade nodded in agreement, but Tyler could see from her bright eyes and the two red spots on her cheeks that she was still fired up.

"Calm down," he cautioned her. "Are you ready for them to be seated?"

"Yes. But place Miss Pike far away from Irena, you hear?"

Tyler laughed again. "Got it."

He was glad when he entered the sitting room to see everyone engaged in conversation and a contented look on Irena's face as she listened to Eddie. Emma was keeping Miss Pike occupied by talking about teaching, and Simon and Rex were discussing something about farming, while the twins... Tyler grinned. The twins were vying for Irena's attention by making silly faces at her then ducking behind their father. And Irena... Tyler's eyebrows shot up. Irena was making faces back!

It was easy to let Irena know she had been caught. When she glanced up at him in the doorway, Tyler made a quick, silly face at her. Her cheeks blazed, but

Tyler saw that she was trying to contain her laughter. He couldn't be more pleased.

"Ladies and gentlemen," Tyler pretended to appear formal. "You may be seated in the dining room. *Dinnah* is served." He made a mock bow to Irena. "May I escort you, madame?"

Irena took Tyler's arm and they watched in amusement as Simon mimicked his brother-in-law and gallantly offered his arm to his wife. They each took a twin's hand, and Eddie, following suit, ran to grab Irena's free hand. That left Rex with Miss Pike. Irena and Tyler couldn't resist a glance over their shoulders.

Balancing Pamela on one arm, Rex approached the schoolteacher. "May I escort you, Miss Pike?" It was obvious that he was overdoing the gallantry on purpose as the others had done, but Deborah Pike seemed to be taking the attention quite seriously.

"I'd be honored, Mr. Newly." She rose regally and took his arm. The others couldn't believe it when the woman actually fluttered her eyelashes at Rex.

As the gentlemen seated the ladies, Miss Pike commented on the beautiful table and chairs. Tyler saw her take notice of the expensive china and silver as well.

"What lovely things you have, Mrs. Newly," she effused praise on her hostess. "It's unusual to find such quality outside of the city."

"Many of our things are gifts from a friend in Chicago." Jade nodded to Tyler to say grace, and only moments after he finished, the teacher spoke again.

"The children will dine with us?" That she was offended by this arrangement was clear.

Tyler could see Jade was making an effort to be polite, because all she said was, "As Emma said, Miss Pike, we are pretty informal around here," and left it at that.

"Speaking of being informal," Rex put in, "I noticed you ladies keep calling me *Mr. Newly*. How about you just call me Rex? That way Tyler and I won't get confused which one of us you're talking to. May I call you by your name?" he asked Irena.

At Irena's "Of course," he smiled and turned to Miss Pike. "And Miss Pike?"

Obviously flattered by Rex's attention, the teacher gave him a coy smile. "Of course, you may call me Deborah, Rex."

Rex nodded his approval.

"Here, Deborah, may I serve you some of Jade's delicious roast chicken?" Tyler held the platter ready, waiting for her reply, but the disapproving expression on the teacher's face made it obvious that while she was giving Rex permission to use her name, she hadn't intended everyone to have free license to do so. But it didn't dissuade Tyler. He was enjoying putting the snobbish teacher off balance.

"I have to tell you, Deborah, that my wife can bake the best pies in Grandville. You are in for a treat tonight."

The meal was wonderful, and Irena ate more than she had intended. She said as much to Jade.

"It's the baby making you eat more, but I'm glad you enjoyed the food. Thank you. Do you think you'll have room for pie?" She asked the question so hopefully that Irena laughed.

"Oh yes, and I'm not even going to ask you to make it a small piece. I know how good your pies are!"

Jade refused the offered help and removed the dishes and served the dessert in short order. When she resumed her seat so that they all could begin on their pie, Deborah Pike commented, "You did that so efficiently, Mrs. Newly, but I'm surprised that you don't hire help for your dinner parties."

The use of Jade's formal name did not escape the other's attention. "I enjoy doing the serving myself, Deborah, and I'm quick at it because I had lots of practice when I was a maid."

Miss Pike set her fork down and turned to her hostess. "A maid? But I heard that you were from a wealthy family."

"Oh? Who told you that?"

"Well, I just heard and—and your step-father is the banker!"

"Yes?"

"Well." Deborah Pike looked around the table. "I see."

"What you *see*, Miss Pike," Tyler spoke gently, "are people who are all created equal in God's sight. It doesn't matter if we're rich or poor, farmers or bankers, lumbermen or lawyers." He folded his arms across his chest and nodded his head at Jade. "My wife *was* from a wealthy family. She used to live in a mansion in

Chicago; I've seen it. It was beautiful. Then her father lost the family's money and when he died, he left them practically penniless. Jade went to work as a maid for Palmer Granville's brother Amos, and that's where I met her.

"I had some lofty ideals at that time," Tyler continued. "I wanted to be rich and live in a fancy house like Amos Granville. At first I couldn't see past the maid's uniform Jade was wearing to realize what a wonderful woman she was. But thankfully, God opened my eyes. Status means very little to us out here, Miss Pike. It might mean something to city people, which is a shame, but here we respect a person for who he really is on the inside."

The schoolteacher remained silent, so Tyler looked around the table. "Well, these little ones look like they're about ready for bed, and that's Irena's second yawn, so I guess we better call it a night and let these people get home to their beds."

Irena blushed. "I'm so sorry."

"No, Irena, Tyler is just teasing you. It's the baby that makes you tired. Believe me, I know."

"You should have twins sometime," Emma joked. "I'll tell you, I was tired then and I'm still tired!"

The three women laughed together as they carried the remaining dishes to the kitchen.

"Nels would have loved twins," Irena said softly. "He wanted a big family."

"Oh, Irena!" Jade pulled the small woman into a hug, not knowing what to say, but Irena smiled at her.

"I'm glad I have this one," she said with her hand in front of her. "God has been good."

Jade turned to her other guest who was standing nearby. "I'm glad you could come tonight, Deborah. I hope you enjoyed yourself."

"Thank you, Mrs. Newly—Jadyne," she corrected herself. "You have been most kind, and you have a beautiful home." The woman's words were stilted and forced, so Jade just smiled.

"Tyler should have the buggy about ready, so I'll get your things."

Tyler and Rex came in from outside. "Brrrr. The temperature's dropping," Rex said. "I wouldn't be surprised to see snow soon."

"It *is* November, after all." Simon came in behind the other two men. "Jade, do you think we could borrow an extra blanket for the kids for the ride home?"

"Of course! I'll get another lap robe for you ladies too."

"Oh, I forgot about this." Tyler reached into his coat pocket and pulled out a letter. "I picked up our mail before I went to the hotel. It's from my father," he explained to Miss Pike and Irena. "If you don't mind, I'd like to take a minute to read it before we go, so if there's any news Emma and Simon need to hear, they can get it before they leave."

"Yes, of course," Irena agreed, and Miss Pike nodded.

They all watched as Tyler scanned the letter, and by the frown that appeared on his face, they knew there was some bad news.

"What's wrong, Ty?" Emma asked.

Tyler looked up at the others while he handed the letter to his sister. "Looks like Ma broke her arm."

"Oh, no!" Jade stared at her husband.

"Pa says that the cold weather froze the puddles in the yard and she slipped and besides the broken arm, she bruised her hip pretty bad, so she's not getting around too well."

Emma took up the story. "He says that Dorcas has been over to help. That's our sister," she explained to the two women, "but they think Dorcas needs to be home with Cavan and Leon, so they're hoping to get a neighbor girl to come and stay at the ranch and help out for a while." She looked at her husband when she was finished reading. "Oh, Simon, I wish we could go, but now with the farm…" Her voice trailed off.

"I'll be going home tomorrow," Rex announced. "I should be able to help."

But Jade shook her head. "No, she needs a woman's help for times when your dad can't be there. Do you think I should go, Ty?"

Tyler thought for a few moments then shook his head. "I'd hate to have you and the kids go. You could end up there all winter if we get heavy snows. I know my folks wouldn't want that just as they didn't want Dorcas and Cavan to be apart. Pa even says so in the letter. He thinks they can manage."

They all stood and pondered over the problem. Then, quietly, Irena spoke up. "I could go."

She almost smiled at the blank faces before her.

"Lucy said there wouldn't be much work at the hotel for the winter, and I'd love to be able to help your mother."

"But you could end up there all winter," Tyler warned.

"I don't see that being a problem."

"Well, I don't know—" Tyler began.

"I don't need your permission, you know." Irena shocked them with her teasing. "Besides, Sky told me to come for a visit any time. Why not now?"

"I should really be the one to go," Emma protested. "I'm her daughter."

"But your parents don't want your families to be separated and"—Irena paused—"I have my family with me."

Jade looked from Irena to Tyler. "Your mom would love to have Irena there, Ty, and when she's all healed up, she'll be ready to help Irena when the baby comes."

"That would be good," Irena admitted. "But perhaps I would end up being more of a burden to them than a help. I hadn't thought of that."

"Don't even worry about that, Irena. My mother would love to have you there when the baby comes. I know she would," Emma said.

Rex spoke up. "Could you be ready by tomorrow, Irena? That way you could travel back with me."

Irena nodded, happy that they agreed with her.

Deborah Pike had remained silent through the discussion, but at this announcement she said sharply, "Alone? A widowed woman traveling alone with a single man? I don't care how informal you people are. That is just not proper!"

Chapter 33

Grandville

Rex rode along with Tyler and the women on the way back to the hotel. He wanted to be with Tyler when he told their sister Lucy about their mother's news and also to help Irena if she had any questions about the trip.

"All you really need are some clothes for yourself and what you have ready for the baby. Knowing Ma, once her arm is better, she'll be knitting all sorts of things for it.

"My house isn't quite done yet, so I planned on spending the winter with my folks too. I hope you won't mind having me hanging around. And don't worry, the house is huge and there will be lots of room if you do want to bring something big with you like your crib and rocker."

Irena thought about that. "Would you have room in your wagon?"

"Plenty of room. We stored them out back at Buck's, right? I'll load them first thing in the morning, then."

Irena smiled her thanks and beside her on the buggy seat she heard Miss Pike mumble something.

"Excuse me?"

But the woman didn't answer.

Rex helped the ladies out of the buggy and said good night to Irena, but as he held out his hand for Deborah Pike, he said, "May I speak to you for a moment, Deborah?"

The teacher was all smiles. "Yes, of course, Rex."

Irena walked on into the hotel but glanced back before entering. Rex had his head rather close to Miss Pike's as he spoke to her. Irena wondered if perhaps he was interested in the young woman. No matter, it was no concern of hers.

It was later that the two women met again in the hallway. Irena moved aside to allow Miss Pike to pass her, but the teacher stopped.

"He plans to court me in the spring." She made her declaration with her head held high.

Irena wondered what sort of reply was expected of her to this announcement. "I see."

She began to walk on, but Miss Pike held up her hand.

"He made his choice, so you better stay away from him." Satisfied, Miss Pike moved on to her room.

Irena was stunned. *Does she think I'm looking for Rex's attention? I love Nels!* Irena felt physically sick to think anyone would think such a thing. She debated if she should even ride with Rex to his folks' place, but then she remembered that Sky needed her. Miss Pike didn't represent the feelings of the others in Grandville. She shook her head as she continued on her way to finish her packing. *I am not going to let that woman bother me.*

Lucy was tearful the next morning when she said good-bye to Irena. "I was looking forward to your having the baby here, but I know my mother will take good care of both of you."

Irena laughed. "I'm going to take good care of her too." Then she was serious. "Thank you, Lucy, for helping me get through the dark days. I will never forget your kindness."

The women hugged, and as Rex finished loading Irena's things, she went to say her goodbyes to Philippa.

Philippa, too, was in tears. "We'll both have our babies the next time we see each other!" She wiped at her eyes. "You have been such a dear friend, Irena. I'm going to miss you this winter. You better come back to us in the spring!"

Irena was also having a hard time saying goodbye. "Please tell the Tuckers goodbye for me too, and you take good care of yourself and your baby." She sniffed. "And I want you to know that I'm going to take your advice and buy a house here next spring."

They hugged again, then Rex was there with the wagon and he bundled Irena up in blankets and put a hot rock at her feet. She waved to Lucy and Buck in front of the hotel and to Ralph and Philippa in front of their store. She sniffed a few more times as they left the small town behind, but Rex kept quiet and let her cry.

A while later he asked, "Are you warm enough, Irena?"

"I'm very comfortable, but how about you?" She was wrapped in several blankets, but he was only wearing his coat.

"Now that you mention it, you could quit hogging all those blankets and at least share *one* with me."

Irena was so startled by his teasing that she just stared at him with an open mouth.

"C'mon, Irena! Share!" he commanded, and with a laugh, Irena slid one of the blankets over to him. She had been a little worried about riding alone with Rex after Deborah Pike's outburst, but she could see that she needn't have been. She and Rex were going to get along just fine and if he was interested in the schoolteacher, however much she wanted to question his judgment, that was his business too.

———

Cora was sitting at the table peeling potatoes when Deborah Pike stuck her head into the hotel kitchen.

"Good morning, Miss Pike. Is there something I can do for you?"

The teacher stepped farther into the room and glanced about her. "I suppose that since Mrs. Jenson is gone, you will be doing my laundry and pressing my dresses now?"

Cora laughed as if the woman had told her a joke. "You suppose wrongly, Miss Pike. I have enough to do with the cooking." She paused in her peeling to look at the teacher. "I thought you were doing your own laundry. Do you mean that Irena was?"

"Of course."

Cora resumed her task as she thought about the way the woman had just replied. *Of course,* as if it was expected that Irena would do her chores. "Well, there's Grace Morrison. She'll be coming about twice a week to help out. Maybe you could hire her to do it. What were you paying Irena?"

Deborah's eyes shifted away from the cook's. "That's no concern of yours."

Cora immediately understood. "You mean you expected her to do it for nothing?" Cora's laugh was without mirth. "You weren't paying her?" she repeated.

"That will be enough of that!"

"How dare you tell me what to do!"

"What's the matter?" Lucy asked as she entered the kitchen and heard the raised voices.

"Miss Pike has been having Irena do all her washing and ironing this whole time *without paying her for it.*" Cora stressed the last part of her statement.

"Miss Pike? Is this true?" Lucy studied the schoolteacher, but when the woman remained silent, Lucy continued, "I clearly explained to you when you moved in here the living arrangements we would have. Was there something you didn't understand?"

"You had a servant. I gave her servant work to do."

"A *servant*? Irena?" Lucy was outraged. "Miss Pike, I assure you, Irena had a job here, and she is my friend, not a servant."

"Once a servant, always a servant."

"Excuse me?" It was evident that Lucy was shocked at the woman's words, and she and Cora watched in disbelief as the teacher turned to leave. They looked at each other and shook their heads.

"Oh, Cora." Lucy snapped her fingers, finally remembering why she had come to the kitchen. "Do you know where I left the cash box? I can't seem to find it anywhere."

"I knew it!"

Both ladies swung around to see a triumphant expression on the schoolteacher's face as she stood in the doorway. "She stole it from you, didn't she? She stole it and ran off."

"Who? What are you talking about?"

"That servant! Your precious Mrs. Jenson!"

Cora could hardly contain herself as she laughed and pointed her paring knife at the outrageous woman. "Lady! Irena Jenson is one of the wealthiest women in Grandville! She wouldn't need to steal from anyone!"

"But…" Miss Pike was suddenly confused.

Buck walked in just then and handed Lucy a tin box. "This what you were looking for, honey?"

Lucy nodded and moved toward the teacher. "Pack your things, Miss Pike. You are no longer welcome to stay here."

Chapter 34

Way Station—Sand Creek

By the time Rex reined in the wagon at the way station, Irena was chilled to the bone. Melody and Leigh hurried to wrap warmed blankets around her and had her sit close to the fireplace. In minutes she held a hot cup of coffee in her hands, and she watched in amusement as the ladies ministered to Rex's needs in the same way while their husbands took care of the wagon and horses outside.

The children gathered around them, all curious and wide-eyed.

"You must be Jason," Irena guessed, as he was the only boy.

Jason nodded shyly.

"Eddie told me to tell you hi for him, and he wants you to know that he named his pony Shotgun because sometimes it *shoots* out from under him."

The children giggled, and soon they were telling Irena about the horses at the way station. Her teeth stopped chattering, and she was able to unwrap some of the blankets by the time the men came inside. Rex had put off explanations until they were all together.

After hearing about his aunt's condition, Gabe said, "I'm sure my ma has been over to help too, but it will be good for Aunt Sky to have Irena there all the time. Thanks for going, Irena."

Irena smiled. She hardly knew the couples at the way station. She and Swede had stopped here on their way to Grandville, but much of that trip had become a blur to her. The couples had attended the anniversary party in Grandville, but Irena met so many people that day that she barely remembered being introduced to them.

They knew about Nels and his mother, and each in turn expressed their sympathies to Irena. She thanked them and had to wipe at the tears that fell of their own accord.

"When is your baby due, Irena, if you don't mind me asking?" Leigh sat down beside her.

"In the spring, around April, I'm guessing. It may well be that I'll still be at the Newlys'."

"Oh, Sky will love that!" Melody exclaimed. "Did you know that she used to work for the doctor in Sand Creek? You'll be in good hands, Irena."

They left early the next day, well bundled against the cold. Despite the conditions, Irena was enjoying the ride. The day before, Rex had filled her in on all that he had done at the farm and how he and Simon had set things up to continue the deliveries into town. At first she had just listened, and at one point Rex asked her if it was bothering her to talk about her former home.

"It is a little hard," she admitted. "When I was on my way here, to America, I kept thinking that I would finally have a house of my own, well, along with my husband, that is. I was never made to feel that I belonged at my aunt and uncle's house in Norway, and of course, the Cavendish house wasn't my home."

Irena was thoughtful. "At first I was surprised that Mother Jenson was going to share our house with us, and then I was glad because I was awfully afraid of being alone with Nels." She laughed softly at her private memories. "Still, I never really felt like it was *my* home."

She stamped her feet and cuddled further into the blankets. "But when I go back to Grandville in the spring, I'm going to buy a little house in town for the baby and me," she announced proudly. "I'm finally going to have my own house."

"That's great, Irena. We have that in common; I should get my house finished in the spring and I'll have my own home too."

On their second day of travel, Rex told Irena something that touched her deeply.

"I have to tell you, Irena, that I really envy the marriage you and Nels shared. On the times that I was out to your farm on business, I could see that you two had something very special. My folks have it too. I can see it in Tyler and Jade's marriage and my sisters' also. I'm sure the Lord is the reason, but it's also that two people who are just right for each other find each other and they make it work. Now, Bernadette and me…" Rex's voice trailed off.

"Do you know what Nels said to me the last time I visited you?" Rex continued, unaware that Irena was holding her breath at this unexpected statement. "He said he thanked God for you every day and—"

Suddenly Rex realized that Irena was sobbing. He quickly reined in the horses while he berated himself for being so inconsiderate as to open Irena's wounds again. Cautiously he put his arm around the grieving woman.

"I'm so sorry, Irena. That was thoughtless of me. Will you forgive me?"

Her sobs were quieting down and she wiped at her face. "Oh, wonderful! Now I'll have icicles forming on my eyelashes."

Rex looked at her in astonishment, and she gave him a wobbly smile. "Don't be sorry, Rex. I needed to hear that. Do me a favor, will you?"

"Anything."

"Remind me what Nels said from time to time. I don't think I'll ever forget, but it's nice to hear it."

"Of course."

She looked up at him again, and Rex could see the ravages of the tears on her face. "What else were you going to say? You said, 'and…'?"

Rex blinked. "Are you sure you can handle more? I mean, you kind of had me scared there."

Irena laughed and sniffed at the same time. "If you don't tell me, I'll just keep wondering, so we better get it all out now."

"Okay." Rex unconsciously tightened his arm around her. "He said that every man wants a son to carry on his name and a daughter to keep his heart soft."

He watched her closely. She didn't sob this time, but huge tears rolled down her cheeks, and she just let them fall as she stared at him.

"Thank you," she whispered.

They were almost to the Newly farm, and Irena was freezing again. Their conversation had remained in a much lighter vein, and Rex found himself enchanted by the hidden humor he was finding in Irena. It was like finding the filling in a layer cake. It was already sweet and then it got even better.

"If you were any kind of a big brother, you wouldn't let your little sister freeze like this! Give me that blanket back." Irena tugged at the blanket over Rex's knees, but he was sitting on it and was not about to let it go. They had been sparring back and forth about it for the last mile.

"Quit your whining or I won't take the shortcut home."

"No! Take the shortcut! Please, take the shortcut!"

"Okay. Here we are." Rex stopped the wagon.

"What?" Irena popped her head out of the blankets and looked around her. They were in front of a huge white ranch house, and Irena could see Russ Newly putting his coat on as he stepped out onto the porch.

"Rex! Why didn't you warn me?" Irena whispered to him. "I look like a papoose! What will your father think?"

Rex roared with laughter while his father approached them. Russ turned up the collar on his coat and thrust his hands quickly into his pockets. "Thought you'd be back soon," he said to his son, but he was looking at Irena, and when he discovered who she was, he smiled with pleasure.

"Irena Jenson! Won't Sky be surprised to see you! Come in; let's get you warmed up. No, you go in too, Rex, you look like a block of ice. I'll take care of the horses and join you soon."

The men were unloading the wagon as Russ talked, and they set everything on the porch by the time Irena got up the steps. She heard Russ ask his son, "Did you get the news about your mother?"

"That's why Irena came along, Pa. She's going to stay for the winter and help Ma, and most likely she'll have her baby here in the spring."

Russ climbed the steps to where Irena was still standing. "Thank you, Irena. Sky will be so pleased. I can't tell you how glad I am that you're here."

The men helped Irena into the house, and Rex walked her right to the kitchen stove while he pulled a chair along and gently pushed her into it. Irena heard Russ go into another room and talk to Sky. In a few moments he came back to the kitchen.

"Sky knows you're here and can hardly wait to see you, so after you get some warmth back into you, go on in and see her. I'll be back soon."

Rex pulled up another chair by the stove and joined Irena. He held his hands close to the stovepipe and stamped his feet. Grinning, he studied her, still wrapped in her blankets. "A papoose!"

Irena shivered. "If I'd have known you were going to be such a bully, I wouldn't have come."

"Here, start unwrapping those blankets so the heat can reach you." Rex stood and began peeling the layers off Irena. At first she clutched at the blankets, thinking he was teasing her again, but he said, "C'mon, trust me, Irena. Rex knows best."

She laughed as he stood her up and unwound blanket after blanket, spinning her slowly in circles. She unbuttoned her coat and opened it to the stove's heat but still didn't remove it.

"Ready to go say hi to my mother now?"

She nodded and followed Rex through the large sitting room to the bedroom beyond. The larger room was cooler than the cozy kitchen, and Irena shivered and rubbed her hands together.

"The bedroom will be warmer," Rex whispered. The door was open, but Rex knocked on the doorframe before entering.

"Anyone home?" he called.

"Rex! Come in! And Irena!" Sky was propped up in bed; her right arm was wrapped in plaster and lay elevated on a pillow in front of her. She reached out her free arm to accept Rex's hug as he bent over her. He looked into his mother's blue eyes and saw excitement sparkle from them, but he saw pain lurking there as well.

He moved aside as Sky beckoned to Irena. "How good to see you again, my dear! And what a surprise!" She pulled Irena close to her and squeezed her hand.

"Rex." Sky nodded to the chair in the room. "Bring Irena a chair. No, put it on this side of the bed close to the fireplace."

Rex did his mother's bidding then stood back. "I'm going to give Pa a hand getting our things inside, so I'll let you two ladies visit."

Sky reached for Irena's hand. "I think we have quite a bit to visit about." She smiled at the young woman, and Rex left them, thinking that their visit would help the healing process in both of them.

Chapter 365

Sand Creek

Irena couldn't believe how contented she felt. It hadn't taken long for her and Sky to set up a routine. The household chores were no problem for Irena. The cooking they worked on together once Sky's hip had healed enough for her to move around again. She helped Irena with her free hand while the broken arm was held immobile in her sling.

When Russ was not available to help Sky, Irena assisted her with the more personal needs Sky couldn't handle with only one good arm. Things like getting dressed and buttoning buttons; using a chamber pot or washing, brushing, and styling her hair. Sometimes Sky would apologize for her helplessness, but Irena's quick, efficient ways made each task go smoothly and without embarrassment, and the older woman was deeply grateful for the nursing Irena provided. Once, after Irena had finished washing Sky's long blonde hair and then brushed, braided, and styled it, Sky had laughingly remarked, "It never looked this nice when Russ tried to pin up my hair!"

She turned to see the results in the mirror. "Why, it never looked this nice when I did it either! I am so glad you came, Irena! You have been such a blessing to me."

Getting away from Grandville turned out to be a mixed blessing for Irena as well. In a way it was a relief to be away from the familiar places and faces, for they evoked memories that were painful for her, yet she found herself yearning for the people who had become so dear to her.

It had bothered Irena to leave the church in Grandville and Pastor Malcolm's clear explanations of God's Word, but she quickly came to appreciate the Sand Creek church that the Newlys attended and was delighted to find Violet Gray in attendance there as well and eager to greet her.

Sky introduced Irena to the other ladies in the area, and she became friends with the Newlys' other daughter, Dorcas. When the weather permitted, the church ladies gathered together in different homes for their sewing circles and Bible study times. It was a soothing time for Irena.

Often when Irena and Sky worked together in the house, Irena would gather up her courage and ask Sky questions about things she had read in her Bible that she didn't fully understand. When Sky realized the depth of Irena's interest, they decided to do a Bible study of their own and often talked and prayed together, sometimes losing track of time and delaying supper preparations. Irena grew closer to the Lord, and though she didn't understand all the reasons why God had taken Nels from her, she was learning that God cared and was providing for her every need.

"It astounds me," Irena told Sky one day, "that I can have the absolute confidence that God will take care of me through eternity, and yet sometimes I doubt that he can show me what to do with my life today, next week, or next year."

Irena learned a lot about the history of Sand Creek and Grandville through Sky, who relished sharing the stories with her. Irena was fascinated to hear about Sky's adventures—being stolen away by Indians and pursued by an English gentleman who was after her inheritance money. When the subject of money was brought up, Irena told Sky her concerns about the money Nels had left and how she planned to use that money for Nels's child. Sky considered Irena's words carefully before she answered.

"I wanted nothing to do with the inheritance money left by the Baron even though it was through his brother that I received it. It took some time and prayer before I could accept it; and Russ and I, and of course my brother, Evan, discussed what to do. We finally decided to use the money with the Lord's blessing. We put most of it away, and after we had all our children, we divided what was left among them and gave it to them when they became adults. It has turned out to be a blessing in each of their lives too, and for that I'm thankful.

"Money can be so dangerous, Irena. People can be swayed to do things they never thought they would when they find wealth in their pockets. Remember that it's the Lord's money, and he's just letting you use it while you're here on earth. Use it wisely for him."

Irena appreciated Sky's advice. She found the counsel of an older, mature Christian woman to be just what she needed in her quest to become a godly woman. One day Irena told Sky about her encounters with Deborah Pike, the Grandville schoolteacher. "I found myself disliking her and though she was the one being rude to me, I wanted to fight back with angry words of my own." She refrained from mentioning anything about Rex's interest in the obnoxious woman, though she still wondered what he could possibly see in her.

Sky gave Irena a knowing look. "You should have been on our bride train to Sand Creek twenty-five years ago. Violet and I had some conflicts then and many more in the years that followed. It's only now that she's gotten saved that we've finally been able to talk as friends and come to appreciate one another. What a difference having Christ in our lives makes! But back then…" Sky paused, searching for a way to explain. "It is good to not answer back when a person is rude to us, but I believe there is a time to stand up for ourselves. The Lord doesn't expect us to take abuse. When there is something unfair happening, it is perfectly all right to stand up and fight back. As Christians we need to maintain a testimony that pleases the Lord, and I believe we can do that without letting people push us around."

Sky went on to tell about the incident when Randi Riley dumped a bucket of water over Violet's head. The women laughed together, and Sky continued, "Violet was furious with us, but she learned to respect us too, even though she didn't like us. And now, many years later, we're friends."

Christmas was only days away, and despite Sky's handicap, they decided to have guests for the holidays as the Newlys had done for years. At first the Trents offered to have them all at their place to make things easier for Sky since her injury, but when Irena heard about the traditional gathering of the Trents, Rileys, and Newlys at the Newly home, she insisted that she could handle the preparations.

"Everyone brings food," Sky explained, "but the burden of setting up beforehand and cleaning up afterward would be ours, and I'm afraid that's asking too much of you."

"I'll help her," Rex volunteered. "Pa and I will do all the heavy work, and I promise to even help wash the dishes." He grinned at Irena as he placed a hand over his heart while making his pledge.

"I will keep you to that promise," Irena teased. "No sneaking off like you did the other night." Irena wagged her finger at Rex's innocent face. "You can't fool me, Rex Newly. I saw you run and hide in the barn."

Sky watched in amused pleasure as the two bantered back and forth. She and Russ had lain in bed at night and discussed the possibilities of a romance blossoming between their son and the young widow living in their home, but Russ told Sky, "I teased Rex the other day about Irena to see what kind of a reaction I'd get, and he couldn't have been more shocked that I had thought such a thing. He said that Irena and Nels had a perfect marriage and he doubted that she would ever want another husband in his place. In fact, he seemed sure of it. The idea appeared to have never even entered his mind."

Sky was thoughtful. "And when I said something to Irena about Rex finding a wife someday, she said that she hoped and prayed that God would bring the right woman to him because he was the nicest 'adopted big brother' she'd ever had. There wasn't even the slightest hint that she thought of him in any other way."

Russ adjusted his arm so Sky could lay her head on his shoulder. "I wonder how long it will take before they realize that they're perfect for each other."

Sky laughed softly. "Give them time, and we'll just keep them in our prayers." She snuggled closer and said sleepily, "She's already like our own daughter."

Russ chuckled. "And you've got your heart set on being that baby's grandma."

Chapter 36

Sand Creek

"It's your turn to open a present, Irena." Dorcas smiled at Irena and handed her a rectangular package.

"Again?" The glee on Irena's face was a delight to everyone in the room. When it was discovered that Irena had never before received Christmas gifts nor even celebrated the real meaning of Christmas, the Newly friends and family had gone all out to make this a special event for her. Since the evening before with the beautiful Christmas service at church to today's dinner and presents, Irena had been under a spell.

Sky had been worried that Irena was working too hard on the preparations, but Irena insisted on doing everything to get ready that Sky would normally have done if she were able. Irena cleaned the already clean house from top to bottom, and she baked all the treats and delicacies that the Newlys enjoyed. She helped prepare the big Christmas meal that would be shared with Dorcas and her family; the Rileys, Hank and Randi, and their sons; and the Trents, Evan and Ella, and their son, John. The Trents' married daughters joined them as well: Esther and her husband, Dexter Riggs, and Martha and her husband, Rob Tunelle.

The other sons and daughters of the three families were either in Grandville or at the way station, and they would all be getting together in Grandville. Abel, the Newlys' youngest son, was staying in Boston where he was attending medical school. The Newlys were responsible for the hot foods, and the other families brought the rest, including the breads, the salads, the pickled beets and sweet pickles, and the desserts. Irena prepared the beef roast and the roasted chickens, the mashed potatoes and gravy, the sweet potatoes and rutabagas and the corn.

Irena was enchanted with the decorations for the house and the tree, and she spent hours sewing and knitting presents and wrapping them to place under the tree. She even had Rex take her to town one day in the sleigh, and she made purchases for the people on her list and shopped for things Sky needed as well.

Irena was ecstatic when she found what she believed was the perfect gift for Rex. It was in Nolan's Store, hanging on the wall in the back. It was a wall plaque. In a gilded gold frame the Bible verses Proverbs 3:5-6 were handwritten in beautifully scrolled penmanship:

> "Trust in the Lord with all thine heart;
> and lean not unto thine own understanding.
> In all thy ways acknowledge him, and he shall
> direct thy paths."

She hurried to get Jonas Nolan and asked that he lift it down for her.

"It's beautiful," she said reverently as she studied the words inscribed behind the glass. "I'll take it, please, but could you wrap it so that Rex doesn't see it? I want it to be a surprise."

The storekeeper looked at her oddly, Irena thought. Then she remembered that he was Bernadette's father, and she wondered if by mentioning Rex's name, she had given the man a painful memory of his daughter. But Jonas smiled kindly at her.

"I'd be very happy to, Mrs. Jenson. I'm sure Rex will be more than pleased with the gift."

Now as Irena looked at the package on her lap that Dorcas had brought to her, she read that it was from Rex. She looked up to find him smiling at her. Bashful that every eye was on her, she began carefully peeling the paper away and suddenly she glimpsed a gilded gold frame.

Oh, no! She thought as she turned the plaque around to read it, but to her surprise the words of Joshua 1:9 were written on it, not Proverbs 3:5-6. Her hand flew to her mouth to cover her astonishment as she read the words:

> *"Have not I commanded thee?*
> *Be strong and of a good courage;*
> *be not afraid, neither be thou dismayed:*
> *for the Lord thy God is with thee whithersoever thou goest."*

She turned the plaque for everyone to see.

There were *ooh's* and *aah's* and she somehow managed to choke out a "thank you" to Rex, who assumed her downcast eyes meant she was overcome by emotion. She couldn't believe it when Dorcas picked up the package Irena had wrapped for Rex and headed toward him.

"From Irena," Rex announced, and curiously he balanced the gift in his hands and felt along its edges. His eyes flew to hers, and he could see she was hard pressed to keep from laughing. "You didn't!" he accused her.

Rex tore the paper off quickly and looked at the plaque in his hands.

"It's the same thing he got Irena," someone called out, but Rex turned it around for all to see and said, "No, it's a different verse. See?"

Irena was laughing now, and the others joined in. Dorcas took Rex's plaque and held it up next to Irena's. "They're a set," she exclaimed.

"I thought it was perfect for your new house," Irena explained to Rex. "Now I understand why Mr. Nolan looked at me so strangely when I said it was for you. He knew you bought the other one."

"And I thought the one I bought would be perfect for the house you hope to buy someday." He smiled at her, and their eyes held for just a moment. Irena felt something stir in her and she turned away.

Fortunately, Dorcas passed out the next gift and attention was taken away from Irena. Rex watched the blush steal over Irena's face and wondered if he had embarrassed her. The pink in her cheeks certainly made her look lovely. Suddenly he realized what he was thinking, and he looked down at the floor.

Though the others in the room were interested in watching the next gift being opened, Sky and Russ continued to watch the bent heads of the young people across the room from them. Sky felt Russ squeeze her hand.

Chapter 37

Sand Creek

Irena was still confused when she prepared for bed. Rex had been nothing but his usual self the rest of the evening, even fulfilling his promise to help with the clean up, although Ella Trent and Randi Riley had already done most of the work, shooing Irena and Sky out of the kitchen.

But she was relieved too. She wasn't sure what had happened to them in that brief moment when they had looked at each other; she was only glad that everything was back to normal.

Sky's cast was finally removed, and though the doctor told her that it would take some time to regain all her strength, Sky declared that she was ready to switch places with Irena and take care of her now. Doc Casper had checked on Irena too while he was at the Newlys' home, and he chuckled at Sky's announcement.

"Irena is doing well, Sky. Don't go coddling her now. Both she and the baby will be happier and healthier if you let Irena continue to do whatever she feels capable of doing." Then he cautioned Irena. "Just don't go doing anything foolish, young lady, like lifting something too heavy or breaking in one of Russ's wild horses."

Both ladies laughed, and Irena poured the doctor more coffee.

"When do you think the baby will be born, Doctor?" Sky asked.

The old, white-haired doctor was the man Sky had worked for when she came to Sand Creek as a bride twenty-five years earlier. His veined hands were becoming gnarled, but there was no shakiness to them, and he still had a twinkle in his eye.

He gulped down the hot liquid in his cup before replying. "I'd say about April, wouldn't you, Irena?"

Irena smiled shyly and nodded. That's what she had figured as well.

"Do you expect any complications?" Sky questioned further.

"Irena is small," Doc Casper admitted, and Sky nodded, indicating her concern. "But unless her baby is terribly big, there should be no reason to worry. Irena is also strong and in very good physical shape, not like some of these young ladies who have to ride in a buggy or a sleigh everywhere they go and couldn't walk a mile without having a fainting spell." He laughed. "I wish all my patients took care of themselves like you do, Irena."

The doctor stood slowly and shrugged into his overcoat. "Well, I'm headed to the Grays next. Taylor's had a bad winter cold, and Violet's worried about him getting pneumonia. I'll be glad when Abel is through with his training so he can be my partner; there's getting to be too many people in Sand Creek for only one doctor."

Sky hastened to wrap some bread, and she pointed to one of the pies on the counter. "Irena, will you put these things in a basket for the doctor? And here's another basket for the Grays. Would you take it to them, Doctor, and tell Violet we'll be praying for Taylor?"

The doctor watched as the ladies bundled up the food items. He shook his head at Sky. "I still can't believe the change in Violet. It's a miracle that God finally got through to her."

"It's a miracle he got through to any of us." Sky laughed. "We're all so undeserving."

"Amen." The doctor picked up the baskets and waited while Irena opened the door for him. Pausing beside her, he gave her some parting orders.

"Now don't you let Sky trick you into thinking she's all healed already. She still needs to take it easy with that arm for about a week, you hear?"

Irena smiled and nodded.

"Too bad you're not looking for a job, Irena. I could use a good nurse like you around."

Irena was pleased with the doctor's praise, but when she closed the door and turned back to Sky, she said, "I don't think I would like being a nurse and taking care of just anybody. I like helping you because you are my friend. Do you suppose that's selfish of me?"

Sky laughed. "No, I don't. When I worked as a nurse, I felt much the same way. And now I get to take care of you finally. Just think, only a few months to go. Are you getting excited?"

"Yes, but I'm also a bit scared," Irena admitted in her honest way. "I remember how much pain my aunt Dagne endured, and I used to wonder how she could go through it year after year, having one baby after another."

"You were only a child yourself then." Sky shook her head. "And you say you helped with your aunt's deliveries?"

Irena nodded. "Three times the doctor did not come in time and I had to help. But I was so glad that the doctor was there when one of the babies died; I would have felt responsible." She was silent a moment. "I think about that little dead baby sometimes and I start to worry, 'What if something happens to Nels's baby?' I would feel that I had failed him somehow."

Sky pulled Irena into her arms and let the young woman cry softly.

"We know that God is in control and that you and the baby are in his care." Sky hesitated, then as Irena calmed down, she said, "This is *your* baby too, Irena. It is a blessing that you will have a child to remind you of Nels and the love you shared, but it is all right for you to open your heart to new love. Someday you may wish that you again have a husband to care for and a father to help you raise your child."

Irena moved away from Sky and sat down at the table where she could face her. "I don't know. Wouldn't that be shaming to Nels's memory? I loved him, and he was so happy to be a father."

"And Nels loved you too. That's why I think that it would please him if you found happiness again, if you found love again. You've been alone so much. I don't believe he would want you to live your whole life alone."

Sky sat down across from Irena and searched for the right words to say. "I'm not saying that love is something you should go looking for, Irena, but it is something you should not turn away. At least pray about it and see where the Lord leads you. It may be that he wants you to remain single. Just pray that he would show you the desires your heart should have."

Sky stood and began clearing the table, leaving Irena to her thoughts. She hoped she hadn't said too much. Silently she prayed, *Lord, I want to help this precious girl, but I don't want to interfere with the plans you have for her. Please give her peace about her future.* Sky continued to pray for Irena and the baby and the coming delivery. She was startled from her thoughts when Irena took a frying pan from her hands.

"The doctor said that you are to take it easy with that arm for another week. This pan is much too heavy for you to lift."

Sky sighed audibly. "Yes, *nurse!*" She relinquished the pan and put her hands on her hips. "But I'll pay you back when it's your turn, you know."

She was relieved to see Irena laugh, and they joked as they worked together cleaning the kitchen. *Thank you, Lord,* Sky prayed.

The door opened, and both women turned to find Rex grinning at them.

"You two ladies feel up to a short sleigh ride?"

"To your house?" Sky asked eagerly.

Rex nodded, and Sky clapped her hands. "Oh, good! I've been anxious to see how far you've gotten. Do you feel up to it, Irena?"

"Yes, of course."

Rex could tell by the excitement on the women's faces that they were ready to get out of the house for a while. "Well, bundle up good. The weather's not too bad and the ride isn't far, but I know Irena will be stealing your blanket from you, Ma, if she gets too cold."

Rex ducked as Irena threw a dishtowel at him. The ladies hurried into their winter coats, and Sky asked if Russ was coming along with them.

"No, he's over at the Riley's, remember?"

"Oh, that's right." For just a moment Sky debated about staying home and letting the two young people go on their own; then she saw that she was trying to play matchmaker, and she immediately dismissed the thought. *I have to leave them in the Lord's hands,* she decided.

Rex handed the ladies up into the back seat of the sleigh and spread a blanket over them. "Hang on to your share of that blanket, Ma." He winked at Irena as he spoke, and Sky was quick to notice Irena blush.

"Rex, you just be nice to poor Irena today," Sky scolded her son, "or I'll see to it you don't get a piece of that pie she made."

"I'll be on my best behavior."

Irena relished the sleigh ride. The crisp, cold air stung her face, but the white frosted trees and fields were so breathtakingly beautiful that enduring a little cold was well worth the view of the scenery.

"God provides beauty for us to enjoy everywhere, doesn't he?" Sky commented, and Irena could tell she was enjoying the outing just as much.

"I can't decide which season I like the best," Sky continued. "They each have something special to offer. I feel sorry for people who live anywhere else but in the north."

Irena nodded. "It reminds me of Norway, yet I feel that this is really my homeland now."

Rex led the sleigh down a tree-lined path, and Irena could see smoke coming from a chimney beyond the treetops. Soon the house came into view, and Irena blinked in surprise at the size of it, yet she remained silent. As was normal for her, she formulated her thoughts before she spoke them, but apparently Rex was too eager, too impatient to know what was going on in her mind, and he asked, "Well?"

He turned to look at the women after he halted the horse. Sky waited a moment for Irena to speak. Then, as the girl beside her continued to remain silent, she said to her son, "I love the dormers over the upstairs windows, Rex. They add so much to the look of the house. It's really charming."

Rex grinned at his mother's praise, but he swung back to Irena. "What's the matter, Irena, *cat got your tongue?*"

Irena smiled. "It's so much bigger than I imagined. Why, it's as large as your house," she said to Sky.

Sky nodded. "Russ advised Rex to build large enough at the beginning then he wouldn't have to add on later like we did if he should have a large family someday. And even if he has a small family, he will have room for family events here, like we had at Christmas."

Rex jumped down to help the ladies out of the sleigh, and Irena saw that he had shoveled a path to the porch, and he made sure he set the ladies down on a cleared area so they weren't in deep snow.

"The stove and the fireplace are both going, so let's get you in and get you warmed up. Then I'll give you a tour. But first"—he pointed at the out buildings—"the barn—obviously—the milk house, the ice house, and the chicken coop." He held onto an arm of each of them as they walked. "Don't slip now, Ma. You don't need another broken arm. And you hang on tight, Irena. We don't want to take any chances with you in your condition." He smiled down at Irena, and she shyly gripped his arm, thankful for his support.

The house was pleasantly warm and smelled of newly cut lumber. Two lone chairs were sitting by the kitchen stove, and Rex led the ladies directly to them.

"Warm up before I take you around. You better keep your coats on, though, because the rest of the house is pretty cool."

Irena looked around the kitchen appreciatively. The big cook stove looked like it could handle any family gathering. Rex already had a handsome icebox in place and there was a water cistern in a large sink. Cupboards were built along the wall with a counter and worktable under them, and there was a wood box beside the stove, and she could see it was filled. The only thing she couldn't picture in the room was Miss Pike. Irena shook her head as if trying to dispel the image. She hoped Rex knew what he was doing.

"This would be the only room that I guess you could call furnished." Rex laughed. "Are you warm enough now to see the rest?" There was a boyish eagerness in his voice that made Irena smile. He led them into the dining room and indicated the location of the future table and chairs. Next he showed them into the sitting room, which was large and boasted a bay window overlooking the frozen lake. Irena walked to the window and stood looking at the scenic view. Sky joined her.

"Oh, Rex, this is lovely!"

Rex spoke from behind the women. "This room was going to be two rooms—the sitting room and a formal parlor. That's what Bernadette wanted." He paused, and the ladies turned to look at him. "But I don't care for formal parlors, so when Bernadette...changed her mind...I changed the house plan." He grinned. "No formal parlors for me!"

Sky laughed at her son. "We rarely use ours anyway," she admitted. "Most of our guests prefer the sitting room or even the kitchen."

"What about you, Irena? Do you think my house needs a formal parlor?"

Irena looked around the bare room. She could visualize it filled with furniture and laughing children. Then her eyes moved to where Rex was standing in the middle of the room, his hands on his hips as he appraised his house.

The winter sun was low, but it spread sunshine throughout the room, filling the space with light. Irena thought of the small formal room that Mother Jenson referred to as the parlor. It was dark from the heavy drapes on the windows and decorated with feminine doilies on the backs and arms of the chairs. She couldn't recall ever seeing Nels sit in that room.

"No," she finally spoke. "Your house suits you, Rex. You don't need a parlor."

Rex grinned.

"This will be the downstairs bedroom," Rex continued his tour, "and the stairs here lead up to four rooms. I can close the door here and not have to heat the upstairs at all while it's empty, which may be for some time. Maybe I could take in boarders," he joked, "and I could send them to you for meals, Ma."

Sky just rolled her eyes at her son's teasing while Irena walked through the bedroom. Irena noticed with interest that the room also had a large window in it that overlooked the lake, and she smiled her approval to Rex. She sensed that he needed to not feel closed in. The ladies climbed the stairs and exclaimed over the generous-sized rooms and closets they found there. Rex was beaming.

They returned to the warmth of the kitchen, and Irena noticed a doorway by the icebox that she hadn't seen at first.

"What's in there?"

Rex opened the door to allow her to see inside. "It's an extra pantry and a place to keep the bath tub. In the summer it can be used as a bathing chamber, but in the winter I imagine I'll pull the tub into the kitchen and keep it close by the stove."

Irena nodded. "You seem to have thought of everything. I think it's a fine house, Rex."

"You've done a wonderful job, Son. I'm just sorry that you won't be living at home much longer, but if you have to move, I'm glad it's not so very far away." Sky smiled up at her tall son.

"I'll be getting my cows from Simon this spring and some from the farmers around here, so that's when I'll probably start staying over here, but you can bet I'll be showing up over at your place around mealtimes."

"I hope so." His mother laughed.

Irena couldn't help but wonder as she listened to their exchange how different it would have been for Rex if he had married Bernadette as he planned. He hadn't mentioned his decision to court Miss Pike to anyone that she knew of, so perhaps his trip to Grandville in the spring meant more than bringing home cows. It looked like the house was all set up for a woman to start housekeeping. Maybe Rex wouldn't be taking his meals with the Newlys much longer. Miss Pike and Rex… Irena shrugged. It wasn't her business. And yet, she and Rex had shared that look.

Chapter 38

Sand Creek

It was getting closer to the time of the baby's arrival, and Irena needed to go into town to pick up the rest of the things she wanted to have ready for the baby. She mentioned it to Sky, who agreed to go along with her.

"I can finish getting the things on my list too," she proclaimed.

Irena knew Sky wanted to be with her to watch out for her, as she was in the final weeks before the baby was due. Irena appreciated the protective care and concern and had grown to love the entire Newly family. She wondered how she could ever repay them.

Sky handled the reins on the buggy, and they moved along at a leisurely pace over the hard road. The snow was nearly all gone, but the frost remained in the ground. Soon the roads would be soft and muddy, making travel difficult again.

They went to Nolan's store first, and the ladies began gathering the items on their lists. A woman came from the back of the store, and Irena recognized her as Bridget Nolan. Bridget welcomed the ladies, and after greeting her Irena went back to her shopping, but she noticed Bridget pull Sky off to the side and whisper to her. Sky shook her head at Bridget and appeared to be calming her down. Then Sky put her arm around the woman. Looking over her shoulder at Irena, she called, "I'm going to have a short visit with Bridget while you shop, Irena. I hope you don't mind."

"Not at all." Irena watched the two women walk to the back of the store and wondered what was wrong, but she went back to finding the items she needed.

She was near the front of the store when she happened to look out the window. The day was cold, but the sun was shining, and Irena enjoyed looking out at the town of Sand Creek and watching the people move about, huddled against the chill. She grinned to herself when she spotted a couple embracing around the side of one of the buildings.

Either they're having a romantic tryst or they're trying to get out of the wind. Irena smiled at her thoughts. She knew she shouldn't be spying on the couple, but they seemed oblivious to watching eyes. Then the woman pushed away from the man and ran away from him. *Oh, oh! Trouble between the lovebirds.*

Irena was about to go back to her shopping when the man turned and walked down the boardwalk. Her hand flew to her mouth in dismay. *Rex!*

Rex reined in his horse as he entered Sand Creek. He needed some building supplies and wanted to get them ordered as soon as possible, so he ran up the steps to Nolan's store and felt the blast of warm air that greeted him as soon as he entered the building.

"Hi Jonas," he called out a greeting. He strode over to the potbelly stove in the center of the store and warmed his hands as he told the store owner the items he would need.

"I wrote it all down on a list I'll give you as soon as my frozen fingers thaw enough to get it out of my pocket," he joked.

Jonas nodded but didn't speak, causing Rex to raise his eyebrows at the man. "Something wrong, Jonas?"

"Bernadette's here." The man's voice held a note of apology.

Rex looked down at his hands as he rubbed them for warmth. He should feel some sort of emotion, he supposed, at hearing Bernadette's name, but he wasn't feeling anything.

"I'm sure you and Bridget are happy to have her here for a visit." He made the comment as nonchalantly as he could. He certainly didn't want Jonas to think he had been pining for his daughter since she left him.

"Her husband didn't come with her."

Rex hesitated before replying. "Then you'll have more time with her. Greet her for me, okay? Now, about the things on my list…"

Rex concluded his business with Jonas and headed outside and down the boardwalk toward Clyde Moore's place. He needed the blacksmith to forge some hinges for a fence. He stepped around a building and ran smack into someone.

"I beg your pardon…Bernadette!" He held her by the arms while he steadied her. It was a shock to be face-to-face with her, and he didn't know what to say. His arms dropped to his side, and he was about to bid her a good day and move on, but there was something in her face he couldn't ignore.

"Is something wrong?"

Bernadette burst into tears and threw herself at Rex. She sobbed into the front of his coat, so that he felt he had to comfort her. He patted her back and tried to soothe her, but he was at a loss to know what was wrong.

"I should have married *you*, Rex!" Bernadette sobbed.

Rex stood rigid. "What?"

"Steven is gone all the time and he never takes me with him and I'm always alone and I hate the city and I miss you and I wish I had married you instead of running off with him." Bernadette caught her breath. She stood away from Rex but still held his arms. "If you still want me, Rex, I'll marry you!"

Rex was dumbfounded at first then disgusted. He tried to brush Bernadette's hands off his arms, but she held on tight and pleaded with him.

"Stop this, Bernadette! You're a married woman, and I'm no longer in love with you. I doubt I ever was."

At Bernadette's gasp, he explained. "We were infatuated with each other and the idea of being in love, but you never really wanted *me*, did you? You wanted a home and a husband, and I was available."

Bernadette looked down at the ground.

His tone softened. "You married Steven Rowan. You must care for him."

Rex waited for an answer, but the woman before him refused to look up.

"You don't want to ruin what you have, Bernadette. You can decide to make your marriage work or you can go on being miserable in it. But, please, do what is right before the Lord. I want you to have a happy life."

She looked up with tear-stained eyes. "I know," she admitted. Her shoulders slumped in defeat. "I never should have said that to you, Rex. I'm sorry. It's just that…it isn't turning out like I thought it would. I…I do love Steven, but…I…I thought things would be more exciting and romantic away from Sand Creek, but they're not."

Rex watched as Bernadette wiped at her eyes and stood straighter.

"I had a weak moment when I heard your voice in Papa's store and I thought maybe I could have it all back again. You know, the romance and the adventure. I was wrong. But you were right, Rex, as always. I do love Steven, and I should be a better wife to him. I still have a lot of growing up to do, I guess."

It always had surprised Rex how quickly Bernadette could change from one subject to another or from one emotion to another. It reminded him that one day she was promised to marry him and the next she ran off and married someone else. She did it again now. "It was good to talk to you, Rex." She hugged him briefly then said, "It's cold out here! Good bye and thanks!" And she ran off.

Rex didn't know if he could bounce back from the emotional upheaval Bernadette just put him through as quickly as she did. He turned and headed down the boardwalk not knowing where he was going, just wanting to move away from his encounter with her.

Father, you protected me from a marriage that was doomed to fail, and I thank you for that. At the time I was devastated, but now I rejoice. Bernadette wasn't the one for me, but I pray that she and her husband will mend their broken marriage and be happy together.

Rex found his horse and left town, deep in his thoughts but light in his heart.

Irena was silent on the ride home as she listened to Sky chatter on about not finding the right fabric she wanted. She huddled into the blanket wrapped around her and thought about what she had seen.

Rex with a woman. She hadn't expected that. Rex seemed so perfect, so caring of others, and thoughtful. This sneaking around behind buildings just didn't seem to fit with the Rex she knew. The moment she realized it was Rex she saw hugging that woman, she had felt a physical pain.

She hadn't really been listening to Sky's ramblings until she heard a name that caused her to perk up and pay attention.

"And that's why Bridget wanted to talk to me. That Bernadette! She was always a handful even as a little girl, and I have to tell you, I was concerned when she and Rex started courting, but she seemed to have matured by then. Anyway, poor Bridget! Here Bernadette comes home without her husband and tells her folks she's running away from him because she's unhappy with her marriage. Well, since Bridget asked for my advice, I told her..."

But Irena's thoughts overrode Sky's words. *Bernadette!* Was that the woman she had seen with Rex? Would Rex really take back a woman who had left her husband?

Irena's heart was heavy. She had begun to think quite highly of Rex, but apparently she didn't know him as well as she thought she did.

Chapter 39

Sand Creek

The late March day began in much the same way as all the other days since Irena came to live with the Newlys. She was up early and stoking the fire in the kitchen stove to prepare a hearty breakfast for Russ and Rex before they headed out to begin the ranch chores. Sky laughingly complained that she could never seem to beat Irena to the kitchen in the mornings, and Irena was secretly pleased that she was able to get a head start on the work and take some of the load off Sky.

Irena had been distant to Rex for a while since that day in town, but he remained the same. She was puzzled. Was he waiting for Bernadette to divorce her husband and come back to Sand Creek? He gave no indication of having an interest in the woman. Would he? Irena knew from her studies with Sky that the Lord didn't approve of divorce, that marriage vows were for life.

Surely Rex knew that. Somehow she couldn't picture Rex disobeying God's Word in such a blatant manner.

Because Rex continued on as before, she decided that maybe her fears were false, and she decided to put aside thoughts of Bernadette and let the Lord have first place in her thoughts. It was easy then to enjoy Rex's company once again.

Today the March winds were blowing and the clouds were gray and heavy in the morning sky. Irena lit a lamp to work by and soon had coffee, potatoes, eggs, sliced ham, porridge, and bread ready. Sky sniffed the delicious aromas appreciatively as she entered the kitchen.

"Mmm. It smells good in here! You spoil me, Irena." With practiced ease, Sky guided Irena to a chair and set the bread and a knife in front of her while she took over the work at the stove. All the while Sky kept up a stream of conversation, and Irena smiled secretly at the not-so-subtle maneuver and Sky's attempt to hide it. Sky had been babying Irena for the last two weeks, and Irena allowed it because she knew it made Sky feel better. Still, it was good to get off her feet.

"I do hope Violet and Taylor made it to Grandville by now." Sky continued to ramble on. "The weather today looks like a storm could blow in, and they wouldn't be able to travel at all if they were out in it." Sky studied the view out the window. "They left three days ago, so I should think they would be there by now. I know Violet is just beside herself about having a grandchild, and she was determined to be there when it was born. Duke and Angelina, that's Ralph's parents, remember?

They're planning to wait until after the birth to go. Duke says he can't leave his farm indefinitely to wait for a baby to arrive." Sky stopped her monologue when she noticed that Irena's eyes were closed. She worked quietly but kept an eye on the young woman's face. Eventually Irena opened her eyes and slowly let out the breath that she had been holding. That she was trying to hide her pain was clear.

"How long have you been having pains?" Sky asked gently.

Irena looked up in stunned surprise. "How did you...?"

Sky just smiled as she stirred the porridge.

Sheepishly, Irena smiled back. "They started around midnight," she admitted.

Sky's hand stilled. "How often are they coming now?"

"I've had three since I started breakfast, but—" Irena broke off speaking when Sky pulled the porridge pot off the stove in one quick motion and slapped the lid on it. She hurried past Irena, and Irena heard her call Rex's name out the porch door.

Presently Irena heard Rex's boots clump on the porch steps, and as the next pain began passing through her, she heard Sky's voice giving orders. There was a loud crash, which made Irena jump, and then in a moment Rex was kneeling beside her, his face only inches from hers.

"I'm going for the doc, Irena. You just hold on until I get him here, okay?"

When she didn't speak right away, Rex looked frantically at his mother. "Ma! Something's wrong!"

"No, she's fine. It's just another contraction. But you need to get the doctor now. Tell him the pains started at midnight."

"Midnight! For goodness' sake, Irena! Why didn't you wake me?" Rex stared at Irena while she finally took a breath and then smiled at him.

"And miss seeing you act like this?" she teased. "What fun would there be in that?"

His astonished face nearly made Irena laugh, but Sky gave her son a push to the door. "Are you going or should I send your father?"

"I'm going." Over his shoulder, Rex shouted, "I'll be praying for you, Irena, but you just wait for the doctor!"

Both women laughed as Sky put her arm around Irena's shoulders.

"What was that loud noise on the porch?" Irena asked.

Sky gave an unladylike snort. "Rex was bringing in a load of firewood for the kitchen, and he was so excited when I told him you were in labor that he dropped it all on the steps."

Irena began to laugh again then drew in a sharp gasp as the next pain began.

"Okay, just take it easy, honey. When this one passes, we'll get you up to your room and get you ready."

Russ opened the door to the kitchen and waited quietly while he watched Irena close her eyes and bite at her lower lip. Sky's face echoed his anxious look, but she smiled at him. "She's doing fine."

Irena's eyes flew open and seeing Russ, she started to apologize in embarrassment, but Russ stopped her. He pulled out the chair across from her and, reaching for her hand, he began to pray, "Lord, be with Irena this day as she brings a child into this world. Help her have courage and strength and may she feel you close beside her. Help her to know that she is never alone."

Irena felt tears slide down her cheeks as she thanked Russ with grateful eyes. Sky helped her to her feet, and Russ walked behind them as they ascended the stairs; then he left them. They waited through another contraction before Sky helped Irena undress and slip into a nightgown.

"See, I told you I'd be taking care of you soon," Sky teased her. Then Sky set about putting out the things she knew the doctor would need and laying out the baby's garments and blankets. She checked the heating stove in the room and laid a basket of things nearby it to have them warm and ready for the newborn.

Then they waited.

Downstairs they could hear Russ in the kitchen, and they both smiled when they heard him bring in the firewood. Sky rubbed Irena's back and read to her. They talked when Irena felt like it and they were silent while she rested.

The wind howled outside, and Sky saw big, fat snowflakes start to fall. Her first instinct was to worry about Rex and the doctor getting through the storm, but she prayed and asked God to help them.

"My aunt's babies came much faster," Irena groaned impatiently.

Sky was sympathetic. "The first babies usually take the longest. After that each one seems to come a little faster."

"How long did it take for you to have Tyler?" Irena spoke through clenched teeth.

Sky hesitated. "Try to relax, Irena. Don't fight against the pain; it only makes it worse."

"You didn't answer me."

Sky laughed. "I went through a night and a day like this," she admitted but quickly added, "but everyone is different, and you are certainly progressing well. In fact, I'm thinking that the doctor and Rex better hurry."

"If they don't—"

"Don't worry, Irena. I'm sure you and I will do just fine, but I'd really like Doc Casper to be here. He has more experience than I have—" She stopped, stunned at what was unmistakably a giggle from Irena.

"You've had six children. I'd say you were pretty experienced."

Sky shook her head at Irena's teasing, and then as another pain gripped the girl, Sky let Irena squeeze her hand and she gently talked to her until the pain eased.

"Something happened!" Irena pulled aside the sheet. "The water broke," she said with wide eyes on Sky's face.

"Then it won't be long now," Sky assured her cheerfully, but relief overcame her when she heard Rex call out from downstairs.

"We're here, Ma! How's Irena doing? Can I see her?" Then to the doctor, "Here, I've got your coat. No, you can warm up later!"

Both women laughed in relief, and Sky shook her head. "Rex is just tied up in knots worrying about you!"

Less than half an hour later, a baby's cry stopped Rex's pacing in the kitchen. Russ had kept vigil with his son, silently praying not only for the delivery upstairs but also for the anxious heart of the man waiting downstairs. A huge smile crossed Rex's face.

"You hear that, Pa? That's good, right? That means it's all over and Irena's okay?"

Russ smiled his relief. "We should be hearing very soon."

Rex stared at his father. "You mean something could still go wrong? Like what?"

"Settle down, Rex. It just takes time to clean the baby up and to make Irena comfortable. You've certainly delivered enough foals and colts to know that."

Rex rubbed a hand over his face. "It's just that—if anything happened to her—" He stopped as if realizing that he had spoken aloud, and he turned to his father.

"I know, Son. I know."

***

"It's a girl, Irena!" Sky cooed to the newborn as she wrapped her in a warmed blanket and began cleaning her with the washcloth she had ready. "Oh, she's so beautiful!"

Irena couldn't take her eyes off the bundle in Sky's arms. She was exhausted and exhilarated at the same time, and though she was impatient to see inside the cocooned blanket, she was content to let the doctor and Sky continue their care. Secretly she had hoped for a boy, someone to carry on the Jenson name for Nels and to remind her of him.

Somehow she knew Nels would have wanted a son. But God had chosen to give her a girl. What was it that Rex had told her that Nels said, *A daughter to keep his heart soft.* She blinked back tears as finally Sky placed the bundle in her arms.

"She's so tiny!"

"She's a small one," the doctor agreed, "but she looks healthy enough. Sky will help you get started feeding her. She's had some experience in that area."

He missed the amused look that passed between the women. "I suppose that son of yours will let me have some coffee by the fire now, eh? He was in a mighty hurry to get me here—took me from the breakfast table, in fact."

Sky called after the doctor, "I'll be down in a few moments to feed you." Then she looked at Irena. "Let's get you cleaned up. Something tells me you'll be having visitors."

A quick wash, fresh nightgown, and clean linens made Irena feel like a new person. She reached for the baby as Sky tucked her in.

"Have you thought of a name?"

They both watched in awe as the little one tried getting her fist into her mouth. Her face puckered up in frustration until she got her mouth around the two middle fingers and began sucking in earnest.

"She'll want to eat soon. How about if we let the men get a peek at her first?"

Irena reached for Sky's hand before she could move away, and Sky waited expectantly for the new mother to speak.

"I want to name her Anika, after my mother."

"What a lovely name!" Sky exclaimed.

Irena smiled down at her daughter. "And I had thought that I should use Nels's mother's name too, but—"

"What was Mrs. Jenson's first name?"

"Ingeborg."

"Oh."

Irena looked imploringly at Sky. "She doesn't look like an 'Ingeborg'."

"Well…" Sky cocked her head to one side as she studied the infant.

"So, if you don't mind…I'd like to name her Anika *Sky* Ingeborg Jenson." Irena asked shyly.

"Oh, my!" Sky was unprepared for the tears that sprang to her eyes. She bent down and kissed Irena's forehead. "I'm honored, Irena." And she left the room, wiping her eyes.

Sky was still dabbing at her eyes when she entered the kitchen and came face-to-face with her worried son.

"What's wrong? The doc said Irena and the baby were fine!"

She was startled at the anguish in Rex's face. "She *is* fine. If you settle down, I'll let you go up and see for yourself."

"Then why are you crying?" Rex demanded. "Did something happen?"

"No, nothing's happened." Sky cast an amused glance at her husband. "I'm just happy." She explained about the baby's name.

The doctor was sipping coffee at the table with Russ, and Sky moved to the stove to prepare some food. "Why don't you go up and see her now?" She suggested to her son. "Then she can get some rest."

As Rex hurried to the stairway, the three adults in the kitchen grinned at each other. "He's worse than most fathers I get." The doctor laughed.

Rex slowed his steps and knocked on Irena's door. He wiped the palms of his hands down his pant legs and quietly opened the door when he heard her answer.

His relief at seeing that she was all right nearly caused his knees to buckle, but he managed to make it to the bedside and sank into the chair nearby.

Irena's eyes never left Rex's face, and she was moved by the emotion she saw there. She was thankful for his concern and felt warm and protected by it. She held Anika closer for his inspection and watched the wonder cross his face.

"She's little," he said softly. He watched in amazement as the baby sucked her two fingers, and he gently rubbed his large finger over her tiny hand. "Hey, there, little Anika Sky," he whispered.

Irena felt a lump in her throat and tears sting her eyes as she watched Rex talk to her daughter. When his eyes swung to Irena's face and he smiled, she could barely manage a wobbly smile in return, and a small sob escaped her lips.

"Oh, honey," Rex said gently. "I'm sorry. You're tired." He softly wiped the tears that dripped from her lashes with his fingertips. "You have a beautiful daughter, Irena. Nels would have been so proud."

Her eyes closed at his words, and she was astonished when she felt him place a soft kiss on her forehead, much as Sky had done. She felt him move away, and she opened her eyes to watch him leave. He turned at the doorway for a final look at her then lifted his hand in a wave and closed the door quietly behind him.

"Oh, Nels," Irena said softly. "I think I'm falling in love with Rex."

Chapter 40

Sand Creek

Sky was in her element caring for Irena and Anika. She enjoyed fussing over them and baking special treats for Irena to help her get her strength back. She never turned down an opportunity to hold Anika, and sometimes there was playful rivalry over whose turn it would be next. Russ and Rex both demanded time with the baby, and Irena laughingly reproved them, saying that they were spoiling her child.

Rex returned to his normal way with no signs of the loving tenderness he had shown when Anika was born, and Irena didn't know how to handle the emotions she was feeling. She knew she should be concerned about feeling anything for Rex when he appeared to be interested in two other women—one of them a married woman. She prayed for the Lord to give her the desires her heart should have as Sky had told her to do, but it seemed that her love for Rex grew stronger every day.

Yet she told herself that she would accept God's will, even if that didn't include a life with Rex.

One day she came to a decision.

"I think it's time Anika and I think about getting back to Grandville." She brought up the subject as she sat nursing Anika in the rocker while Sky knitted in the chair across from her. Leaving Sand Creek would be difficult for her, but staying and seeing Rex love someone else would be even worse. She didn't know what she would do if he came to Grandville to court the teacher. One thing at a time, she told herself.

Sky put her knitting down and looked at Irena. "You know I love you like you are one of my own daughters," she told her. "I wanted to prepare myself for when this day would come, but there is no way to shield my heart from the sadness I will feel when you leave."

"I feel the same way," Irena admitted.

"Then why—"

"It's time," Irena said the words softly, but Sky heard and understood.

"Besides," Irena continued in an attempt to lighten the mood, "I can hardly wait to see Philippa and Ralph's little boy."

Sky wiped away a tear as she followed Irena's lead. "Violet was so excited when I saw her in town the other day. She had just gotten back and it's been, what—a month now? She told me every detail and then she wanted to know all about you and Anika. She calls the babies 'the twins' because you and Philippa gave birth on the same day, which really was amazing. It's a good thing you had Anika here; poor Dr. Arnett had his hands full with Philippa's delivery and Violet's vapors."

Sky paused, and she and Irena just looked at each other and they both knew that a chapter in their lives was ending. "I am going to miss you."

At the supper table that night, Irena casually made the announcement that she and the baby would be leaving in a week or so, depending on the stage and the road conditions. She was careful not to look at Rex.

Russ was truly saddened at the news, and he glanced at his son briefly before he spoke to Irena. "You are going to leave a big, empty place behind in this old house, Irena. I don't know if Sky and I are ready to be on our own, but apparently you are." He caught her eye, and she nodded. He understood.

"I better get to the chores." Rex stood and left abruptly, and his departure made more than one person in the room wonder what was going through his mind.

The next day Irena asked Sky if she would watch Anika while she took the buggy into town for supplies she needed. She also hoped to find a special gift for Sky as a thank you for all that Sky had done for Irena in the last several weeks.

Russ was in the barn and helped Irena hitch the horse to the buggy. She didn't see Rex and was curious about him since he had left the breakfast table early just as he had done at supper the night before. She was surprised when Russ said, "He's over at his house."

Her face turned pink, and she felt like she had been caught red-handed doing something wrong. Russ seemed pleased with her embarrassment.

"He was in to town earlier and said he needed to be alone because he had some things he needed to think over."

Irena wondered why Russ felt it necessary to share that information with her, but she only nodded and said, "I see."

She had some things to think over as well, she thought. As she drove the buggy, Irena admitted to herself that leaving the Newlys was very hard for her to do. They had become family. And Rex—Irena wondered what exactly Rex did feel for her. In her honest, straightforward way she felt like just asking him, but she knew she would be too mortified if she found that he truly only saw her as a friend and didn't want the relationship she felt they could have. And, she reminded herself, there were those other women.

At Nolan's Store, Irena studied the items on display, searching for something special for Sky. She had just spotted a delicate brooch when she heard a voice behind her.

"Excuse me, are you Irena Jenson?"

Irena turned and saw a lovely red-haired woman smiling at her. "Yes?"

"I knew it. You are exactly how Rex described you. We were talking just this morning and he—"

"Bernadette!" A man's voice called.

"Oh." The red-haired woman turned at hearing her name. "That's my husband. I better see what he wants. Excuse me, please."

So that's Bernadette, the woman Rex was holding in his arms that day. Irena stared after the beautiful woman for a moment then she caught a glimpse of herself in one of the store mirrors. She shook her head slowly. No wonder Rex called her his little sister sometimes. Next to that beauty, Irena felt dowdy and plain. She stopped her thoughts. "Well, that's that," she mumbled.

"Did you say something, Mrs. Jenson?" Mr. Nolan stood behind the counter waiting for Irena to finish her purchases.

"No. Oh, I'll take this too, please." And she added the brooch to her other items.

Irena was subdued by the time she got back to the Newlys. She was also in a hurry because it was Anika's feeding time, and she didn't want to make the baby wait and have her become fussy for Sky. Not seeing the men around, Irena worked on unhitching the buggy herself. Then she led the horse to its stall and was just finishing up when she heard Russ and Rex enter the barn.

"You're not going to let her go, are you?" she heard Russ ask, and for some reason she didn't understand, she ducked down in the horse's stall.

"How can I stop her? I have no right!"

Irena was perplexed by the frustration she heard in Rex's voice.

"Admit it—you love her."

"I do!" Now Rex sounded tortured. "But it isn't right! Even this morning when I saw her, I could hardly bear to look at her. She's so lovely and sweet. She's leaving soon and there's just nothing I can do."

"Why not?" Russ demanded.

"Because she's still in love with her husband!" Rex burst out.

Irena's heart was pounding as she crouched against the stall. She heard Russ speak to his son again as they left by the back door of the barn, but she was no longer hearing the words. Her ears were filled with what Rex had said, and her mind was rebelling at the very idea of Rex still being in love with Bernadette.

Somehow she managed to get out of the barn, and she stopped by the buggy and picked up her parcels. Her legs felt heavy and wooden as she climbed the porch steps and entered the house. She could hear Sky humming softly, so she knew that Anika had become restless and needed her, but she could hardly make herself move forward. She desperately needed to sit down.

Sky heard the door and came into the kitchen balancing the baby on her hip. One look at Irena's face, and she rushed to her side.

"What is it? What's happened, Irena?"

"He still loves Bernadette!" Irena blurted out the words then clasped her hand over her mouth when she realized she had spoken them out loud.

"What? Who? You mean Rex?" Sky searched Irena's face while she waited for answers.

Irena nodded miserably while Anika began to howl.

"Here. Take Anika and start feeding her while I try to figure this out." Sky waited for Irena to get settled in the rocker with the baby. She handed her a handkerchief and waited until the young woman stopped sniffing. Sky's mind was working rapidly while she studied Irena.

"Now, why do you think Rex still loves Bernadette?"

Between sniffs, Irena rattled on about seeing Bernadette in Rex's arms and then seeing her today in the store and how beautiful she was and how plain Irena thought she was and...

By the time Irena finished telling about overhearing the men's conversation in the barn, Sky was smiling broadly, but Irena was unaware of it because she was unhappily wiping at her eyes.

"I told the Lord that I wanted his will and that I would obey whatever he said, but now I'm all upset and I don't mean to be and I don't know what's wrong with me because I never act like this!"

"Oh, Irena!" Sky shocked Irena by giving her a hug and laughing. "Having a baby does some strange things to women, and I'm so thankful it caused you to break down and cry and tell me what was in your heart. I could only hope and pray, you know, that you were in love with Rex."

Irena stared dumbfounded at Sky.

"Now are you finished there?" Sky asked, indicating the baby.

Irena nodded.

"Then you just wait right here. Don't you dare move."

Irena stared after Sky, wondering what the woman was up to and what she meant about hoping Irena was in love with Rex. She never said she was in love with Rex! Did she?

Suddenly Irena heard Sky call to Rex from the porch. Irena panicked. She couldn't face Rex! Not now, not knowing about his feelings for Bernadette! Beautiful or not, Bernadette was a married woman and…and—it was wrong!

Irena stood and laid the baby in the little cradle by the rocking chair. She wrung her hands together as she moved toward the door.

"No, you don't, Irena Jenson!" Sky caught her before she could flee and led her back to her rocking chair. "You are going to sit there and hear what Rex has to say."

Irena glimpsed Rex standing behind Sky. He wore an odd, unbelieving expression, and he had trouble making eye contact with her.

"Now, I've told Rex what you heard or rather what you think you've heard, and he's going to explain it to you."

"Sky!" Irena was horrified that the woman had told Rex about her eavesdropping, but Sky only smiled and left the room, leaving the two of them alone except for the sleeping infant.

Irena stared at the floor, too embarrassed to look at Rex. He seemed unsure where to begin, but finally he sat down across from Irena and asked, "Did you really think I was still in love with Bernadette?"

Irena nodded, but she did not look up.

"Bernadette's married." Rex said the words as if puzzled that Irena could even think such a thing, so it gave her courage to respond.

"But you told your dad that you loved her, only that she was still in love with her husband."

"Oh." Rex nodded while he studied her bent head. "I was talking about you."

Irena looked up. "But I'm—oh!" And then again, "Oh!" She stared hard at Rex, while his eyes never left her face. She was stunned; she was delighted; she was ecstatic, but…still…She decided that now was the time for honesty between them.

"I saw you that day in town when you were hugging her."

"Hugging? Oh!" Rex shook his head. "I'm sorry you witnessed that, Irena. It was not my doing. Bernadette only wanted to talk to me and we got some problems straightened out. I don't love Bernadette, and just so you know, she hugged me, not the other way around."

Irena felt her heart grow lighter. *He was talking about me! Thank you, Lord.* But then her face clouded. "What about Miss Pike?"

"Who?"

"Deborah Pike, the school teacher in Grandville. She said you promised to court her this spring."

Rex's eyebrows drew together. "No, I didn't."

But even as his words elated Irena, she wanted to be absolutely sure. "When you and Tyler brought us to the hotel that night after the dinner party, you asked to speak to her."

"Ah, yes. Eddie wanted me to tell her his pony's name, and I promised him I would. That is all I told her."

He smiled at Irena. "Now let's talk about you. I said what I did to my dad because I know you still love Nels and as much as I love you, I am afraid of getting in the way of that love. I don't ever want to hurt you, Irena."

Irena felt joy flood through her. "I do still love Nels, Rex, and I always will love him…in my memory." She forced herself to go on. "But I love you too, and I have for quite a while."

Rex reached for Irena's hand and held it tenderly while he smiled at her in relief. "I love you, Irena. I've wanted to say so many times, but I didn't feel that I had the right. You and Nels were so happy that I thought you'd never be interested in another man."

Irena reached out her other hand to Rex and clung to both of his. "Nels will always hold a special place in my heart, and I'll want Anika to grow up knowing about her father, but the rest of my heart will belong to you, and I'll want Anika and…any other children we have to love you too."

There was a moment of silence as they looked at each other, and then Rex grinned. "Did you just propose to me, Mrs. Jenson?"

Irena laughed. "Well, I wasn't asking you to be my big brother."

Rex's hearty laugh was heard by Sky and Russ in the kitchen, and Sky breathed a sigh of relief.

"You ended up match-making after all, didn't you!" Russ teased her.

Chapter 41

Sand Creek

The wedding was set for May, and Rex decided the best thing for him to do was to move into his house until then.

Their courtship was different from anything they had imagined. They already knew each other very well, but now they were learning the personal things that engaged couples discover about each other. Anika was always with them, and Rex teased Irena that he was getting two for the price of one. Irena could see that he loved the baby, and she was so glad that Anika would have such a wonderful father. Somehow she knew Nels would have approved.

The spring was a busy time for both of them. Rex had the cattle and fencing and planting to take care of and a multitude of tasks as he got the farm up and running. Irena worked at the new house nearly every day. She wanted to get a garden in, and there were so many things to take care of setting up a home.

They laughed sometimes at the idea of sitting in a parlor to court, but as busy as they were, they took time for quiet picnics and private walks. It was a glorious feeling to have peace about their decision to spend their lives together.

Everyone in Sand Creek took part in the wedding preparations. They hadn't had a big wedding in town for quite a while, and they were always looking for reasons for a celebration. All the ladies were pitching in to bring food, and the Nolans were setting up tables inside and outside their hotel for the big day.

Sky worked happily on a charming ice-blue dress for Irena. She attached a veil to the matching hat and the results were stunning. Even Anika would be wearing a dress made from what was left of the beautiful fabric.

Rex and Russ put all their extra efforts into getting furniture built for the new house, and Sky and Irena sewed curtains and made rugs. Soon, Rex's house was becoming a home.

Nearly all the couples in Grandville came. Irena had written Philippa and asked her to be her Matron of Honor, and Rex asked Abel, who came home for the occasion, to stand for him as Best Man.

Irena walked down the aisle on Russ's arm, and she and Rex stood before Pastor Malcolm Tucker, who shared the ceremony with the Sand Creek pastor.

Irena couldn't help comparing this wedding ceremony to her first one. Then she had been a shy, nervous young girl, taking a step into the unknown. Now she was a young mother, still shy, still a little nervous, but confident that she was taking the path the Lord had laid out before her.

The ring was placed on her finger, and Rex kissed his bride for the first time. Then they turned to the applauding audience and were introduced as Mr. and Mrs. Rex Newly; but instead of walking down the aisle, they waited with smiles on their faces as the Sand Creek pastor made one more announcement.

"You are all invited to join the wedding celebration following at the Nolan's Hotel. As a special surprise, we will be honoring today the following couples from Grandville, who will celebrate their fifth anniversary of marriage this summer. As the pastor read off the names of the ten Grandville couples, there were cheers and laughter.

Later, before Rex and Irena and Anika slipped away from the group, Irena pulled Jade and Lucy aside. "I tied the bows on the gift baskets just the way Mother Jenson taught us," she told them proudly, and Rex, who was never far from her side, grinned at the women.

"Hey, were you surprised?" he asked.

Hearing the question, Tyler joined the group. "Not only did you get us here without us knowing about the surprise anniversary celebrations, but we were all dressed up to boot!"

Irena tucked Anika into her cradle, stopping to caress her soft cheek. She turned to find Rex watching them from the doorway. He was leaning against the doorjamb with his arms crossed in front of him. Irena smiled as she moved to his side.

"She's out for the night. I think there was a little too much excitement for our girl today."

Rex opened his arms, and Irena slid into them.

"I love you, Irena Newly."

She tilted her head back and to one side. "I like the sound of that."

"No regrets?"

Irena knew Rex was wondering if she was thinking of Nels today on their wedding day. Truth was, she had thought of him several times, but always as if he were smiling at her, pleased with the choice she made. Over and over she thanked the Lord for bringing Rex into her life.

"None, Mr. Newly. And you?"

His arms tightened around her. "I want us to hold on to each day, each moment, and not let them get away from us. I am honored that you and Anika will share your lives with me. I..." Emotion stopped him from continuing, so Irena reached up and put her hand alongside his cheek.

Without even cracking a smile, she said, "You're just worried I won't share the covers with you."

Rex blinked at her serious expression before a slow grin creased his face. "Irena Newly, life will be a joy with you."

For more information about
A Newly Weds Series or
author Margo Hansen, visit her at
www.margohansen.com

Margo would enjoy hearing
from her readers. Send your
comments or questions to
margo@margohansen.com

Other books by Margo Hansen:
Sky's Bridal Train, Jade's Courting Danger,
and *Emma's Marriage Secret*